22

CW01671750

Madibaland

Madibaland

Denis Beckett

PENGUIN BOOKS

PENGUIN BOOKS

Published by the Penguin Group
27 Wrights Lane, London W8 5TZ, England
Viking Penguin, a division of Penguin Books USA Inc, 375 Hudson Street, New York, New York 10014, USA
Penguin Books Australia Ltd, Ringwood, Victoria, Australia
Penguin Books Canada Ltd, 10 Alcorn Avenue, Toronto, Ontario, Canada M4V 3B2
Penguin Books (NZ) Ltd, 182-190 Wairau Road, Auckland 10, New Zealand
Penguin Books (South Africa) (Pty) Ltd, 1A Eton Road, Parktown, South Africa 2193

Penguin Books (South Africa) (Pty) Ltd, Registered Offices:
1A Eton Road, Parktown, South Africa 2193

First published by Penguin Books (South Africa) (Pty) Ltd 1998

Copyright © Denis Beckett 1998

All rights reserved
The moral right of the author has been asserted

ISBN 0 140 27456 1

Typeset in 11 on 13 pt Life
Printed and bound by National Book Printers, Drukkery St, Goodwood, Cape Town

Except in the United States of America, this book is sold subject to the condition that it shall not, by way of trade or otherwise, be lent, resold, hired out or otherwise circulated without the publisher's prior consent in any form of binding or cover other than that in which it is published and without a similar condition including this condition being imposed on the subsequent purchaser.

Contents

Heads & Health

Between May 1995 and July 1997 I presented 74 episodes of a TV programme called Beckett's Trek, which aims to offer a free-thinking approach to matters affecting the present state and future prospects of South Africa.

This book arises from experiences connected with the last 25 of those episodes. It is not a blow-by-blow account and not a diary. It is an idiosyncratic selection of observations that struck me in the course of wandering around the country, and beyond, armed with a licence to question.

Initially it was envisaged, by author and publishers, as a sequel to *Trekking*, which appeared in November 1996 and was a 'book of the series', of the kind that in Europe or America would be hugely marketed under 60-foot banners saying

AS SEEN ON TV

and would sell a million copies to people searching for a Christmas present for somebody who already has too many ties or chocolates.

We didn't quite plug all the promotional cables into the neon-light sockets, which was fine by me as I am edgy about the celebrity circus. But Trekking sold about 7 000 copies, which counts as biggish in the South African pond. The book you're holding was going to be named, until the last minute, *Trek Two*, and it was intended to consist of more of the same – light-hearted tales of what the screen didn't see sprinkled with tangents of soft sociology.

For good or ill, however, Trek Two acquired a life of its own as its pages took shape, and with the publishers tearing their hair and threatening harm to my kneecaps, and the Christmas trees filling the shopfronts and the Jingle Bells jingling, the penny belatedly dropped that actually it was a book of a fairly different stripe. It contained a higher quotient of the perspectives on the State of the Nation, not all of which are restful; a good deal less of the inside stories on the making of a TV series, and practically zero of the media philosophising which led the Sunday Times' review to mixedly bless Trekking with the edict that 'it should be prescribed for journalism students'.

So now you have *Madibaland*, not so much a Son of Trekking as a second cousin once removed. 'Madibaland' strikes some chords that ring right to me. Slightly cheeky, affectionate, very specifically located in a particular time and a particular place, and intimate in the sense of expressing a belonging. It's a name that only South Africans will ever call South Africa, and at that only those South Africans who identify with it and claim it, and at that, even they will only do it now during this weirdly wondrous window in history while we teeter on the fulcrum of the see-saw, precariously vacillating between coming down on the First-World side and coming down on the Third.

Nelson Mandela (ah, what a good name to drop[1]) once told me that to call him Mr President was all right but those

[1]He was my guest on a Radio 702 talk-show.

who 'really want to get to my heart' would call him by his clan praise-name. Well, I really want to get to the heart of the country which in these closing days of the millennium he so colossally bestrides. So there you have it, Madibaland, and too bad if some people say 'hm, could that be somewhere in the Northern Province?'

If you didn't read Trekking, if you never came across the TV series, welcome and feel at home. No qualifying course required. I hope you'll find a bit of insight and a bit of entertainment of the kind you would meet if you spent your working days having to get to the most unlikely combination of places you could think of, and a little thought on how we might bet more boldly on the see-saw coming to a First-World landing.

If you did read Trekking you will encounter overlapping references here and there; you will certainly find a heritage in the way of writing and the way of seeing, and you will recognise the same fundamental approach to South Africa, namely that I belong here and love the place and its people, warts and all. But I here upfront offer you a dutiful Health Warning Notice. Madibaland goes a long way further than last time into the ringing of alarm bells, and contains assorted comments which might endanger the red corpuscles.

The new South Africa is 30% older now and we're 30% wiser, which usually means more sombre. I for one am somewhat more than 30% surer that the road we're on is the road to the poorhouse, the same road as is known to the rest of Africa and for the same basic reason, namely that we have taken the ideals of liberation and equality beyond the realm of reason and into the realm of fantasy. I am still, however, just as 100% sure as ever that there is a life to be had in South Africa, a life which the people of South Africa will embrace with confidence, and that to get to it is mainly a matter of looking again at the road-map. In these pages I do a fair amount of jumping up and down and gesticulating at signboards.

In the introduction to Trekking I said it was essentially a djol into which a smack of politiek had crept. I hereby say that Madibaland is essentially a social perspective from which I hope the djol has not been lost. To readers who want less dilution of their fun&games factor I can only say (a) there are plenty of fish in that sea, and (b) after another year of crime and decline, distortion and pretence, I feel more motivated than before to blow a whistle or two.

So there is what the lawyers would call the Heads Of Argument, or colloquially the Heads, which by unhappy coincidence is the same word as that which sailors use for the place they utilise just before they shave and shower. The body of the case follows herewith, and if after perusal you feel that the naval metaphor applies, well, there is a debate at hand here, a debate on where a nation goes, and I'll be pleased to hear from you whatever your reply.

As before I owe many thanks. To my co-Trekkers – our principal cameraman, Richard Burnett, with Justin Ingham, Ian Miller, Brett Shaw and others as back-up. The soundies – Brett, Ganief Stellenboom, Morrison Nonyukela, Kathy van Rooyen, Len Nzoyi, Ted Levin, Louis Ndlovu & Co; the editors like Donovan Marsh and Nadine Zylstra and Francois Gerke and Rupert Troskie and Mike Cadman, and the multi-faceted production manager Michael Modena. To Hannatjie Fourie and Christa Joubert and Louis Raubenheimer and the team at SABC3, who found us a spot on their schedule and a corner in their budget and a deep and wide range of friendly greetings on our calls to the blue building in Artillery Road, even including the calls which put us on the carpet. To Alison Lowry and Pam Thornley and Claire Heckrath and their colleagues at Penguin for their great wisdom in putting Madibaland on their schedule and their great patience in keeping it there whilst gritting their teeth at the author's missed deadlines. To Gill Murray at Sidelines for help way beyond the call of duty and for almost suppressing her rightful rage at her editor's missed deadlines. To the innumerable good people who made time to speak to us and our intrusive camera, especially (and apologetically) those who thought 'What! Is that all!' when they flashed by in micro-seconds on the programme as broadcast. To Keith, pillar of consistency and sense. To Sheila for proofreading and half a century of motherness. To Meave, Emma and Matt for humouring a dwaaling father wandering around the house with experimental sentence revisions on his lips.

To Gael, for so much.

1

Not About Australia

Australia was Keith's idea. Keith Shaw is my partner on the Trek and the Shaw of Shaw Pictures, the production house which marshals the fancy equipment and the copious personnel required to get a weekly documentary onto the airwaves. And it is Keith who with alarming frequency picks on the subjects which resound the loudest.

Our first 46 Treks had been broadcast over 15 months with a few erratic breaks of one week here and two weeks there, usually when the SABC bumped us to make space for something like a Youth Day special. In mid '96 we got a real break – three months. This was also – heh-heh – to be the beginning of a new arrangement, three months on and three months off for the indefinite future.

The beginning of October we were to Re-Trek. We wanted a blockbuster kick-off, but couldn't think what the blockbuster was. Various good and decent Friends of the Trek argued that we should do some heavyweight investigation into some good juicy apartheid atrocity. I thanked the suggestors for their suggestions and replied that this would be a fine idea but that:

- TV was already wall-to-wall apartheid atrocities.

- The Trek was to a future, not a past.
- Jacques Pauw held copyright.
- Man-made corpses made me sick.

Other well-wishers thought the blockbuster ought to be a social problem programme – drugs, prostitution, or the like. Fortunately Patricia Glynn, whose 'Point Blank' had filled in our time-slot for the three months, had focused well and truly on this area of enquiry and thus obligingly enabled me to make my excuses without having to confess how little I wished to dissect the seamy sides.

It was a lot easier ducking the phoney blockbusters than selecting the un-phoney one. Then up came Keith with Australia: let's see this place to which SA's best and brightest were flocking in tidal waves; let's talk why they quit; let's talk what they find.

I worried a little. I thought we'd end up becoming emigration recruitment officers. Without having to be there, it was easy enough to know that Australia would be neat and orderly and peaceable and nice and there would be several painfully telling comparisons with home. But no alternative blockbuster presented itself, and truth to tell I was intrigued to catch a glimpse of this land of milk and honey. The closest I had ever been was Durban Bluff.

So the dawn of spring saw us heading eastward, courtesy of SA Airways, whereby hangs a slight preliminary tangent on the subject of money.

This was the first time we received any kind of sponsorship for the Trek. Offers had not been lacking but I was Calvin's little brother on the subject of tied editorial. Anybody who suggested a retainer subject to the assurance that I would from time to time mention the merits of his mousetrap or shoe-polish received a flea in his ear.

Most times there was no major moral courage involved in

despatching the flea, because most times the offers were quite bizarrely out of line. An advertiser would be paying the SABC tens of thousands of rands for a minute of air time on my programme, and some smoothie would want to get not only air time but endorsement daarby by giving me two crates of health-drink. And they wondered why they got a short answer.

As it happened, the short answers turned out to be very good practice for the few occasions when genuine temptation came into the picture. The health-drink merchants and their ilk made things so nice and blunt that they erected concrete walls on either side of the path of rectitude. You doubtless know the Bernard Shaw story about the lady and the price:

He (cruel sod) says to a beautiful and flattering young groupie: 'Would you sleep with me for a million pounds?'

'Oh Mr Shaw,' she gushes, 'I'd be honoured.'

'Okay,' he says, 'would you sleep with me for two shillings?'

She recoils, offended. 'What do you take me for, a whore?'

'We've already established that,' he says. 'Now it's just the arithmetic.'

There are various nice lessons in there, one of the less obvious being that for the story to work you have to tell it that way round – the million pounds first and the two shillings as denouement. If you start off with the derisory sum, you forewarn your victim. Had somebody come forth right at the beginning with a great succulent mouth-watering offer . . . well, I trust and hope I would have offered the short answer anyway, but it's also true that the answer to the big question becomes much more obvious when there have been lots of little questions before it.

When temptation did finally grin its grin in the form of an offer to present a TV advertisement – no lies or anything, you understand, just a little stretch or two and a statement as fact of a bit of unprovable hype – saying No was extremely easy.

I worked out afterwards, as a strictly academic exercise,

that the sum involved was slightly more than the total I had paid myself from 1980 to 1985 inclusive. That was partly because in those years I had been trying to save the nation (which paid no attention but saved itself anyway, politically speaking) and took it as natural to go broke in the process, so the comparison didn't mean as much as it would in most people's case. Even so I could have used the loot, and been not much ashamed of the stretches and the slice of hype, and only felt a little bit prostitutional while I enjoyed the spending. But I would have still felt that same little bit prostitutional long after the spending was a memory and its products had faded or sunk or been lost, so I am glad that the health-drink ouens had told me the Bernard Shaw story the right way round.

Still, the arena of what to receive and what not is clouded with ambiguities. I have for example a shirt with a windmill on the chest. This is a plain regular shirt that my wife bought me in a shop like she's been buying me shirts in shops for 24 years. Except that it's (a) a spectacular shirt, not to say unusually indigenous, and (b) it has the name Climax upon it, on the windmill's vane, just like every second windmill you see on every second field from Beit Bridge to Cape Agulhas. So what happens is of course that the viewer thinks: ah, I wonder how much Climax has to pay for that. And the kind of viewer who produces a staff T-shirt with his company name and logo emblazoned upon it thinks: hmm, if I send him a shirt . . .

So I acquire an industrial T-shirt supply that would be Guinness Records material but for the fact that most of it exits fairly soon after it enters, mainly in the direction of the local domestics and builders' labourers and dustbin men who as a rule are happier than I to turn themselves into walking advertisements for Joe's Slasto Paving. But then, I also get nice shirts, subtler shirts, shirts with actual aesthetics instead of just contact numbers, and what do I do? I keep them, and wear them. One day there'll be a declare-your-assets process for TV mense, such as was recently started for politicians. I'll have a lot of T-shirts to declare, even if not the windmill one. (The boss of Climax phoned to ask where I got it. My wife steered him to the shop, which had closed down. He's still looking, as far as I know.)

This issue would come at you from every side. Keith's brother Colin runs Hi-Tec shoes. From time to time he gives Hi-Tecs to everybody in Keith's company. Brotherly solidarity. I'm an Hon Member of Keith's company. These are shoes that traditionally I would admire briefly, glance at the price tag, and then turn to a cheaper shelf. Right now I'm wearing Hi-Tec boots, the best bits of footwear I've ever known. Is this right, wrong, compromising? Until somebody explains, I'm enjoying the boots.

What of the hard cases? Like free meals? When the mayor of Witbank or the ambulance drivers of Vereeniging invite us to partake of the municipality's munificence, no problem hoegenaamd. When a Boksburg pizzeria proprietor loudly insists that two Margheritas and Castle Draught are on the house, beginnings of a problem. Particularly when I'm anyway there as someone's guest, and the disregarding of his money is offensive to my host (in this case an ex Special Branch cop who wants to tell me the bits the Truth Commission isn't hearing such as how he conducted his political policing precisely the way he would have liked God or his mother or the dominee to have seen).

But when you're there with camera and crew, and filming the village, and the darn café won't let you pay . . . big problem. Is this supposed to be a sweetener? I can never know it's not. How can I accept? I can't, in conscience, but then there are places, like the thriving Maputo restaurant at which expatriates gather to swap violent ribald tales of African disasters, where the attempt to pay a bill causes such a federal case that in the end you give up and too bad about conscience.

I could have given the price of the meal to the beggars, you might say, but the funny thing is that when you are wholly and absolutely surrounded by destitution, not only does conscience take a nap but the milk of human kindness curdles. That's my experience anyway. The places where the soft heart ought to be sharpest pierced by the upturned hand, the appealing eye, the sniff of misery . . . these are in fact the places where the soft heart turns to granite. It's mainly a self-defence, I suppose, but it's also a disgust. So the moral price of a good free meal at one of the best restaurants in Maputo is still nestling in my pocket, and the question in my mind is: why does the world work so you only get offered free meals when you no longer need them?

Issues of ethics and moral compromise hummed constantly along in the back of my mind, mainly painlessly like the traffic on a distant highway. Then up comes the Oz prospect and now this is not free-meal territory any more, this is trans-continental air tickets.

Could we ask, could we not, was it begging, was it an abuse? Keith was pushing me to at least ask the airways. I was reluctantly assuming we'd have to zap it from the Trek's budget. Finally I had a brainwave. The whole point of the Trek was that it was supposed to be honest comment, no holds barred, without fear favour or prejudice, etc. So, let's in effect sell SAA a piece of the Trek, no holds barred.

I wrote to Leon Els, about to resume his role as head of SAA public affairs after several months as No 2 to Felicia Mabuza-Suttle, and set it out:

> The quid pro quo would be that I make, on the box, a reasonably substantive comment on the flight.
>
> By 'reasonably substantive', I mean the comment will be distinct and definite. I do not promise X minutes or Y

minutes. I do promise it is not sommer a throwaway.

The comment, in keeping with the nature of the programme, will reflect what I have felt about the flight. It will not in any way be a scripted advertisement. If the flight was awful I would be free to say so. In the more likely event that it is not awful, the comment will be designed to in some way – which way, I can not know in advance – convey an insight or perspective on SAA which I can expect viewers to find fresh, authentic, thought-provoking, or preferably all of these.

This approach spoke well to Leon. As he said, the potential in here was in its way more persuasive than the regular ad which everybody knew was not what anybody actually meant so much as a pre-scripted, pre-approved, pre-refined praise-song. Leon got very enthusiastic about the idea of a genuine endorsement, and very wry about the risk factors. Thus was the Trek's budget relieved of a large proportion of its overstrain (a lot of overstrain was left, paying Aus $$ for everything from the internal Aus flights to the back-up from local journos and injecting added spice to my first exposure to the one-country continent).

This was a challenge. The flight would have to be fairly darned awful before I would kick a gift horse outright in the teeth. I didn't expect to have to. My worry was how to give due acknowledgement without defaulting on the straight-talk factor.

In the end . . . Well, the trans-Indian flights weren't in every respect state-of-the-art. The greying and the balding among us recall with appreciation that great human break-through the in-flight movie, but we do not necessarily wish to keep recalling it through all of our days. Certain further break-throughs have occurred without the nod of SAA, such as choice of channels and individual screens freed of the back of the next guy's head. Plus it does not strike a wholly correct note to give your passengers a metal knife in tandem with a plastic fork.

Yet I would happily pick SAA against Emirates or Qantas or Cathay Pacific etcetera for two simple reasons: (1) it's ours, and (2) its service culture is respectful rather than obsequious. Some passengers, no doubt, go in for the yes sir no sir kiss your feet sir treatment. For me, thank heaven for the SAA way of treating one with more politeness than reverence.

So I said all this to the camera, more or less (and showed the offending knife and fork, which the crew later gave me as mementoes).

I won't say it worked for everybody (perhaps including Leon who preserved a daunting silence on the subject, but came again to the party when we went to Britain nine months later) but it worked for me and in my view it vindicated the point about the impact of non-advertisement advertising. It became one of those statements (some programmes had none, some had several) which constantly echo back as I catch a lift or round a supermarket aisle. They aren't necessarily echoes that say 'ah, yes, I shall be sure to book SAA next time I travel'. They often say: 'Gee you were a bit hard on SAA that time with the knife and fork.' Some say other things, sometimes the opposite. What they say matters less than that they constituted a mini-debate and thus some return for the benefactor, and established a way, unequivocally satisfactory to me, of creating a legitimate trading chip out of playing straight.

The questions about the economics of producing a TV documentary are endless albeit usually roundabout. People are generally too constrained to say straight out 'Do you get bribed?' or 'What do you make?' but they tickle intently at the edges. Actually the economics of TV are lunatic, in keeping with the First Law of Human Affairs which specifies that **there**

shalt be no correlation between effort, value and reward or any two of the above. One programme works out slick and smooth and hitch-free and settles the rent arrears. The next goes awry and causes brain damage as well as abject grovelling for credit extensions, and either or both or neither might turn out to be the best or the worst or the mediocrest. What's new? This is a world where Joe might toil through honest months for half the return that Jack pulls in from concluding a telephone deal; where Jim might throw out with the garden rubbish an item which John will feel lucky to have as the roof over his head. Media economics offers its own peculiar brands of weirdness, but their degree of weirdness is no weirder than the norm.

So there is how we got to Australia, and failed to fall in love . . .

2

Omoland

Cabramatta road is Sydney's used car precinct, and not the place a first-time visitor would normally select to see first light of Australian day. But it happened that a young ex Seffrican whizzkid was flying his private plane out of a small-plane airfield that morning, and the only time we could see him was crack of dawn after the night we arrived.

In the end, we didn't use the whizzkid, who had not much to say other than that it's nice to be rich. But driving back down this long long road, it struck me that something was wrong. It took a while to realise what. It was that the proprietors were washing the cars.

On the used car roads better known to me and, probably, you, you'll see a different sight in the scratch-and-burp prelude to the business morning. You'll see the whites sipping coffee in the sales kiosks, feet on the table, while outside the blacks wield the cloths and buckets.

On Cabramatta road, nobody in the kiosks, and in each lot a middle-aged white guy cleaning cars or sweeping the yard.

There's Oz for you. Everybody stands his man. There is no segment of society which expects to be fawned upon, and there is no segment which expects to be given perpetual direction. People do it themselves. The guy who designs the circuit also carries the ladder. The plumber digs his own holes. The builder totes his own bricks. And the gate guard uses his own judgement.

For them this way of life is obvious and unexceptional. Through South African eyes it is tantalising, mouth-watering, Treasure Island. It made me queasy with envy, and of all the many admirable features of Oz this one left the biggest clout on my mind.

Not that there was a shortage of competition.

Everything works, for a start. Everything is clean, too. You can go into any public toilet any time and bet on finding not just the basics such as that the last guy pulled the chain, but real smack-in-the-head unknown cleanliness. The last guy will have also dried the basin. And he will have deposited the paper towel in the bin, and there'll be a full supply of towels on hand, and nobody will have stolen the soap, let alone the loo paper . . . and it can turn a South African onlooker pale with awe and green with envy.

Recently, when the cement was scarcely dry on the new Johannesburg station, I was there to drop a child and accompanied a younger child to the loo. That there would be no soap, no paper, and liquid floors awash with stompies and chip packets, was expectable and thus only mildly sickening. But that all the seats and most of the doors should be either broken or stolen seemed rough. Moments like this I flashback to Aus and to its reading on that most revealing barometer of society, the state of public conveniences, and experience a wave of despair.

A few months earlier the Trek had taken us to Zambia, and I had come back with a vivid image of the Unworking society. Now in Aus I acquired the opposite. Funny that, the A–Z factor. Maybe we should call South Africa Azania after all, (although Mozambique and Tanzania suggest that the Curse of the Z might not depend on being the initial). I see Australia as the metaphor for effectiveness, and South Africa as on a cusp or a see-saw. We're halfway between the capacity of Australia and the incapacity of Zambia, and we're surely going one way or the other. Which one? Any bookmaker will give you ten to one that we're heading towards Zambia. I'm not prepared to leave it at that. I keep faith in the belief that things can be turned, things can be changed; humans make their societies, humans can make choices. I join the bookmakers in assessing the likelihoods at ten to one. But rather than taking the bet I feel inclined to do my bit to change the odds.

Which is where certain tensions arose.

Many of the people we saw in Aus were ex South Africans, and not a few of these went heavy on the 'my heart belongs with you' line. There were people whose hearts were in the Bushveld, in the Drakensberg, in the Kruger Park, in Plettenberg Bay, daar onder in die mielies by die groen doringboom, wherever. One family had named a daughter after the Outeniquas, and whilst 'Teniqua' is a heck of a pretty name, and I wish I'd thought of it, it doesn't hang all that easy upon a child growing up a bolthole ocean away.

This finally is what these guys were there for. They'd bolted. The peculiar thing about emigration from South Africa is that it is seldom the emigration of adventure, the emigration of opportunity or the emigration away from class oppression, as most emigration from most countries at most times has been. There's plenty of adventure here, no lack of opportunity, and about 98% of the emigrants come from society's topmost drawer. It's the emigration of escape, and what they're escaping from is the blacks.

All right, in the old days they could say it was an escape from immorality to morality, and some people meant it. But one of the bluntest bits of honesty I ever heard was from an emigrant in Durham, North Carolina, the day I arrived at the

Greyhound bus station. She is a family friend. She was waiting to meet me and she was all het up. I approached with normal greetings at the ready and she stopped me abruptly. 'No,' she said. 'No. No. No. Before you say a single word there's one thing you've got to know. We didn't leave because of all the terrible things we were doing to the blacks. We left because of all the terrible things the blacks were going to do to us. So there.'

I burst out laughing and she was most surprised. She was used to the standard cocktail righteousness of emigration – 'iniquitous system . . . impossible for decent people to live under . . .' She saw her confession as a major admission of guilt. I saw it as a breath of fresh air. It'll never be known how many of the anti-apartheid émigrés confessed the same thing to their priest or their dreams or the bottom of their whiskey glass. What's easy to know is that the current incarnation of post-apartheid émigrés – brothers and nieces and old mates, from the same schools and suburbs and clubs, the same upper-class fix in the social spectrum – have dropped the whole pretence. It's hard to believe how quickly and wholly the ethic changed. Today's departers are unabashed: 'I'm leaving because the blacks are going to bugger it up.'

I don't for a moment deny their right to quit, for reasons good, bad, inbetween or unspecified. But several features bug me, of which the greatest is the practical one that every pair of skilled hands leaving a country as skills-short as ours is another nail in the coffin. When one takes the view that the country can be regrukked, that it can be pulled right and made good, you want all the regrukking capacity you can get, and the guys crossing the Indian Ocean represent a horrifying quantity of lost capacity. The flip side of the practicality is the moral angle on the same question: when you've had your start, your education, your background, all formed by Country A, with measureless quantities of hard-acquired public expenditure on your acquisition of skills, I for one have difficulty about simply taking it all off to give to Country B, where it's two a penny.

Yeah, yeah, we're all dancing to the global beat, with free trade and crumbling borders and the barrierless planet allegedly on the rise (although I'll take good odds that this fad, too, will change in another year or ten), so all this talk of obligations is supposed to be outdated and irrelevant because everything will even out in the wash. I'd pay more attention to the even-out theories if I saw more of the departing dentists heading for Malawi, or the contract-hopping sportsmen on their way to Ghana. As it is the world's skills-shifts proceed from places that can't spare them to places that don't need them. Aus is so oversupplied with medics that one specialist we met – he was at Wits with me and thus qualifies as 'young' in terms of productive capacity albeit not of glamour – has been required as the price of entry to lay down his scalpel. He is now the immensely unfulfilled house-husband of a stock-broker wife, with loads of leisure and oceans of opulence but a great crater in the Meaning lobe of his life.

An extraordinary proportion of the oversupply is thanks to the University of the Witwatersrand School of Medicine, and when one looks at the equation from the eastward side of the water – 'Ja, Pete is down the passage in radiology and you remember Andrew with that souped-up Cortina well he's pretty much the main gynae around and Rob is running a heart clinic and of course ol' Mick jeez he was a wild bugger hey well he's Dean of Surgery . . .' – one pictures a daunting image of the ships sailing one way laden with the lounge suites and CD collections of the nation's first team, and returning with food parcels.

Nor had it ever been quite so clear to me how the sports regime of the 21st century is shaping up: the US, Germany, and three or five other white, western and rich countries sharing the honours, by courtesy of an ever-increasing complement of imported players. We've seen the Navratilovas, the Allan Lambs & Co leaving unpromising home countries to enhance the scoreboards of stabler second homes. Speaking to Chris Smith, ex Natal cricketer, on the field of the Whacker, which is how everyone pronounces the Western Australian Cricket Association of which Chris is general manager, I couldn't help envisaging yesterday's trickle becoming tomorrow's flood. Chris made no bones of seeing it that way, although he expressed it a whole lot more delicately than another formerly Seffrican sports administrator who told me off camera that: 'In another generation all kids with potential will be on scholarships here, and your national team will be in the same league as our country villages.'

So there's a happy thought, reaching further than only to those who get bothered about who wins sports matches. For me in Aus, what was more bothersome was that I was having barneys with everyone I spoke to. Yes, they were entitled to run out. But I was also entitled to say I didn't like them running out, and this got under the skin, sometimes about three feet under.

Some heated exchanges featured on screen, and so did some extremely poignant ones. Michael White in Perth, ex Nataller and journo, had left home specifically for the purpose of keeping the family together. He had wanted to avoid that day which gives so many parents their worst nightmares – the day when the kids say 'sorry, mom and dad, there's no future here so I'm quitting, but don't worry, I'll visit every few years'.

To avoid that day Michael had undergone numerous privations, had sacrificed friends, community, clubs, customs, interests, and a goodly chunk of career. And now where was his son? Back in Johannesburg.

Josie Brouard, in her glorious panorama flat on Bondi Beach, was as straight as you could ask for, a walking SoWhat!

and fazed by nothing. I remembered Josie's days as a semi-political reporter, politically correct for her day, although the phrase hadn't been coined yet, and full of conscience in more of a gentle way than the heavy-lefty style. But she had darem been among those who had been saying change, change, change, and I for right or wrong suffer from a sense that those who said change, change, change belong in the place where they made the change, back among those they persuaded to change and who were living the change. One of Josie's works was particularly memorable. Alongside a vivid picture of her holding a heart-wrenching malnourished baby there was an urgent article about human misery and the need for all good people to support the eradication thereof. Now here was Josie as sharp and smart and sexy as ever plying her energies in an environment where for most people misery meant there was a holding pattern over the pizza oven. Was there a certain inconsistency? I raised the thought and with a disdainful shrug Josie said: 'If I'm in a shit relationship I get out. If you don't like that, pfft.'

Well, there was an unequivocal statement for you, and the way Josie said it, totally upfront, you couldn't even take offence. Moreover, there was a logic to it. If you're in a bad relationship you do get out, eventually. Usually, though, you first go to some effort to rectify the relationship, and if it is a relationship that means much to you, a relationship where the good elements also come on strong, you go to a lot of effort. Everybody must reach their own conclusions about when the effort is no longer worth the return, and maybe in the end there is no great principle involved in this debate, merely a haggling over quantum. Nonetheless I got upset about what seemed to me to be a light and easy turning of the back upon Africa and upon its people and therefore also upon me.

In Wits days I had been much frowned upon by the anti-apartheid establishment for being soft on the Boere and for bothering to make puny efforts to learn their language and for trying to talk to them on the error of their ways rather than screech at them from a high horse. Once when I was chairman of the Law Students Council there was one of the innumerable stand-offs between protesting Witsies on the campus side of Jan Smuts avenue and counter-protesting lawanorder types on the other. I committed the heinous offence of crossing the road to request the latter to desist from stuffing stones inside the tomatoes they were throwing at us. Inevitably I ended up arguing the case for why it was that we were protesting about whichever apartheid law we were protesting about. I had a fairly chilly hearing from the tattoos and the beerboeps, but it was a mantelpiece of warmth in comparison with the deep freeze from the lefty set when I recrossed the road. For long after my ears rang with denunciations of my lack of discipline, lack of strategy, and general lack of commitment to the cause of freedom and justice and the oppressed.

Okay fine. Just one question: howcome the purists are now sailing their yachts on Sydney harbour while I'm still riddled with hang-ups about freedom and justice and the oppressed? Maybe they grew up faster. Some of them had been hastened on their way by banning orders or Dirty Tricks Departments and threats real or imagined. Even then, though, I was stupefied by some of the justifications. One fellow had been not only a boyhood friend in my life but also a very major guru in very many lives of which mine was far from foremost. This was a guy who headed half a dozen student clubs and organisations, mastered bucketloads of productive hobbies from woodwork to photography, learned foreign languages in his spare time, excelled at every sporting arena from the chessboard to the athletics track, took on four extra courses in his Bachelor's degree so he wouldn't get bored, and got Firsts for all fourteen. The mind boggles at how much contribution this pair of hands had to make. The heart sinks at how it wasn't made. I drive nowadays along Jan Smuts avenue and every week there's another beggar. Every week there's another placard, No Job No Food. The oppressed come in all shades now, and they come in legions. No one will ever know how fewer they may have been had a brain of this magnitude stayed on to create order and industries like its owner's forebears did. That the beggars would have been fewer, none can doubt.

Now here in a pleasant living room in a pleasant part of a pleasant city, I hear that the reason he took the long flight out is that 'a clearly articulated black response forced us to recognise that we were not wanted in South Africa'.

Hmm. A 'clearly articulated black response'? Yes, there is a certain lame-brained black category which says: 'Let these whites go, then we can move into their jobs.' But that is a tiny category of ideological morons, certainly dwarfed by those who – whether rationally or intuitively – know that white flight means small economy, and hopefully dwarfed too by those who genuinely consider whites to be fellow South Africans. And even if there were an unmistakably articulated black response, why take note of any such racist claptrap? We paid little attention, back at the ramparts in Jan Smuts avenue, to some very clearly articulated, and distinctly majority, white positions. We talked about rights for all, freedom for all, the non-racial world. Now we're supposed to say: 'Oh dear, a black voice tells us to leave, dig out the passports'?

So a sense of duplicity ran close to the surface right through our travels among South Africans in Aus. And the rhythm in the background was an altogether startling sense of the whiteness of Aus.

One knows of course that Australia is essentially a white country. It's patent. You know this stuff in the same way as you know that a Scottish accent is hard to understand or that

Japan's subways are packed. But knowing it in the abstract is not much preparation for seeing it in the reality. The reality is that the place is so white – or at any rate so non-aboriginal – that it is a consistent shock. Moreover, when you do come across aboriginal people . . . well, you have living fulfilment of all the stereotypes.

When Cook set foot in Aus in 1788, there were by modern science's reckoning some 500 000 indigenes in the continent. (The number dropped right then and there when some locals met the musket in the course of trying to deter the setting of foot.) When the Brits annexed the Cape not 20 years later, there were by modern science's reckoning some 500 000 indigenes south of the Limpopo. There are now 200 000 in the one place and more than 30 000 000 in the other. Something was done differently, and in a nutshell that something was genocide. The wicked South African racists somehow didn't get the hang of it. So now South Africa's First-World segment is about 20% of the population and is haemorrhaging rapidly in favour of places like Australia, where the First-World segment is about 98% of the population and handles the upkeep of the rest as a taxpayers' budget item like the upkeep of a museum or national orchestra.

Upkeep? Harsh, huh? Yep. I would never have thought of it that way before I went looking for aboriginals, a task which is not much easier around Sydney or Perth than looking for gold in Johannesburg's pavements.

(And the word is aborigin*als*. Aborigin*e* has fallen into disfavour, like imposed ethnic terms invariably do. Attempts to replace it with the separate names of the dozens of tribes smashed against reality. Aboriginal is the current respectful term.)

In Perth we met one of the most calmly impressive social workers it was ever my pleasure to find. What is more he is my goombol, right down to the single n. His name is Denis

Eggington and he introduced me to the aboriginals' special relationship with the namesake. For one, you never call your namesake by his name. You call him goombol. Which technically means just that, 'namesake', except that in English you do not use 'namesake' in the second person à la 'Namesake, please pass the sugar'. My goombol had a professorial air and non-aboriginal features, and did not himself experience much uphill. His wife and kids, however, looked just like the aboriginals of the picture books, and had numerous depressingly familiar stories. They take his smart new project-supplied car into town, and somebody's going to think they've stolen it. They go to a shop to buy tennis shoes, and the attendant will hover over them lest a pair leap up and jump into a handbag.

Denis was social worker to, of course, an aboriginal community, and as he and others made clear, that is about the only work any aboriginals have. The public purse gets hold of the brightest and soberest members of the race and pays them to administer the public upkeep that gives their cousins houses and vouchers and keeps them out of sight. You can tramp the streets of Perth for days and, as one of our interviewees contentedly said, 'never see a blackfellow'. We did tramp the streets for days and we saw one family, of four women. A mother, two little girls and a very ancient grandma were lying in a public park, in a position of such abject forlornness that the hoboes hanging around a South African bottlestore look in comparison like champions of dynamism. They were visiting a relative in hospital. They had no place to stay. They had walked umpteen miles because no taxi would pick them up.

In Sydney aboriginalism takes a different manifestation from Perth. It all hangs out, in a suburb called Redfern. Redfern is all aboriginals, and aboriginals are only in Redfern, Australia's Soweto, the aboriginal capital of the world, and a hell of a bitter joke. Redfern is by Australian standards a slum. By South African standards it is not. It's an old, small, semi-inner city precinct, occupying perhaps a fiftieth or a hundredth of Sydney's land area. It has a magnificent view of the gleaming distant spires, a smell of booze and urine, and severalfold more junk lying around its yards than the rest of the city put together. Its commercial, industrial, and business component consists of a handful of publicly sponsored welfare projects. There used to be two tourist shops selling boomerangs, but one is abandoned – you see the wares through the dirty window – and the other moved to an upmarket quarter where the whites wouldn't feel scared – or ashamed? – to bring their foreign friends in search of a little Australian culture.

I'm sure there are fine people living in Redfern, trappees of dependency and prejudice trying valiantly to punch their way out. But they're hard to find. What we found was cliché from start to finish. Our normal game and gung-ho guide Caro suffered cardiac arrest when I raised the thought of going to Redfern, like her Joburg counterpart would do if a guest asked for a ride around Alexandra. The aboriginal 'self-help' agencies were mainly run by white lefties and (with one exception) were as curt and unobliging as is possible short of actively asking for a fight. Nearly everybody we met was drunk and the rest were full of the pathetic big words of ideological excuse-making and anachronistic Che Guevara slogans. Redfern didn't go down big.

What went down like a brick in a mineshaft was the incredible Oz chutzpah. In desperate search for something to pass as a national culture, they've latched on to the aboriginals. They use aboriginal words for their placenames, and the distinctive aboriginal dot paintings for their logos and symbols. They're advancing the phenomenon by the day. Just before we got there a very lovely chunk of parkland changed its name from Long Nose Point to Yuralbin Park, complete with an extensive mawkish plaque explaining the etymology of 'Yuralbin'. (Some unimpressed local had scratched it over with koki-pen; a wildly radical protest for Oz.) At long last they're creating an Australian culture and a symbolism to replace the corks on the hat, but they're creating it out of a culture which the average Australian views with undiluted contempt.

In one sense we're as bad. We too are creating a South African symbolism out of the artefacts of a subsection, viz the Ndebele. The creating and the marketing is by sharp operators in Sandton and barely features actual Ndebele people other than as gimmicks, but at least the people whose artworks are being stolen can walk tall, more or less, around their nation. In Oz, it's the ultimate adding of insult to injury.

All of which is about as disturbing to your average Seffrican emigrant as a daffodil is to a glacier. That's the reason they're there: no blacks. What they do in compensation is to make a fetish about their multi-culturalism as regards Asians.

Every good liberal emigrant mum in the seaward suburbs will proudly tell you how very multi-cultural the school is. A class list will feature names from Vietnam, China, Cambodia, Thailand, Japan, Korea, and Burma. Usually, one name each. It's like the attitude in the Democratic Party corners of South Africa five years ago, when the mums were delighted at the broadening arrival of a Maseko or Moloi among the Joneses and Cohens, but if this is multi-culturalism the Pope's a Buddhist. It's the Kyis and Myungs and Changs enduring their compulsory dose of Straailian before heading back to their ethnic ghetto to further the invasion upon the Straailian economy.

The suburb of Cabramatta, at the end of aforementioned used car road, is known to the so-called Dinky-Die Aussies (the guys whose ars sound like motor-car hooters and whose conversation is the analysis of rugby tests) as Vietnamatta. There are Korean, Thai, and Laotian areas, mainly with aboriginal names, and of course a Chinatown, named, funnily enough, Chinatown. And when Kipling figured that east is east and west is west and never the twain would meet, he only had the half of it. The separate eastern ethnic enclaves might as well be cast-iron sub-compartments.

I'm not suggesting that no transcending takes place; let alone no affection or respect or group-hopping or love, of whatsoever character. I'm sure it must. But for the Aussie establishment to present their relationship with the Pacific cousins as a model of multi-culturalism is a self-delusion of bizarre proportions. They all do it – everybody who claims to be cultivated or sophisticated or edjamacated. I think it's a manifestation of a certain secret guilt over the absence of the missing 29 800 000 indigenes. Meanwhile the Dinky-Dies sound like so many AWBs. The average Aussie employs a bluntness of appellation on ethnic matters such as has not been known in South Africa for years. He refers to the Orientals as Slopes and the aboriginals as Boongs (and for that matter the Seffricans as Yarpies, although this is fairly affectionate – after all they're white and play rugby). While it's hard to see what he's got against the aboriginals, whom in most cases he never claps eyes on unless he accidentally bumps into the ethnic channel on his TV, you can see why he says things like 'Strewth, maite, Ah'd raither hairve the bloody Ku Klux Klan than the bloody Slairpes.' Namely, because he suffers from the not unreasonable dread that in a few years his country is going to be an outpost of Asia.

The Number 1 topic of bar talk is the progression: Anh or Tho or Duc arrives on Monday morning from Ho Chi Minh City, one of 80 in the rowing boat, bedraggled and miserable and with his backside hanging out his trousers and not knowing whether this is Vladivostok or Santiago or Copenhagen or what. Tuesday he gets a barrow, Wednesday he starts a stall, Thursday he opens a supermarket and by

Friday he's into downtown real estate. This is Competition with knobs on; and not a formula for mass popularity. It's also so drastically removed from the kind of cultural issues that we wrestle with in Africa that after a few days of hardening indignation, I was disgracefully curt with Australians who started pulling the righteousness trip on me.

Then there's another small thing, which can make an oke a bit um er tongue-tied in the mentioning, which is that the Orientals are drastically unAfrican in another way too. 'Inscrutable' is the respectable word, but perhaps not the most honest. Honesty says that there's a certain coolth, which is a little bit offputting and is a long way removed from the easy acceptances of Africa. I thought for a while that in my case it might be mere familiarity, that I was used to African openness and beaming African smiles. But I doubt that now, having learned that many an Aussie, too, feels edgy and unsure of his ground in the company of the Pacific Tigers.

This generalisation, like all generalisations, is regularly belied by the wondrous diversity of flesh-and-blood. But as a generalisation it is also, like most generalisations, a reasonable reflection of statistical probability. And we can't understand our world accurately if we are to treat honest generalisations as unmentionable. If one generalisation is that the Orient has a fix-it capacity which is not marked in Africa, its obverse is that Africa has a friendliness capacity which does not trip easily from the Eastern countenance. If you ask the way from a passer-by in Sydney's Chinatown, you might get very meticulous directions but you might also get a look to make you sorry you spoke. In South Africa the answer will be all grin and warm heart and long-lost-brother, and it will make your day even if it does not quite get you to your destination.

Aus was a stark lesson in the Beginner's Course in Understanding Race, that unexpectedly lengthy learning curve within which we are all floundering. It's a pity for the Aussies that the lessons from our somewhat more heated laboratory have so little bearing on the opposite brand of ethnic muscle-flexing that is coming their way. They can legitimately take comfort in the certainty that the problems of being out-performed are less awesome than the problems of being throttled by under-performance, but for myself I would find it hard to trade the fantastic personal relationships that Africa offers for the thinned lips and expressionless glowers that seem to be part of the portmanteau that the high-performers carry.

For most of my former compatriots the ethnic issues flowed from mind like rain down a drain. For the first time I acquired a real sense of the comfort some people find in homogeneity. As a good South African boy I had always taken it as simply natural to have other kinds of people around. By the time I got around to realising that the world didn't always work like this I'd developed a taste for diversity and an affection for the various groups who comprised our homegrown diversity. (Which is to my mind the key to living contentedly in South Africa. If you set yourself apart from the other lot – Boers, blacks, Indians, whoever – you're always finding things to get your knickers knotted. Embracing them as your own makes life easier and richer.)

So whereas the monochrome character of Australia comes across a tad pallid in my eyes, in the eyes of other beholders it's the Real McCoy. One ex Seffrican, David Thomas, a delightful guy and your classical Packer For Perth, a one-time parliamentary candidate for the Progressive Federal Party whose moneyed liberal constituency was much mocked for its propensity to emigrate, put it straightforwardly: 'We're boring people, which is why we choose to live in a boring society.' There's something in David's comment, but there's something else as well.

I ate one night with David and his Aussie lady, Barbara, in their quaint house in a quaint street in a quaint suburb called

Balmain, all terraces and balconies and old wood like a magnified best of Woodstock or Salt River. Afterwards I walked back to our guest-house in Potts Point. This was a ridiculously long walk, and took all night, and donated half my shoe leather to the Municipality of Sydney, and left me schizophrenic in bittersweetness.

The high side was: what a wonderful, natural, simple pleasure – to walk free and secure and content under a beautiful sky through a beautiful city. The low side: what a sorrow that the equivalent excursion in my own city would be a thing of anxiety and threat and the neighbours saying: 'What!? You mad!?' I got the feeling that this business of boredom vs excitement, comfort vs challenge, is not sorted out yet. South Africa hasn't found the formula, but neither have the Aussies.

In many ways the orderliness of Oz is more orderly than my stomach can take. We tend to picture Aussies – Crocodile Dundee, kneed testicles in the scrum, sheep-stealing forebears etc – as a rollicking, swashbuckling breed. The dreary truth is that this is a nation that waits for pedestrian lights. The clammy hand of infinite regulation hovers over your collar-bone every time you draw breath. The urban landscape is a forest of By Order notices instructing the dutiful citizenry as to where, when and how they are permitted to walk, to talk, to run, to jump, to eat, to drink and to pick their noses, and with which finger. Out-of-order characters are called 'ferals', which they pronounce ferril to rhyme with Beryl. A feral is looked upon with much wrinkling of the lip and a frisson of nervous excitement, and a feral might be a guy with a hole in the knee of his jeans – a white guy of course, Asians never have holes in the knees of their jeans and aboriginals would be treated as ex officio honorary ferals even if they were wearing tweed pinstripe. It is streng verboten to allow your dog to bark. To disobey the pedestrian light is to attract glares of righteous disapproval and suspicions of feralism, even if there is not a vehicle for two miles in all directions. What got my goat, to the point of strangulation, is the signs on the airport trolleys to prohibit the pushing of kids. For my kids in their toddler years the ride on the airport trolley was a birthright and an ecstasy, and I'd have difficulty living in a society where so innocent an enjoyment is a criminal act. I'm all in favour of a law-abiding world, but there can be too much of a good thing.

I needn't have worried about falling in love with Oz. It wasn't even a temptation. A fundamentally admirable society, for sure; a lovable one, no thanks. I came away with a new sense of the admiration, a renewed conviction that South Africa needs to point itself in the Australian direction, and a reinforced confidence that the fundamentals of South African life offer a human wealth and a dimension of purpose that compensate for our statistical and material drawbacks. To be in Australia would to my mind mean a sacrifice.

3

Cape to Karoo

After the heady experience of crossing continents – first time the Trek ventured out of Africa – a return to eie bodem seemed called for, and no bodem is more eie than the Cape Flats.

What we really wanted was a programme about coloured people. Coloured people had been generally as under-featured in the Trek as in the South African discourse as a whole, and lots of them were letting us know it.

'When are you going to do a programme about us?' was a standard question from all sorts of quarters, and the '*us*' could mean a thousand things – *us*, waitresses; *us*, civil servants; *us*, the youth; *us*, the aged; *us*, gays; *us*, Freemasons; *us*, the citizens of Riebeeck Kasteel . . . However, when it came from people of one particular complexion it always meant the same thing. Whether they were conjurors or engine drivers or disabled or octogenarians or bungee jumpers, what they meant was '*us*, coloureds'.

We tinkered with a kind of general ethnic travelogue – going out with fishermen and the usual. One drawback was that from sore experience I knew that, never mind that we'd be bogged down interpreting into English for the viewers, I wouldn't even understand the fishermen's Afrikaans. The

Western Cape is bilingual in one language. When coloureds, especially outside the city, speak the local Afrikaans it might as well be Urdu as far as the Highveld ear can grasp it. If you're lucky someone can translate into Received Standard Taal and if you're not you're reduced to baffled non-committal uh-huhs, terrified that a 'ja' or a 'nee' might mean anything from insulting someone's mother to contracting to purchase a spliff.

In any case we wanted a question, an issue we could get excited about rather than a foreign-correspondent-style Window on the World. Plus we sought a delicate balance. We wanted the coloured guys who said 'do *us*' to feel that we were indeed doing *them*. But we didn't want to be too blatant about it. 'Doing coloureds'? – a little crass in this day and age, wouldn't you say? We would never 'do blacks' or 'do whites'; people would just come into things in the course of doing a programme on a theme.

So maybe we should make the theme something kosher and un-ethnic like 'State of the Cape' or 'Whither the Mother City', and just coincidentally happen to have so many coloured people on screen that the do-*us* contingent would be sufficed.

Sies, what weasel thinking! I'm ashamed to recall that we were tempted. In the end we dropped it. It belatedly occurred to me that there was a fundamental difference. No black people and no white ones ever asked us to 'do them' *because* they were black or *because* they were white. Coloureds asked us all the time. Plain reality said there was a difference here; something to do with minorityism, no doubt. So we did coloureds. We even named the programme, unabashed, 'Three Colours Brown', which although founded on a reference to a hi-falutin' trio of 'discerning' movies nonetheless ranked as one of our better titles.[1]

[1]We'd had some that held their heads up, like Scatterlings on the émigrés of Aus (and Omoland on the Aussies of Aus), and some excruciating ones. The programme on SA artists was somehow inflicted with Far-Art, leaving me with my head held anywhere but up.

What is more, we had our question. From about 1983 until about 1991 the in thing among the with-it crowd had been great disdain for the notion of 'coloureds'. Coloureds were supposed to be black, and to identify with their brothers in oppression. I don't think the average coloured guy on the pavement ever got to know that he was actually black, and of those who were apprised of this new development some were wont to demur in short sharp words. But in the circles of rectitude it was a big thing. It was a badge of liberatory honour to never use the word 'coloured' without putting dismissive quote-marks around it. That wasn't only in writing the word, but also in speaking it, so that if from a distance you saw a discussion going on with people repeatedly raising their hands as if to scratch dust specks from an imaginary pane of glass, you knew that the subject was coloured politics and the discussers were of the persuasion that would now be called 'politically correct'.

The fashion started fading even before the wallop when the bulk of coloureds voted incorrectly in the Mandela election, and there has been a corresponding rise of the formerly dismissed debate over 'coloured identity'. One night I was at a function where a group of coloured people fell into furious debate over an article (by a white writer) telling them to reaffirm the black side of their ancestry (apparently it's okay to dump on the white side), and there was our question: What is this thing called 'coloured identity'? Where is it pointed?

It took about seven seconds in the Adderley Street flower market to discover that the thing had a lot of bark. The flower ladies didn't need any second invitation. As soon as they heard we wanted to know how they felt about the unfolding South Africa, the vloekwoorde flew. There, and later when we took the same kind of dipstick readings in Athlone and Bellville and wherever, practically everybody came up with the one-liner that has become the ultimate cliché of coloured life in the new times. 'We used to be not white enough,' they said, 'and now we're not black enough.'

On paper it looks like a slogan. Hearing it over and over from a vast variety of mouths, it became a sadness. What I'd thought the great endeavour was all about, back in that past aeon of solemnly standing up for the verities of freedom, was creating a society where colour didn't count. Here in Athlone, in that selfsame Klipfontein Road where they had not merely stood up for the cause, they had flung bricks and spilt blood for it, was the last place you could say 'well congratulations on achieving a society where colour doesn't count'. They'd think you were making a cruel joke.

Not that they were themselves exactly colour-blind. Every second person had some caustic 'them' comment – *they* take our jobs, *they* piss in the street, *they* bring the crime. I suppose these two things feed on each other. The more the *they*, *they*, *they*, the more the resentment from the *them*, who resort the more keenly to numbers and political power to achieve their objectives, and who thereby get more of the *they* treatment.

The wide range of spokespeople we met – the academics and editors and politicians and priests and teachers – were a different story. I've never known so much or so real a wrestling with roles. And to think we'd thought the ethnic issues would fade away.

I felt we handled the coloured-identity thing with reasonable discretion and tact. However it wasn't finally a cerebral matter; it was an emotional one. It had certainly left me feeling emotional anyway, emotionally on the side of the people who feel themselves the jam in the sandwich.

A little later we went back to terrain which outwardly features similar people, the Karoo. I realised for the first time that although the people look the same and are called by the same name, they are really radically different communities – far more diverse than say the white English-speakers of

Gauteng and the white English-speakers of Natal or the Eastern Cape, who mainly differ by which rugby team they support and whether they pronounce i-words such as pin or ship with an ee, uh, or ur. The Karoo people are different people in a different world, in which they are clear majority, which gives them a certain psychological security, I suspect, but not a lot in the way of blankets, baths or toilet bowls.

A Karoo trip is so starkly scenic and inherently fascinating that you can't really mess it up even if you try. It's impossible to imagine how you can take a video camera to the Karoo and not come away with programme-worthy footage.

Unless, unless . . . unless you have no tape. We had, as always, plenty of tape – several hours in a part-used box and a whole extra box for five hours worth of insurance. We ran through our first few tapes at normal rate and picked up a nice range of Karooisms. There was the beautiful young Boerevrou in the marvellous oasis farmhouse that had been built on continuously since 1848. I said it must be a fantastic feeling to live in such a sense of continuity. 'You're joking,' she said. 'With the ghosts of seven generations of mother-in-law around me, I feel like a sinner if I want to as much as re-position a chair.'

There was the sad mayor of Victoria West, a Xhosa guy with no English, not much Afrikaans, and a big worry on his mind: 'When we were still fighting for our liberation,' he said, 'we believed that when we had power we would fix everything and make all our problems right.' He gazed wistfully away from his little general dealer store across to the excavations and the rusting half-installed pipes of a drainage project that had now been months on hold. 'But,' he said, 'now we have the power and nothing happens, because we spend all our time arguing with each other.'

There was the commercial traveller in a yarmulke, who had purposefully chosen the Karoo route because he had assigned himself to keeping check on the old Synagogues. They were all unused now, in the small dorps, and had become barns and warehouses and the like. He would visit where he could, and clean up, and do whatever possible to maintain respect.

There were the hopeful towns like, appropriately, Hopetown, experiencing property booms and a return from the city. There were currently crumbling towns like Britstown, where in the presence of the mayor a large group loudly insisted that stealing sheep was the only possible occupation for people such as them. There were virtually crumbled towns like Merriman, and pluperfectly pre-crumbled towns like Deelfontein, now reduced to masonry. (I'm sitting, in the cover picture, on the garden wall of Deelfontein's hotel.) At Deelfontein we met a coloured lady sheep farmer, who grazes her sheep entirely on the strips between the roads and the roadside fences. At Merriman we had a terrific argument with a local community leader about why the people were wrecking the station. The station building was a work of art, with mahogany beams and pressed steel ceilings and all, and was being trashed for target practice. Couldn't this be a kind of community centre, I asked? Well it could have been, he said, but now it was all messed up. At Merriman we also came across a heartfelt testimonial to the one and only local farmer who, in the view of the local peasantry, made an effort to help them with loans and with water and expertise. They sang this guy's praises until his ears must have been ringing, and I found it touching to see how much appreciation there could be for just one person in power who stoops to contribute, and how much difference one man's efforts could make.

All through the Karoo, we were also hearing about Vosburg. You must get to Vosburg, people said; don't miss it. I wasn't quite sure why we needed to get to Vosburg, but had the general impression that good things were happening there. We kept intending to get to Vosburg, but kept getting to elsewheres on the way. Then we discovered that our five hours of spare tape was not actually five hours after all. Somehow a mistaken set of tapes had got into the box, and our five hours had shrunk to little more than five minutes. Was it worth going all the way to yet another distant dorpie for a bare flash of the camera's eye? We debated. We went. I was glad we did. At Vosburg there is a Dr Vos, grandson or great- of the original Vos. Dr Vos was not around. He didn't need to be. Everybody told us about him. They told us how he had retired from some government job in Pretoria and had settled in Vosburg. Looking around, he had thought: 'This place has crumbled far enough, let's take it in hand.' So he had gone to one neighbour and said, Tannie Sarie, if you'll buy some paint I'll paint that barn for you, and then another neighbour and said, Swaer Fanus, I know you're short of cash but if I get you some cement would you be prepared to fix up that wall of yours, and so it went on until the whole town got into the spirit. The hotel jacked itself up. The police station won the national award for purtiest police station. The farmers were coming up with new marketing and promotions plans. In effect, through the efforts of a single individual a town's decline had stopped and turned around.

Five minutes of tape disappears awfully fast. You need pictures of the hotel and the police station and the neat kerbsides and all, and then we climbed the koppie overlooking the dorp from the west, with the sinking sun conveniently behind the camera. Perfect. I just had to tell the tale of Vosburg abnormally short and sharp and fluff-free.

I tried, and it was at least comprehensible. I hope it gave somebody somewhere some inspiration. It had certainly inspired me.

4

Gem Across the Limpopo

Some of our SABC colleagues were never altogether enthusiastic about us 'doing Africa', on the grounds that we'd be constantly coming back with bad news. Yep, this was a problem, but not necessarily a vitiating problem. Africa's vital statistics might look a little glum, but the statistics are not all of life. Everywhere we went in Africa we would find big hearts, which did not always outweigh the evidence of material disorder but did always offer at minimum a consolation.

In Zimbabwe there was much more than consolation. Given the constant doom-&-disaster depiction that prevails about their governmental affairs (and given that I, like awfully many South Africans, had not set foot north of Beit Bridge for decades), it was a large surprise to find a little gem of a nation tucked away on the other side of the Limpopo.

We didn't start off too well, with a good chunk of Third-World bullying at the border post. Richard had been capturing scenes and feel when an officious guard decided that this camera was taking liberties and confiscated the tape, which, if anybody ever got to look at it, would have been less than riveting. Richard did a neat sleight-of-hand and handed over a blank.

There could have been warmer welcomes, but from there on Zimbabwe offered large and surprising attractions. In Bulawayo, for one thing, I was astonished to find no shacks. Bulawayo looked like Joe Slovo's Dream – a place where everybody had a roof and water and electricity. With neat and orderly townships, and a grand classical city centre with the famous roads wide enough to turn a team of oxen and wagon, Bulawayo looked, felt and smelt to me like a pretty powerful success story.

Of course the images become dented with talk and enquiry, and it turns out for instance that there is huge local resentment that the city gets no newer, unlike Harare, which in the standard phrase of the average Ndebele resident 'swallows all the money'. A sense of Ndebele grievance is much more palpable than I had expected (after all, it is more than a decade since the Shona/Matabele contretemps was last news) and so is a sense of some desperation that the vast bulk of local earnings are remitted from Down South. I can appreciate the difficulties when fathers and husbands spend 50 weeks a year in another country in order to bring home the bacon, but the frequently expressed complaint that Bulawayo 'looks old' is a miscomplaint of monstrous proportions. Let Harare keep the cash, and at this rate Bulawayo will in not a long time become one of the world's great distinctive cities.

Bulawayo is old, anyway. Let alone that it looks old, it behaves old, and that is also not a bad thing. In the newspaper office I was astonished to hear a noise last heard in the South African equivalent some 30 years ago – the sound of, never mind typewriters, manual typewriters, with the kerclunk, kerchuuung of the hand shift at the end of the line. In the streets the central conveyance was not just bicycles but big old black steel Rudge bicycles, no less, with tinkling handbells and ornate shaft-linked brake cables. It might have been 1950, even down to clothing, which seemed not to have noticed the technicolour revolution of the last 30 years, to say nothing of the imprinted T-shirts of the last 20.

In one sense the old-fashioned feel is gentle on the eye. In another it is, it seems to me, an extremely major economic phenomenon. I go for example to a steelworks, which is employing hundreds of people to do the work for which your state-of-the-art Gauteng industrialist might use 40 locals and several million rands worth of German robotics. I know there's a flaw in the equation here, and that the Zim way of doing things is not stopping Zim's workers from flocking over the border. But there is more to it than just to say 'you see, you see', as if that is proof that everything has to be up-to-the-minute or else come short.

The steelworks isn't coming short, and its owner, a third-generation Rhodie, is doing fine; in fact extremely fine. He had his wobbly moments, he tells me, while some half or more of his white Rhodie compatriots were upping stakes and shipping out. Since they'd only been about the population of Benoni to start with, the holes in the social fabric were very visible. Now he's happy as a sandboy. He's at home, he's doing what he wants to do, he's making a good living, and he's bringing work and purpose and bread to the tables of several hundred families. You can't come and tell him that economics proves he can't exist; that he can't make out with labour-intensive employment practices and total disregard of modern technology. He does exist. He is making out. And he's making out a good sight better than if he laid off a hundred workmen in favour of a machine, and had them and their families turning to robbery.

We saw several Zim working-places in operation by the end (not all of which featured on screen). They all in several ways shared the same approach. They all did things which the laws of economics, as interpreted by the fashion of the 90s, prohibit. In one clothing factory we were stunned by the sight of a gigantic room filled with seamstresses (and whatever the male equivalent might be; there were plenty of men among them) sewing identical garments for the supermarket racks. At another, the accounts department looked like a scene out of Dickens: a supervisor at a high table at one end, and great ranks of (all male) clerks drawing up documents with pens. I'd have loved to say 'quill pens', which would have fitted the tableau, but the truth is they were mundane ballpoints.

At the same time our straw poll also showed the Zim bosses taking a common approach, not overly familiar to a South African eye, towards their staff. As they walked us through these time-warp scenes, there was constant greeting and exchanging of pleasantries. The managing director of the clothing company, a tall and forceful blonde lady, paused every five seconds to introduce us by name to anybody from a department manager to a guy with a broom. The steelworks proprietor came across someone using a blow-torch in some sort of wrong way, and he dealt with it without even noticing that we were noticing. No shouting at the erring workman; no yelling for some supervisor to come and get his hands dirty showing the right way. Just a quiet, almost unconscious, friendly greeting and moment of private demonstration.

I don't claim that our sight of working life in Zim was necessarily representative. I do say it was impressive. It was also a heck of a booster to a view I have often been beaten back from. I have argued to many South African employers that decent personal relationships mean as much for productivity and industrial peace as formal structures do, and have many times come short. On one occasion a very go-getting industrialist, now living abroad, shut me up with: 'Thank you. When I need socialist propaganda I'll call you.' Well, sir, thank you too, but it does strike me that if you'd brought a bit of ubuntu management into your business, along with your super-smart commercial calculations, fewer South

Africans might be dependent on charity today and your personal medical bills might be considerably lower.

In Harare, one could understand why the Bulawayans were griping about discrimination. Apart from the many large and classy new private buildings, there are many more even larger and classier new government buildings. Some of these, and especially the new Reserve Bank, are highly contentious, let alone in the eyes of the Bulawayans who are so miffed about not getting them, but in eyes everywhere that heads get scratched and brows get wrinkled over the thought: 'A building? For all those millions of dollars, which might have fed and schooled so many people for so long?'

I suppose this has to be a perpetual Third-World dilemma. Do you eradicate pomp and glory so as to cater for the bottomless pit of basics? Or do you spend on cathedrals and culture, on architects and trombonists, and hope to raise the people's sights?

When you have a Third-World city looking as good as Harare does, you see the benefits of the sights-raising argument. Harare, unlike Bulawayo, is full of squatter camps around the periphery, but the city centre is just as beautiful although in a totally different, modern way. It's not only the townscape, it's also the cleanliness.

The common South African explanation for why Zim is so free of the plastic litter that carpets our urban areas is that Zim doesn't have plastic packets that blow and flutter forever; it only has good old brown paper bags which obligingly disintegrate. That always seemed a logically sound explanation to me until we got to Zim and I discovered that it is factually nonsense, which is no doubt the core problem of a good deal of fine logic.

There are plenty of plastic bags. It's just that people put them into bins. It's 'the national culture', as one proud Zimbo said. The effect is certainly a relief, to the point that I'd love to send the South African population for the beginner's course. When you walk around Harare your head is held high. It's clean, it's nice, it's proud, so you keep it clean.

Which doesn't mean it's perfect. There is an endless wail of sirens, which of course is nothing new to Joburg citizens, but these are different sirens. The crime sirens are few and far between the pompous sirens, which deafen the city whenever Robert Mugabe is on his way to or from anywhere, or has a guest or guests which is apparently nearly always. We were in the offices of the Independent, Zim's fiercely maverick weekly newspaper, when the sirens came pompousing past and we had to hold proceedings until they had gone. We were talking to the editor, Trevor Ncube, who put in words what I believe is a common Zimbabwean perception of Zimbabwe: 'We're a fine country despite our government.'

Odd and sad, to look at that former Federation and its liberation heroes. Kaunda, Banda and Mugabe, who all walked on water until their promises withered and the arteries of their egos hardened. Now two down, and the remaining one has descended from On High to the level of a whipping-boy. The redeeming feature is that everyone says what they like about Mugabe, unworried about arrests or beatings or secret police. Indeed from the openness of the castigation in the market-places, they'd be much surprised if anybody were to put in a good word for him. At least there's a liberty about it, but it does not speak high of Africa's patterns of liberation.

What speaks a lot higher, funnily enough, is the whites still around Zim. I don't claim to have met a whole sample survey but those we did come across – several farmers, some shop-keepers, and residents of larnie suburbs like Borrowdale, in addition to the industrialists – were a great surprise.

South Africans have for decades been used to the idea that the really hairy racists were the Rhodesians. We were just in the little league. They had a whole vocabulary of their own for the subject, and attitudes that could make you puke. One knows of course that the old days are old, but you still expect a certain resonance, and I couldn't find it. Practically everybody says things are fine, you just get used to features like the telephone being out for a few days at a time, the water or lights being off for a few days at a time, and things are fine. Even in private and off camera, I was getting the same line. Funny how those who were once the most obdurate became the most willing. It's because they're so close, I suppose. Africa's easier to handle when you're looking at it from the inside, and can feel the subtle webs of joys and mysteries.

5

Can-Do

The Australia trip cost us a whack, despite the munificence of SAA. I don't want to even *think* of what the Lichinga trip cost.

Lichinga was my hang-up, less than avidly supported by my colleagues. Who the heck, they said, not without substance, cares a continental curse about some tuppeny Third-World dorpie that nobody ever heard of? I saw their point but I pushed my case nonetheless.

I was interested, for one. I was interested in Lichinga per se, in the way that I am interested in any place a million miles away from anywhere I've ever been, particularly places of the Southern African persuasion. But then, I don't by definition get to every such place. I was interested in Lichinga more than Kabwe or Ghanzi or Goedgegun or Cuito Cuanavale because it is one of six or eight staging-stations of a novel and gripping phenomenon, the Second Great Trek.

So I for once refused to succumb to the consolidated urgings of the sober heads associated with our own small trek, and the next step was that the valiant Michael Modena, production manager, started figuring out the logistics. Which, when the results emerged, caused wholesale gulping and reaching for the Betablockers.

As the crow flies, Lichinga is a couple of whiskers further than Cape Town. As the human being flies, it's forever. On the Lichinga route there is no obliging big-daddy SAA with a convenient quota of subsidised media tickets. The options were:

- Drive, meaning a minimum three or four days of actual movement plus incalculable heel-cooling at eight border posts. There's exit from SA, entry to Zim, exit from Zim, entry to Mozambique, exit from Moz, entry to Malawi, exit from Malawi, re-entry to Moz. By all accounts an average of two days taking the sun at each dusty control point is par for the course, and that is for upright citizens untainted by the possession of that baggage so alarming to the authoritarian mind, an obtrusive stock of video equipment. We could have been in for two months on the road, there and back, not counting the much warned-against potential of a bandit ambush on the last leg. Not attractive.

- Scheduled flight, meaning five hops, five changes of plane, assorted time-spans of heel-cooling at Maputo, Beira, Nampula, and Pemba, and an extreme lack of confidence in our equipment finally being disgorged alongside our persons at Lichinga airport.

- Charter.

I'm a Joburg boy born (well nearly) and bred. Where I come from it's a strange and unusual experience to hire a taxi. I know it's second nature to half the world, but in my corner of Joburg a taxi is a foreign object. Buses, yes. Combi taxis, a.k.a. black taxis, also increasingly yes, as a kind of alternative bus. But the metered taxi, when you tell the driver where to go and he is in effect your employee until you pay the fare . . . that's a way of life that never penetrated our primitive consciousnesses, and on the once-a-decade occasions where it somehow comes up your typical Joburg boy feels ill at ease and out of his depth. So what does it do to such a bumpkin when he's suddenly hiring an aeroplane? It gives him collywobbles, is what, particularly when the lady at the charter office casually quotes the fare. Gulp is hardly the word. 'If necessary,' she says, detecting a heart stoppage at the end of the phone line, 'we could possibly arrange a flight at a few thousand rands less, but that's a single engine and it flies lower and takes ten hours instead of six and it gets a bit bumpy and you might not feel too good for a while afterwards and we don't recommend it over northern Mozambique because when the bandits take pot-shots you can get a bullet coming through the fuselage.'

So a week and a moderate fortune later we're on the twin engine to Lichinga, which, if you were wondering, is the capital of Mozambique's second most northerly province, Niassa, on the east side of Lake Malawi (which remains Lake Niassa in Mozambique's vocabulary).

Niassa is about twice the size of today's Gauteng or half the size of yesterday's Transvaal, and its flavour is summed up in a sentence from Mike Slater's Guide to Mozambique: 'If you own a four-wheel-drive and like to get away from other overlanders, Niassa is the place for you.' Met ander woorde it is, in the good Seffrican phrase, t'hellangorn. Slater also provided us with handy forewarnings as to the circumstances of the capital city. The power station is 'fired up from seven until ten every evening, after which it is very dark', and 'the hotel has no running water, its food is all right if you like eggs and potatoes'. The Trek had known its moments of five-star living. It did not need Sherlock Holmes, or even Inspector Clouseau, to detect that this episode was not to be among them.

Getting there from Lanseria was only marginally more problematic than it needed to be. We had to check in at Beira,

Mozambique's sole legal port of entry north of Maputo. Our pilot, Brad, had already become stupendously agitated en route when it turned out that he'd understood we'd be back by Saturday, which was his birthday and the night allocated for the biggest bash he'd ever thrown. We'd made it pretty clear, we thought, that the return trip would be Sunday night. This was Wednesday. The poor fellow was about to spend half a week with his bloodstream frozen over in contemplation of friends from far and wide hammering at his distant door, while he sent futile telepathic apologies from a lonely Lichinga night.

The nearer we drew to Beira the jumpier he got. To add to his woes he was developing a growing dread of his imminent welcome. This was not, after all, a respectable cargo such as medics or aid agencies or horsethieves that he was carrying. This was *journalists* – a commodity, he insisted, which the Beira passport ouens would view in the same light as heroin or high explosives or rabid Aids-infested monkeys. Iron bars clanged shut in his mind's ear.

At the start he had not been at all jittery. Like everyone, or at any rate everyone in South Africa, he was picturing TV as a nice kosher thing. Television is fine, television is okay, television equals entertainment, soapies and so forth, nothing unwholesome. But since then there had been a few hours of flitting over the African veld, with snoozing and reading and talking (for a landlubber attuned to staying alert at the steering wheel, it's astonishing to see pilots hibernate through the long straight stretches). What we talked about was inter alia what we were about to be doing, and I could see the warning lights flickering into his cranium as ol' Brad homed in on the conclusion that our business was not to take pictures of game parks but to ask questions, nasty if possible. This, he made it increasingly clear, was not an activity that the bureaucrats of Beira would smile upon.

In vain did I claim that the new-and-improved 90s world,

no longer stuffed with KGBs and Special Branches and Stasis, had put these childish things behind it. No ways, he said. I could read theories in books all I liked, but he was the oke who knew Beira airport and he could tell me for sure that *they* hadn't been reading those books.

Trying to mollify the guy, I reassured him that all was kosher: no less a personage than The Governor had not only ratified our visit but was indeed awaiting us in person. It didn't help at all. Quite the opposite. He expostulated: 'That's the governor of *Niassa*! These guys this side despise the authorities up north! Whatever you do don't try to use the governor of Niassa to twist arms in Beira!'

By the time we made ready for the Beira approach, we had all put each other into a state of nerves. Then nature snapped her fingers to show us who was boss. We were over the Pungwe river and marvelling that a southern African river we'd never heard of could make all the household-name South African rivers look like the product of leaking taps, when Mother Africa flung us a salutary snap storm. One minute the plane felt big and strong and First-World and triumphant. The next minute it was a moth in a waterfall, a bagatelle, bobbing about the sky like a soap-bubble. Legalities and earthly trivia withered to oblivion. For once the phrase 'white men' was entirely accurate. Our complexions could have done pride to a washing-powder advertisement. By the time we drew up alongside the Beira control tower, the storm having died as suddenly as it was born, hearts slowly regravitating from boots to chests, the terrors that mere man might inflict upon us had become laughably puny.

In suitable confidence, thus, we sallied forth to the rubber-stamp domain, and it turned out that the spirit of the deregulated 90s had penetrated Beira to an extent even beyond what I had hoped for. Cameras, shmameras. Who cared? Who, for that matter, noticed? No problem. We completed the technicalities under a huge map showing 'Bechuanaland' and 'Nyasaland'. Refuelled and buoyant we buckled up for the last leg to Lichinga and were firing up the engines when an official came running across the tarmac waving papers: Stop, senhores, your plane has no permit.

I was for taking off regardless. We could be in the air in two minutes, with empty skies ahead, a 100% certainty that no RPG rockets were in a state to shoot us down, and a 99% likelihood that nobody would bother to have the gendarmerie accost us at Lichinga. Brad very sensibly said no, and when I thought about it afterwards, such as at the time of the September '97 mid-air collision in the even emptier skies off the Skeleton Coast, I felt ashamed of having tried to persuade him. So it was off with the engines, unclasp the seat-belts, and into the tower to humbly await the pleasure of Senhor Roculdo, the person laughingly alleged to be 'in charge'.

The flight had been permitted for a particular plane, ZS-MXC. The plane we were in was ZS-MXT. Had there been some transliteration somewhere? Mike Xray Charlie had turned into Mike Xray Tango by some slip of pen or tongue or linguistics? Or was it that a change of arrangements back at Lanseria had been inadequately communicated to Beira? Senhor Roculdo had noticed, give him credit, but for reasons and explanations he cared not a whit. His interest in the logic of the issue was on the same level as his interest in the geology of the Ukraine steppes. All he needed was the say-so of Dr Xualo, the Director of Civil Aviation in Maputo, or his deputy Mr Dalphin de Deus. Whom we were welcome to phone, from the call box at the post office.

And who were both absent. So there was a whirligig of phoning, of scurrying between post office and control tower, of alternate bouts of indignation and pleading, and of Brad's spirits sinking through his kidneys along with his residual hopes of making it to his party.

After a couple of hours Brad's fuse blew, and he let loose a tirade of you-people abuse. You people have no idea what you're doing. You people couldn't run a piss-up in a brewery. You people couldn't organise your way out of a paper bag. You people . . .

Senhor Roculdo responded to Brad's tirade the same way he responded to my rather humbler avenue of enquiry: with total impassivity. Which is to say he obviously had not the faintest idea what to do, and having no idea, did nothing. On the one hand this was a fairly despair-worthy approach to public service, and yet another of those perennially depressing whither-Africa features. And yet, and yet . . . it seems to me that 20 years ago one was used to nearly as much ineptitude from Western civil services as one is from African civil services now. Certainly, in my youth I would expect total boorish obduracy from the average white mini-despot, Afrikaans or English, and that is a thing you now barely meet. Those same guys' sons and even younger brothers have developed a tradition of applying kop and using sav and solving problems and generally figuring out how to put a brand of bureaucratic 'e' on the end of 'human'. If they could come right(ish) in a generation, maybe when Senhor Roculdo's son is manning the control tower sometime in the early 21st century, he'll do it too. Maybe he'll even get a new map.

Also there was this strange thing: no bribes. No hint, even, that a bribe might expedite our progress. At any rate, no hint that I could see. I concede that I may not be the world's most astute bribe-detector. I've never paid a bribe in my life and wouldn't know how to go about it. In South Africa, when people insist that you can't get phones installed, passports granted, fines lifted, etc, without paying bribes, I have no hesitation in saying: nonsense. I've had plenty of phones installed and passports granted. I've also over the years had plenty of fines lifted, or anyway not imposed, by the simple expedient of being purely polite to the traffic cop, and I am confident of my ground when I state that the allegations of rampant bribery are just another of the many areas of conventional overstatement of South Africa's ills. But this was Mozambique, where everybody tells you all the time that bribery is as entrenched a way of life as breathing, and I myself do not know the ropes well enough to rebut the conventional wisdom. So I hesitate to shout the odds.

What I do say, though, is that throughout the whole long argy-bargy with Senhor Roculdo and his assorted minions, no back-pocket money changed hands. If anybody was thinking that it ought to, they kept their thoughts too subtle for the naked eye.

So there was one plus and one minus in the affaire Roculdo. The ineptitude was worse than you might have thought, the corruptibility quotient was better. On the face of it, a stand-off, six of one and a half-dozen of the other, except that for me personally that didn't adequately reflect it. Whereas the ideal would be a society where officials could make decisions as well as a society where they made their decisions honestly, if I had to choose one or the other I'd rather have the honesty than the eptitude. So I was feeling overall quite good about Roculdo's honest incapacity, at least until he suddenly disappeared.

We had arrived at about ten in the morning. Over the next few hours we represented about 98% of the reason why Senhor Roculdo and some 25 other airport employees had a job. Only one other plane arrived, bearing an amiable Hollander who was the accountant for an international aid agency and was paying his employees. He was miffed that he had to lug the wage-packets around the country himself, using a plane at a price he would have rather put into medicines or foodstuffs, but this was the only way to get wages into the pockets of the workers instead of the pockets of intercepting bandits. His plane suffered from no registration irregularities, and was processed in and out in no time.

For the rest, the airport's entire business was ZS-MXT, and you might have thought that even if they didn't know what to do with us they would have given us the benefit of their time. In which case, you're wrong. We were evidently invisible until we actually blocked people's paths. Come 12 o'clock, Senhor Roculdo vanished, without as much as a goodbye or a see-you-later. We thought he was going to the loo. In fact he had gone for lunch, two and a half hours of lunch. Siesta time, to be observed to the letter regardless of the needs of the customers.

By the time he got back I was ready to kill, but waddayaknow, somehow, magically, despite Messrs Xualo and De Deus being no less absent than ever, something had changed, and we were waved on our way. This was no time to pause and ask for reasons. Even less to discuss the meaning of the term 'civil' in the concept 'civil service'. We split.

Late afternoon we descended to Lichinga airfield, which, but for a classy 4x4 parked at the side of the runway with two white children playing next to it, was deserted. As we pulled up the vehicle got into gear and drew up neatly behind our wing, disgorging a surreally tall elegant lady in a long white dress who looked like she might have been Glenda Jackson's sister, playing a role such as the Duchess of Lancaster. The effect was slightly dented when she greeted us in a rresounding Afrrikaans intorrnation, but we soon learned that it wasn't all wrong. Molly Fullard would make a pretty fine Duchess of Lichinga.

* * *

Lichinga is at one and the same time both very exciting and very depressing. The story of Africa. The excitement began with the African residential area. Of course, the whole town is

African residential area now, but the central bit is very visibly bequeathed from the Portuguese. It was the *African* African residential areas that got to my sociological G-spot, and particularly the newer ones.

In South Africa, new African residential areas can make you weep. They consist of 2 parts formal housing developments to 98 parts informal squatter developments. The formal is, with some exceptions, bland and barren and starkly functional, and so devoid of individuality that after two beers on the way home you can wander into a neighbour's yard by mistake. While the uniformity might, for all I know, be a middle-class perception unshared by the residents, who at least are acquiring water and toilets and electricity and brick walls, as a rule the building work is done in a frantic rush and with maximum cost-cutting and under inordinate pressure for numbers of houses to tick off on the 'delivery' balance sheet. If they fall down tomorrow morning, the guys compiling the PR statistics don't need to know.

The informal is, also with some exceptions, higgledy-piggledy squalid chaos. The roads are skinny impassable urine-soaked mudpaths and the dwellings are desperate lean-tos made of cardboard and purloined scraps of roadsign and corrugated iron.

The exceptions, it is true, are not to be forgotten. Aside from the actual outright class of suburbs like Diepkloof Extension, there are places where the sub-economic houses hit a kind of jackpot and there are also places where squatterland is orderly and controlled and encouraging. But the overall impact is the fearsome image of 'proper' African accommodation being both barely liveable and also increasingly eclipsed by the spread of the cardboard and tin alternative.

In Lichinga there was something else: picture-book little village-suburbs scattered around the town filled with houses neither 'formal' nor 'informal' but an attractive synthesis that defies either classification. The streets are straight and wide. The dwellings are essentially made of wood and reed and the produce of the soil, and while this may be not so much by aesthetic choice as because Lichinga radically lacks the detritus of a manufacturing economy with its junkyards and scrap-heaps, the effect is an idyllic contrast with the SA pattern.

I call them dwellings because it's hard to know what else. 'House' is misleading, carrying connotations of doorbells and garden gates, but 'shacks' would be plain wrong and so would 'huts'. 'Huts' makes you picture the dung-and-dagha kraals that still cover such rustic corners of South Africa as have not yet been overtaken by shacks. Lichinga's dwellings are a good deal larger, in terms of cubic metres per interior, and what is more they are urban and they are new. Not many people are putting up *new* traditional-style huts in South Africa. They're doing the formal thing if they can afford it and the shacks if they can't. In Lichinga the newest structures have the nicest blend of old and new – African basis with bits of western technique. They have thatched stoeps and branches for pillars, and although they are fundamentally similar there was definitely no central architect. They are thoroughly individual within their similarities.

I felt oddly like some pioneer of virgin Africa, a Burton or Speke or Livingstone, walking through the suburbs of Lichinga. In one way these places belonged in the 19th century. In another, they held out a profound spark of hope for the 21st.

If you look at the urbanising face of South Africa today you are apt to acquire a furrow in the brow. The vaunted promises of X million houses by the year such-and-such, Y million by some other time, are way out of court. All one can envisage is squatterland everywhere, freezing the genial current of the soul. Look then at Lichinga, and wonder.

Could it be that a new direction may lie ahead, a real renaissance, African style? Could it be that black South Africa could adopt this kind of practical return to roots, and find a contentment and a pride in the creation of an African way of modern living? Even if possible in principle, and that's a long shot already, how might it be led and initiated? By who? That's even longer.

In Lichinga, ironically, this renaissance was caused by war and driven by, of all forces, Renamo. On its home ground Renamo is not perceived as the wicked ogre that our reading tells us it is, or was, but as a kind of people's movement, followed as automatically and instinctively as the Soweto citizen follows the ANC or the Tugela peasant follows Inkatha. Both the fact that the new dwellings exist and the orderliness in which they exist is due to Renamo having resettled rural people in the town during the war years. But if this part of Africa could achieve a desirable by-product from an unfortunate cause, surely others can replicate the by-product without suffering the cause.

Lichinga's homesteads left me conscious that inspiration is at hand, and re-invigorated in the belief that the continent has things to show us. It is not just a matter of we the big powerful industrial southern tip leading the way for the benighted to follow. There's reciprocation to be had, and a long way yet to grow into joint appreciation of African solutions.

For the rest, Lichinga was pretty much all downside. For 20 years the place has languished. Not a cable has been laid, a phone installed, a wall painted, never mind a factory built. The only visible development, aside from those distinctive homes, was a memorial to Samora Machel. The memorial was designed as a series of brick and concrete pillars into which were laid various items of wreckage from the plane in which the fatal crash took place. Now, every one of the memorabilia has been wrested away, and there are only barren scarred pillars with indentations where they were.

The one and only public petrol station is closed and its pumps are rusted. The one and only mechanic, a Portuguese, faces the Herculean task of keeping the government buses on the road against the obstacles of minimal parts and minimal tools. That there are far more ruined and rotting buses in his yard than one ever sees mobile buses on the road suggests that he is having less than Herculean success.

Two doctors, a Nigerian and a Russian, man a decrepit hospital. The Portuguese general dealer says he set out during the war to deal with scrupulous even-handedness – humanitarian help to both sides, no spying or partisanship on behalf of either. Somebody doesn't agree. Soon after the war he received a parcel in the post. It blew his arms off. The other general dealer, an Indian, is at the centre of a storm of local opprobrium over the lavishness of his daughter's wedding. Following a mysterious internal dispute the electricity department has cut off the water department's electricity and the water department has cut off the electricity department's water, which may have a bearing on the Through-the-Looking-Glass supply of both utilities to the rest of the town. The hotel still has no running water anyway, although its geysers hang forlornly from the ceilings in painful testimony to the lost modernity of some previous age. I will say, though, that once one gets the hang of flushing the loo by tipping a bucket into the bowl, it's no hardship. And mastering the art of a tipping the big bucket into the small bucket and using the small bucket as a shower adds a dash of interesting spice to the perpetual learning of life.

There were redeeming features all right. One of them was to sit under the warm evening trees of the beer garden, amiably supplied with the ubiquitous and sometimes cold 2M beer (the product of SA Breweries' Mozambique subsidiary, tasting a lot like Castle in a different can) and unnameable and sometimes hot meatstuffs. Although we could identify our dinners neither by menu nor by the eating, the stomach was not complaining. The market was in its way a redeeming feature too. Over my deceased white western bourgeois corpse would I willingly ingest the produce of this fly-ridden, gob-spattered health inspector's nightmare, or so I thought until I fell to wondering where the hotel's unnameables came from, but it was redeeming nonetheless because it was packed and busy and bustling and, we were told, ten times as active as it had been two years ago – an embryo of an economy on the up.

The reason we were in Lichinga at all was that a couple of weeks previously we'd been in Maputo. Maputo was in many senses in exactly the same position. It, too, looked to the naked South African eye like a wasteland, but it, too, was full of people who said: 'Wasteland, forget it! Two years ago we were a wasteland. Now we're coming right.' And indeed, closer scrutiny showed ways in which Maputo was coming right. There was paint where there had been none before, such as on the grand old railway station recently restored to glory. There was activity where there had been none before, such as in the restaurant precinct on the Marginale, and the one-time red-light-cum-prawn district much beloved as a South African holiday destination before the revolution, subsequently derelict for two decades and now with the shutters turning into shopfronts.

To be sure, Maputo had a horrendously long way to go. Concretely, any place where a major industry is the theft-deterring welding of iron cages around vehicle headlights, indicators and wing mirrors has a long way to go. Symbolically, one could have difficulty betting on a city whose every major street remains named after the heroes of the most disastrous philosophy of mankind's history – the Avenidas Karl Marx,

Mao Tse-tung, Vladimir Lenin, etc. The harbour, whose wharves are firewood and cranes are scrapmetal and water is littered with half-sunken wrecks, handles, its manager tells me, less tonnage per year than its brash young rival Richard's Bay handles per day. The city's roads have pot-holes that could break a neck, never mind a leg, and the distinctive Portuguese metal drain-covers have largely disappeared, leaving trenches that would challenge a tank and causing ordinary vehicles to routinely climb the pavements. Currently the missing strips are being replaced – by poured concrete, which makes the roads passable but the drains useless. Maputo has far to go, but it's pointing in the right direction.

I couldn't get to grips with how much or how little of the mess was to be ascribed to the war. Maputans didn't help much, often treating the war as materially less of a factor – and/or excuse – than I had expected.

With one fellow – a businessman, son of the first president of Angola, Agostinho Neto – I had a gripping exchange. He was going on about restoration and repair and the pains of coming to terms with the fallacies of your own previous positions – his mother was Mozambican and he'd fought the revolution both for Frelimo in Mozambique and for the MPLA in Angola.

After a while I said: 'Look, I appreciate all this honesty and introspection, but I don't understand why you don't take the easy out. Blame me. I'm the white South African whose taxes blew up half your bridges and heaven knows what else.'

He shrugged: 'Ah, you guys were bit players. We actually did the main damage ourselves. However, if you want to make reparations there is certainly something you can do.'

I said: 'Okay. What?'

He said: 'Send us your Boers.'

Send us your Boers. It was a thunderclap, coming from a guy whose life's work had once been to shoot Boers. Of course

I got him to redo the exchange with the camera running, and as usual the second version didn't come half as crisp as the first. But the phrase kept echoing, especially when I found more and more supportive echoes coming from other Mozambicans – editors and government guys and all. Clearly there was a radically different view of these matters in Mozambique to the one which was increasingly emerging in South Africa, where the dreaded white males in general and white Afrikaans males in particular were treated as an unfortunate feature of nature's shortcomings, like mosquitoes or black wattle, to be dispensed with where possible.

In Maputo itself we saw plenty of evidence of the changing ethos, nowhere more than when we called at the mill, a towering cavernous building about nine storeys high and effectively the headquarters of the country's productive capacity, from which we wanted to take a bird's-eye shot of the industrial area. We asked for the managing director, and after a longish delay a burly young white man came bustling along the corridor, holding out his hand to say: 'Sonnekus. Aangename kennis.'

Mr Sonnekus took us for a tour of his domain and explained that the mill had 19 separate functions. Over the first 19 years of liberation these functions had ground one by one to a halt until for the twentieth year the staff's sole job had been to clock in, and eight hours later clock out again. Then a South African firm had taken over and in its first ten months had restored nine functions. The others, he reckoned, would be up and running within another year.

As we walked – and climbed, the lifts had not been blessed with priority attention – Sonnekus introduced us to various of his lieutenants – Coetzee, Van Schalkwyk, Nel; we might as well have been in Lichtenburg. I asked what had happened to the previous management team. 'They're all still around,' said Sonnekus, 'just that they're doing different jobs now.'

Everybody had been demoted several ranks – from managing director to head of the transport department, from deputy MD to supervisor of maize quality, and so on. Sonnekus firmly maintained that the ex-directors liked the new deal and were adamant that these were the levels of responsibility they should have been employed at all along. I would have liked to know whether this was exactly what they said when they were in full spate of free talk. I didn't get to speak to any of them. But whatever they would say there was clearly something enormous – and something problematic – in the turnaround and how it happened.

We met further fortifying evidence elsewhere in Maputo, and we also met a huge amount of reference to a related phenomenon on the go in the north, a phenomenon everybody called Mosagrius, by which Afrikaans farmers were being settled on Mozambican land, and the funny darn thing was that in all these references nobody laughed.

In South Africa, by contrast, everybody laughed. And nobody had heard of Mosagrius (an acronym for the Portuguese of 'Mozambique South Africa Agricultural Co-operation Project'). In South Africa, people had heard of what some called the Second Great Trek and most simply dismissed as an impossibly hare-brained scheme involving displaced Boers moving in on central Africa, and either way they laughed like drains. Me too, to start with.

Intrigued by the very different responses in Mozambique, when we got home I did a little enquiry into Mosagrius and related developments. It turned out there were several of these, bearing startling similarities to the original 1838 Great Trek right down to the fact that the Boere involved were squabbling like wildcats over where to go and how, and under whose auspices. The biggest, it seemed, was a project spearheaded by the Landbou-unie.

We went to see the officer in charge, Dr Chris Jordaan, at

the Landbou-unie offices in Pretoria. Assuming, like I dare say most South Africans, that there was something vaguely right-wing and conspiratorial about this, I expected Chris to be guarded and tight and off-putting. And was entirely wrong on all counts. He was as expansive as could be, and warmly welcoming. Things still seemed all wrong nonetheless. The Boers muscling in on Central Africa . . . crazy. Politically impossible, personally impossible, structurally impossible, economically impossible.

Chris and I talked in an office, under a huge map of Africa. Early on, while I was wondering whether these guys had been smoking wild mushrooms or were just born deluded, Chris suddenly stood up and turned to the map, and drew a huge swathe with thumb and forefinger through Africa's midriff from west coast to east, incorporating great stretches of Angola, Zaire (as it was), Zambia, Malawi, Mozambique and Tanzania.

'In 30 years,' he said, histrionically, 'this will be Boer farmland.'

Egad, I thought, for arrogance this guy gets A+.

Chris looked me calmly and unabashed in the eye as he sat down again, and said 'And it will be feeding Africa.'

I gulped and began to wonder a different wonder. What else, after all, was going to be feeding Africa? The Red Cross? Millions of hardscrabble subsistence farmers eking precarious existences from ever shrinking hillside patches? And of all the hare-brained impossibilities, which had not been present when Messrs Pretorius and Trichardt and Potgieter & Co opsaaled in the Cape in 1838 and pointed the oxen northwards?

We went off with Chris to the nearby Pretoria Botanical Gardens to talk on camera with a bit of visual background. Chris was, rarely, nearly as frank on camera as off about the problems and obstacles, and the smallness of what was happening compared to the largeness of what was intended.

So far his project consisted of exploratory mini-migrations of farmers by the one and two, all embattled, all struggling, some packing in. In particular, he said, two had just gone up to northern Mozambique. Jan Pelser and D C Bredenkamp had set up in a barn not far from Lichinga.

That's why we got to Lichinga. That's how we met the estimable Molly Fullard.

Molly was a living inspiration. A Boerevrou van die Republiek af, finding herself in this unlikely corner of the sub-continent as a result of her husband's work with a Christian agency, she had learned Portuguese in no time and in no time later had won the town's heart. The governor – who told us in unequivocal terms that the Boer arrival was the best thing Niassa could have asked for – treated her like a cross between chief lieutenant and elder statesman. To the peasant multitudes she was Joan of Arc combined with the Pied Piper of Hamelin. They flowed in her footsteps like a giant sweeping gown, politely claiming her ear at every opportunity – 'por favor, Donna Maria, por favor' – to ask for advice or guidance or, especially, for her to put their names down for the awaited explosion of employment with the Boers. Even to the NGO fraternity, to their own great surprise, she was a communal centrepin.

Lichinga was thick with NGOs, leading to some fascinating results such as the sight on the roads. There is a rank order of vehicle ages around Southern Africa. On Jan Smuts avenue in Johannesburg the average age might be three or four years. On the N2 coming into Cape Town, at least double that. Get to, say, the Hammanskraal road to Pretoria and you can add another five years. By the time you reach Lusaka or Maputo, the median is deep into the twenties. By this criterion one might expect as distant a dorp as Lichinga to be populated by Model Ts. Wro-o-ng! Most of the cars in town are barely out of the box, which is because most of the cars in town belong to the aid agencies. So the roads are divided between swarms of bicycles or mopeds and an aristocracy of new 4x4s bearing Swedes and Americans and Brits and Germans behind the logos of the western world's Development Set.

The Development Set is an inherently lefty institution, and while I deeply respect the lefties who for the betterment of mankind forsake the tennis clubs of Hampstead I have also noted that they tend to be a dauntingly judgemental bunch, at least towards whites. If you're white and non-lefty or, worse, wrongly lefty, expect long looks, but if you're an Afrikaner and non-lefty, expect acid. This is the only time the development mob are allowed to get racist.

We met a few development types around Lichinga. One lady flatly refused to talk to us, even as much as to say 'go away'. She shook her head with lips sealed; we were after all the notorious White South Africans upon whose villainies she had cut her developmental teeth. Some of the others were less radical but did seem to feel the need to pinch their noses. Most, however, were relaxed and refreshingly human, and an interesting picture emerged.

At first, we gathered, the NGO fraternity had mainly looked upon Molly as merely a bit of an outsider. But by personality and workhorseship she graduated into acceptance and indeed to become what someone termed 'de facto mayor of the expats'. So far so good. Then word got around that a Boer invasion was about to begin, sponsored by the Freedom Front, an Afrikaner political body that had been in right-wing opposition even in the days of the old apartheid government. Batten the hatches! Then – betrayal! – it emerged that Molly was to be the Hon Secretary and Liaison Officer for the invaders. The Third Boer War loomed large in Lichinga.

It didn't last, at least not for everybody. A landmine removal guy put it nicely: 'For the first couple of weeks we tried to pretend this was New York, that we could pass them in the street and not notice. But they kept on politely greeting us and we got to feel ridiculous. Then one of the Boers fixed somebody's motorbike, and since then we've all been finding excuses to drop in.' Another fellow, in agricultural education, said: 'The real reason some people have difficulty with the Boers is that deep down we know we aren't leaving ripples. We come here with noble intentions, and six months after we hand over the keys our projects will have fallen flat. The Boers come with selfish intentions, and the result will be ploughed fields.'

By the time we met Jan Pelser and D C Bredenkamp we'd had enough build-up, not least from the governor, to expect them to be 8 feet tall at least, and preferably on white horses. The reality was a Toyota bakkie, and a Laurel and Hardy duo. Jan is tall and scrawny, DC is short and burly. Both make jokes all the time.

And like any farmers, I suppose, they aren't shy to tell you how ruined things were before they arrived, and how un-ruined things are becoming now that they're there.

They had a case, one has to say. They arrived at their farm on a Friday night – late, dark, can't see nuttin', they're ushered to mattresses in a barn. Saturday morning they sally forth to find themselves in the middle of a forest of ruined machinery. They estimated R50 000 000 as a round figure for what the stuff might cost if you bought it new now. I suppose they exaggerated. People do. But no matter how much exaggeration, there was also much equipment – hundreds of items ranging from huge combine harvesters to modest tractors and ploughs. Much of it had never been used, as was demonstrated by the manufacturers' protective plastic wrappings still in place – as I saw myself when I was there a month later – on the blades. Most of it was kaput. The tyres were perished – the treads still virgin but the sidewalls gone. The metal was rusted. Even the merest layman's eye, e.g. mine, could see beyond doubt that very little of this cornucopia of machinery was ever going to move again, except conceivably one day on a scrapyard's trailer. Nearly all of it was German – the engines had Zundfolge orders stamped on the blocks – and had evidently been donated to Frelimo by East Germany in a display of comradely solidarity sometime in the late 70s.

That Saturday morning the Boers went through it and came across a bulldozer in repairable condition. By nightfall it was repaired. Sunday for God-fearing Calvinists being prayer day it lay in peace for the most eager 24 of the total 170 000-odd hours of its long rest. Monday, the Boers made a road.

That story summed up the nub of what seemed to be going on here. A can-do element had been injected into a can't-do place, and the implications were large. Jan and DC told the tale in a distinctly chest-beating way, treating themselves pretty much like the arrival of the US Cavalry in a John Wayne movie. Others however, including the very straight-spoken Governor Boniface and several somewhat nose-out-of-joint NGO people, corroborated the basics.

With the surrounding peasantry, whose views on these matters I would much like to have heard, I did not have means of communication. The good Molly was not with us in most of the rural interludes, and even if she had been I doubt we would have got much further. While we on this side of the border picture Mozambique as Portuguese-speaking, in the hayseed areas and especially the isolated northern ones this is less correct than picturing places like Msinga or O'okiep or Sekhukhuniland as English-speaking. They might have English on their signboards and English on their screens, insofar as screens penetrate their world, but they have not a lot of English on their tongues.

Mozambique has ten major vernaculars and numerous lesser ones, and although Molly is, of course, getting stuck in to the local lingos she has a way to go before the point of interpreting sensitive matters of socio-political perspective. Jan and DC relied upon the translation services of an aide – English-vernacular direct – and it was clear that this process barely kept up even with their single-syllable lift-that-barge, tote-that-bale brand of discourse.

So I'm not claiming expert status or in-depth insight. In the months since the trip I've seen a steadily growing flow of reportage that seems very categorical and confident, and since it is nearly all critical if not plain mocking I begin to wonder if I saw things crookedly. I also wonder, though, how the invariably western authors managed to ride so well over the communication obstacles I faced, and there are times I suspect that a totality of the truth might have evaded more eyes than merely my own. A caustic August '97 article on the Lichinga Boers asserts, for example, that 'they only come to the village to buy goats . . . They don't get out of the car . . . they beckon, pay and go, their feet never touch our soil and their skin never touches ours', which neatly strikes the desired note of obnoxiousness but also rings a touch improbable. There can be few white men on the planet who have closer physical contact with black men than the working plaasboer, and having seen Jan and DC at work with their labourers I somehow doubt that they suffer any especial anguish about setting foot on village soil.

Still, Great Trek II is a troublesome phenomenon. For one thing, there is a certain pain in the sight of Mozambique saying in effect 'Sorry, we stuffed up our revolution, now we need whites again.' For another there is a huge level of gross over-expectation, with the Boers being treated as the next best thing to the Second Coming and reposed with hopes that can never be fulfilled.

Jan and DC were categorical about the wishfulness of much of the Mosagrius thinking. Mosagrius was attested by Presidents Mandela and Chissano in some elegant panelled presidential office a long way from the soil of Niassa. Each arriving Boer is supposed, for example, to guide and assist a satellite colony of small farms set up around his perimeter by members of the Niassa Farmers' Union. One difficulty: there are only five members of the Niassa Farmers' Union, four of whom are bottlestore owners doing little if any actual farming.

Nor did the Boers see their role in the world as apostles of liberal non-racialism. On the contrary they were just as categorical about their adherence to the basic old conservative world-view: we're white, they're black, and although the twain may be properly respectful and mutually co-operative they are very damn definitely never to merge. DC was adamant that this was precisely why they were wanted in Mozambique: 'We don't fool with the men and we don't fool with their women.'

At the same time the Boers brought with them an employment outlook that would have fitted fine into the Free State in 1950. When I picked Jan out over the way he'd conducted a briefing of a tractor driver – all brusque command with not a ghost of a chance for the driver to raise any thoughts he might have had on the matter – Jan was sublimely unabashed. That's the way a farm works, he said. You don't consult, you tell. That's why in less than a month there was more development here than there'd been for 20 lost years.

The material evidence was on his side, but the attitude offended my grain nonetheless. I can get sold on the idea that the Boer presence will make groundnuts grow where they have not grown before and tills click where they would not have clicked otherwise. In fact I'll here and now take bets that in 50 years' time this current funny little migration will be generally perceived as vastly more important than that other funny little migration, 160 years earlier, which created South Africa as we know it. But I can't accept that it simply ends up replaying the last century on more northerly territory. There has to be real reward in it for the guys at the bottom of the social pile – reward that takes life beyond sheer body-and-soul survival, reward that generates its own momentum. I get the feeling that the Landbou-unie could usefully install a supercharger in its human-relations seminars.

The day we were leaving Lichinga we encountered a strange sight. Lumbering into town, swaying and reeling on a road best suited to a pushbike, was a 30-ton truck. Behind it, a mini-procession of caravans and bakkies.

This was the next contingent, of whom I don't believe anyone was less than 65 years old. They'd been 14 days on the road, each driver alone in his vehicle, using crackling short-distance radios to keep each other awake. Oom Alwyn, in the truck, told me that his gross vehicle mass was in fact 44 tons, nearly 50% overladen. He didn't know whether he'd prayed harder in South Africa, where a spot check at a weighbridge would have put paid to his safari, or after South Africa, where while crossing any of the numerous bridges he might have become a sad statistic. One of his items of cargo was a green corrugated-iron shed, loaded on the truck like a sentry post. He displayed the equipment inside, and it is not a great exaggeration to suggest that with the contents of his shed he might have doubled the total quantity of power tools in the province of Niassa. His giant generator, alongside the shed, might have done the same for the power output.

Why were they there? Why were any of them there, Jan and DC too? There must be a vast range of personal background circumstances of which some doubtless spoke to the failures, financial, marital or other, which the sceptics are quick to assume. However, they certainly did not all speak of collapse. One of the newcoming couples had left their Bothaville farm to a son. Their dowager cottage was still there, still theirs, an insurance policy to which they could return anytime, but they chose to do something more challenging with their retirement than drink coffee on their stoep. DC was a qualified accountant, but felt the yen to explore. He waxed eloquent on his future plans, which involved the early reunification of the family and later a Cape Dutch manor on a hill, with pool and fishpond and lawn and the productive lands all around.

Two features kept recurring. One was the fertility of the soil, with everybody quoting stratospheric estimates of the yields to be expected from this apparent Eden. The other invariably began with the phrase 'Generaal Constand het vir ons gesê . . .'

Constand Viljoen is a very little-sung hero of the South African transition. At the start of apartheid's last fling he was the commander of the army, and by all accounts one of those officers for whom the troopies would put their heads over parapets without pause, and go down singing the anthem. When the National Party government appeared to be reneging on its traditional commitment to white rule no matter what, Constand quit and set up a new right-wing political movement, the Freedom Front. For a moment it seemed that a coup lay in the offing: Constand would rally the volk and more particularly the military and would pull a Hitler on the constitutional process, putting an end to all this tinkering with treason and establishing a fascist regime to keep everyone in their place by tank and fighter-bomber.

During this moment, incidentally, I came as close as I ever wish to feel to a near-death experience. Constand was holding a rally at Potchefstroom, before an audience who were looking upon him as the White Messiah. I was swanning around among the journos and at one stage I walked through a tunnel slightly out of sight of the main activity. Six or eight drunk Boerseuns, whose guns and swastikas were displayed with prominence, were in the tunnel. They pushed me against a wall and one shoved a gun in my throat so hard that for weeks I couldn't swallow. 'Oom wil kak skryf, nè?' he said. 'Nou gaan oom afkak.' Which means, de-colloquialised: 'You want to write untruth, old man? Now you're going to suffer.'

I didn't think the guy intended to pull the trigger, but I did think he was drunk enough for an accident to happen, and I invoked the name of Constand. I spluttered with as much coherence as my vocal impediment allowed that this was not the kind of hospitality that the general would approve of. They let go and that was it, aside from the bruised throat and a certain slight to my self-esteem. Oom? Dammit they could have been my younger brothers more easily than my nephews. My hair wasn't even grey yet.

By six months later I would no longer have got away with calling on the general's sense of propriety. The rightist heavies would have shot me for insult, and would have rather liked to shoot Constand too. He had taken a radically different line to what anyone expected, and after some extremely shaky moments he turned out to have taken the great bulk of the right wing with him. He led them into the Mandela election, where the heavies had demanded a boycott, and after the election he led them into the paths of loyal opposition, arguing by the means of democracy and abiding by the outcomes of democracy. The blood-and-guts skop-en-skiet brand of fierce rightists hated him even more than they hated De Klerk, which was several thousandfold more than they hated Mandela. They hated him because he had ruined their rebellion.

Now that the ominous pre-'94 memories are ancient history, and the peaceable outcome of the election has itself faded beneath the spectre of crime and decline, the sharpness of that knife-edge is hard to take seriously. I'll bet though that once history is freed of the errors of parallax it will record that two events saved this country from fascist rule and full-scale war. F W de Klerk's much-forgotten 1992 referendum told the righties – to their huge and unfeigned shock – that they had nothing like the preponderance of Afrikaner support they had believed they had. Even so, when it came to the election had Constand not led the body of brown-suit church-going conservatives into participation the tearaway Right would have had sway over the cockpits and the cannon and we'd be a wreck.

But Constand went his unexpected way, and part of that way was into the philosophy that even if his people did finally acquire a patch of Africa to call their own it would be not much fun surrounded by chaos and poverty. So he set out to make Africa work, and that's what all the new pioneers told us: 'General Constand said we must make Africa rich.' I don't suppose that altruism was their central motive, since I didn't see many harps or the fluttering of angels' wings, and I have my worries about 'rich' turning out to mean labouring jobs at rates that translate into fewer dollars per year than an American visitor might spend at the Polana on a evening's sundowner. Nonetheless I can't find it in myself to sniff at the prospect of roads appearing where there was bush before, ploughed fields emerging in the scrub, and cash however small circulating where no cash had been.

The social questions are as large as the practical ones, and in the kind of place where the train runs at three kilometres a day – people walk ahead of it knocking the rails into place as it moves – these are large by any criterion. But I stick to the belief that there is more to admire than deride in the Afrikaner expansion into Africa.

We touched down at Lanseria a couple of hours before Brad's guests were due to descend upon his flat. Pity the bottle-stores were closed, but pilots also maak 'n plan so Brad was a happy man, and I was a changed one. I was getting used to our own small Trek playing havoc with my accumulated book-knowledge on Africa and the universe and all, but never more than this episode.

Our programme ran in almost the least viewer-friendly slot possible – 9.30 pm on Christmas Night. I suspected that our viewership was going to consist of my mother (the Trek's loyalest fan) and the families of Molly, Jan and DC insofar as they were within reach of SABC3's limited footprint. In fact we've received, and it has not yet stopped, an unprecedented flow of enquiries – for copies, for names, for numbers – and also a much fiercer barrage than usual of complaints and ridicule. How, went the common demand of the politically correct gentry, could I take this pathetic affair seriously? Why, it would all be over in a month or two. If the Boers weren't chased out by popular outrage they'd have chickened out under the onslaught of malaria and strain. I have no doubt that all of these factors will take their toll, over and again, but there is a resilience at play that can too easily be under-rated. Writing this book, eight months later, I rang Molly for a situation report. Coming on, she said. No plain sailing, but coming on. Four more intakes had brought the total up to 14 Boers. An agricultural education centre set up and running. Seeds being planted.

6

Oops

At the close of 1996 there were 61 episodes of Beckett's Trek behind us. That spelt approx 650 videotapes covering some 25 metres of shelf space in Shaw Pictures' newly enlarged archives. It spelt about 300 hours of footage, and some 50 hours occupancy of the airwaves (allowing for repeats and for varying durations). It spelt many thousands of combi kilometres and tens of thousands of airborne kilometres. Considering that at the start none of us had seriously expected it to actually happen, and that even when it did happen we expected it to stop happening at any moment, the endurance we had achieved was a shock to the system and the acclaim that accompanied it was a bigger shock.

We were not, after all, supposed to be in this business at all. In my mind I was no kind of 'TV person', let alone those barbarous neologisms 'a personality' or, even worse, 'a celebrity', as people have the distressful habit of calling anyone whose face features often enough on the box.

I was a displaced journalist, and had only been a journalist in the first place because I was a displaced lawyer, and if the truth be known what I really wanted to be was a socio-political explorer figuring out routes towards that elusive target of a nation where everybody would feel welcome and wanted and vorentoe.

So the TV thing was all an accident, although by no means an unpleasant one. To get paid to have fun can't be bad, and the Trek was certainly a useful basis for the exploration. The reviews and the critiques, and letters and the polls, were showing consistent approval. We must have done something right in some previous incarnation, and even if we were not sure what it was, we were feeling fine.

Then came the 1997 season, Series III, and . . . well, it's not exactly that the wheels came off, but we were jarringly jolted back to earth.

Series III went all wrong, not necessarily in ways that the viewer noticed but definitely in ways that we noticed. We lost direction. We ran round in circles, starting programmes which we abandoned mid-stream, producing programmes which we then regretted having produced, missing programmes which we then regretted having missed.

The omens were out of order, for a start. Shortly before the series began there was a bust-up at Shaw Pictures, when most of the black staff were nabbed red-handed in a rip-off scheme. Until then there had been a pretty good sense of team – shared purpose, shared meals, a reasonable sense of the new South Africa flowering in our work.

I said in *Trekking* that I itched for a fuller hand of the newly enfranchised component in the planning and organising. This itch had not been much relieved, but as companions and colleagues the black guys we worked with were great. My worst problem with any of the regular staff was with a driver who could by no amount of preaching, screeching or imploring be dissuaded from his High Noon style of road usage. All other drivers were rivals, and to the end if he thought I was sleeping or distracted and somebody gave him grief such as by wanting to overtake or by riding up our behind, he'd give grief right back in that duelling fashion which is the great failing of our otherwise amiable highways. But the same guy was a paragon out of the driver's seat, and when he and the others were caught in the act of shrinking the inventory it left a sorrowful feeling.

What it also left was one black associate for whom I had very high hopes in the planning-and-organising department, and who I had fingered as a potential director or guider of the programme. After the theft I attached all the more importance to this guy. Not long afterwards he struck an awkward patch and borrowed a car from me and a largish chunk of money . . . and Shakespeare was dead right with that thing about neither a borrower nor a lender be. The car eventually came back looking like it had been in a fight with a concrete mixer. What had been lent was an aged but kempt and approximately roadworthy vehicle. What was returned was mobile scrap-iron. The right side had been squashed against a wall, so entry to the driver's seat was via the passenger door. The back right door was tied to its pillar with wire, which was easy because no obstructive window was any longer there to get in the way. The crushed front fender had been reshaped with sledge-hammer and bolt-cutter. The light-switch had packed in but been ingeniously rearranged so that for night driving – or a quick flash of the headlamps – you would merely reach behind the heater switch and twirl two naked wires onto a fuse connector. This process had necessitated the removal of the dashboard. At least two brake pads had worn to non-existence and the sound of metal biting disc when the pedal was pressed could pierce ears six blocks away.

I half expected that a Leon Schuster candid camera must be mounted in a telephone pole to trap my reaction. But no, my erstwhile partner-designate was proud that he'd brought the car back, two months after borrowing it for 'a day or two'. When I said that it didn't seem to be in quite the same shape as I'd last seen it he put a contemplative hand on his chin and peered carefully. 'Hmm,' he said, 'now that you mention it, I suppose so. But it is still going.'

Well, that was truly spoken, even if in a tone of voice that implied that since it was still going I was therefore churlish to nit-pick.

He rolled out a pile of banknotes, promising that this was the start of repaying his cash debt, and asked if he could borrow the car for another day or two. You've got to have class to have that much crust. In any case, what was I going to do with it? But now the day or two has grown to 200, and no more cash has arrived, and I am greatly grieved – mainly at the loss of a once fine friendship but also at the regression of the Trek into monochrome white hands.

This was in keeping with the state of play across the nation, but that didn't make it any better. The 1994 honeymoon had turned stone cold by three years later, and the famous 'change' was spending as much time in reverse gear as in forward (and zero time in top). Some of this was funny, some of it was sad, most of it was both. You could go to the kind of seminar where for years it had been obligatory to round up a black presence, and all of a sudden it didn't matter any more. Launches and openings ceased to be brain-damage territory for the PR companies and their copious rainbow checklists – confirm a week before, re-confirm the day before, re-re-confirm on the morning . . . They dropped it all and just sent the blacks the same invitation they sent the rest. Those who came, fine; those who didn't, too bad; and if it ended up 99% non-African, no pain. In the Guilt-and-Struggle era there had been an excitement attached to the non-racial endeavour. Now that the guilt was over and the struggle won, there was a hard-nosed reaction.

Back in 1992 I'd spoken to an executive lunch club in the Eastern Cape, and had been struck by the committee's frantic concern to lure black members. They'd had twenty-odd black acceptances and they were like cats on hot bricks waiting for these guys to arrive, barely acknowledging the mere regulars. By half an hour after the scheduled starting time about ten of the blacks had pitched up and the committee caucused anxiously in a corner as to whether or not we could get going. Afterwards their sole concern was what had the blacks thought, were they coming again, were they joining up?

In 1997 I spoke to the same club and noticed that there was not an indigenous face in the room – a few coloureds and Indians, but no Africans. I mentioned to the chairman that things seemed different. 'Oh,' he said indifferently, 'since we made the rules the same for everybody we've got used to being a gathering of minorities.'

That summed it up. Liberation was supposed to mean the erasure of the barriers of colour, freeing everybody to find their own levels and their own associations according to interests rather than race. In practice it has meant a shifting of the barrier. Where there used to be a stark legal line placing the enfranchised whites on one side and the disenfranchised Africans, Indians and coloureds on the other, now there is a subtle unwritten line which has Africans on one side and whites, coloureds and Indians on the other, sharing commonalities of interest, commonalities of speech and commonalities of convention, such as that if you attend a lunch club you pay for the lunch.

So while the de-Africanising of the Trek was in line with the altering trend, this was not a trend that I found comfortable. In my view the whole object of the exercise is to excavate the meanings of South Africanism in all its complex mystery, and this would be a task far better undertaken with at least some concrete sense of the wholeness of South Africa around one. What was worse, for a person who believes as I do that affirmative action is a terrible error, the institutionalising of the appointment of wrong people to wrong jobs for wrong reasons and in the end an act of treason against the nation's central need for growth, there are certain obligations. If you're going to say that artificial colour-coding is a false way of finding fulfilment for blacks, you'd better make plenty of effort to find real ways of fulfilment. You'd better find real opportunities, real routes to real advancement, using real people's real talents. If you have no faith in the stocking of executive suites with phoney directors and out-of-depth managers, you must offer the ordinary guy at the coalface a dashed solid alternative reason to see his ceiling being raised and his sights being heightened.

And where had we got to in this respect? Absolutely no further than the average employer, which is to say, about two thirds of a millimetre. Now such woeful efforts as we had made and such pitiful hopes as we did have were smashed against the rocks of mistrust. The sense of team was overtaken by a sense of fracture. It was not conducive to a good kick-off of a new series, and things soon went from bad to worse.

Much of what we started doing never saw the light of day. Take the SA Bureau of Standards.

What a respectworthy institution this place is, a thing that South Africans treat as an unnoticed part of the social furniture but which, viewed up close, is properly a focus for a great deal of pride. We encountered the SABS somewhat by accident, in the course of getting two pairs of jeans cut to ribbons. In the encounter its merits grew upon me, and we set out to do a whole show on the place.

Hah! A débâcle. The SABS gave us a ton of its time, with infinite generosity and endearing goodness of heart. We were there not once, not twice, not thrice, but fource, at a cost in equipment and personnel that it is bad for my blood pressure to recollect. And in the end not a sole solitary mention of the establishment made it to your living-room or mine.

Let me take the tale in order, starting with the jeans episode.

A lawyer friend had been telling me about the great piracy phenomenon. Commercial pirates were flooding in to South Africa with cheat products – El Cheapo copies of Nike shoes, Levi jeans, Panasonic radios, Chanel perfumes, the famous brand-names in every arena from T-shirts to bulldozer parts. The implications, he argued, were a long sight larger than met the eye, in that not only were legions of unsuspecting consumers about to discover that their proud new VCRs and CD players would pack in by next Tuesday afternoon, but also that the genuine manufacturers would opt out and leave South Africa to the mercy of the junk-product dealers.

It seemed intriguing and we set off on a tour of enquiry. We kept company of a police squad on a fleamarket raid in Pretoria, and it was more than intriguing, it was bizarre. We were at the police station, meeting and greeting and establishing credentials, when a distraught group of German tourists pitched up with a smashed video camera. They'd just been mugged. The woman with the camera had shards of her skin's outer layers hanging down one arm. She'd tried to hang on when the muggers had sought redistribution of the camera, and the result had been total damage to the camera and considerable damage to the arm.

Very sorry about that, said the police, pity our business today is hunting down counterfeits. So the Germans tossed the camera in a bin and went off muttering, and I don't believe they have a second visit to sunny South Africa high on their agendas.

We went with the police to nail the counterfeiters. The first guy we found was a Chinese selling Nikes. Nike's lawyer Marilyn Krige – young, beautiful, Churchillianly eloquent, and a TV programme's dream come true – had no difficulty pointing out half a dozen ways, from the absence of the airbag in the sole to the positioning of the logo, in which this shoe was fake. So the police loaded up a carload of takkies and took the details of the salesman. So far so good, even if I wondered what good the detail-taking could do, and so did the cops. They said that all they could do was confiscate the counterfeits, and next day the guy would have a new stall with another supply.

Unfortunately the flurry did not pass wholly unnoticed, so every Chinese dealer we subsequently saw had a suspiciously bare rack of wares before him, with large expanses of empty shelves, absolutely no big-name brands among his stock, and a butter-wouldn't-melt-in-my-mouth expression.

We diversified our search, and while I was listening to an Afrikaans stall-holder proudly explaining that, yes, of course all his Omega watches were phoney, what the heck did you expect for a hundred rands, there was another commotion right behind me and lo!, the police had rumbled an elderly Scotsman selling Mickey Mouse towels.

A corner of my mind had sneakingly suspected that we were into Mickey Mouse terrain, but this was rubbing it home with a vengeance. The Scotsman was loudly outraged and but for the density of his accent would have been a star on camera. He shouted the odds with vehemence: How was I to know that Mickey Mouse was royal game? Would you cops prefer that I paid the rent by stealing handbags? The cops were zut impressed. This is the law, china. You're infringing copyright. If you don't like it go and tell parliament.

Marilyn and I had a neat little barney on camera. Was this, I wondered, a suitable use of embattled police manpower in a time of rampant crime? Darn sure, said Marilyn, if you let the jungle overrun commercial rights you slipstream into the highway to collapse. Logically I could take her point, but there was still something odd about devoting a team of groot fris Boeresersante to fighting the good fight on behalf of Mickey Mouse.

We followed the trail a little further and discovered in

essence that nothing is what you think it is. You can buy a big-name cassette player for R1000 and it turns out to have fewer and flimsier parts, tinnier sound and sloppier soldering than a no-name player costing R50. The big name might be counterfeit, but it equally well might not.

Nor does the size of the price tag have any necessary bearing whatsoever on the degree of authenticity. Your teenager might find two examples of that inexplicably major status-symbol, the Billabong jersey, and pass up the cheaper to invest in the more expensive as the latter must obviously be the Real Thing or it couldn't cost so much more could it now? Well yes it could. It need not be any realler than a seven-rand note, but it might have twice as solid a fabric as its cheaper, authentic, rival, and twice as thorough a stitch. Alternatively it might fall apart the first time it meets a washing machine. Either way it could easily display an unabashed 'Made in China' in some perfectly undisguised spot that your teenager will never think of glancing at until after she gets home, such as on the back of the neck. When you scrutinise a Chivas bottle with a magnifying glass you might find that it is an unmistakable fraud, yet its whisky might as well taste identical as it might taste like paraffin.

Let alone the counterfeiting factor, the average consumer has next to nil chance of knowing when he's fanning the flames of plain straight theft.

Some cases are obvious, all right. I have for long maintained that there's a special place in hell for the bourgeois motorist who shrieks his fury to the mountaintops when his hubcaps vanish and then happily reaches for his wallet when he is offered an enticingly cheap replacement, but on this Trek I was brought up short.

I was sitting on a wall in the Library Gardens while an attorney, Joe Louw, ran through a string of the exotic mechanisms applied by commercial crooks. All fine and

Captions

1. *Martha and Emmly (sic) Mlambo apply the Ndebele brush to a place where no Ndebele brush has been before. Here in London it was very evident that insofar as we have a national ID in the eyes of the world, like Scotland has the tartan or Holland has clogs, ours is Ndebele art.*

2. *Justin, Louis and a patient Zimbabwean truck driver at Beit Bridge. This was the South African side, he'd been waiting half a day and had only a modest amount to be patient about. The Zim side, there was not so much a queue as the mother of all parking lots. Hundreds and hundreds of 20-tonners were twiddling their thumbs while they awaited the grace of the bureaucrats.*

3. *Keith Shaw and Ben Harber, Witbank's chief traffic cop, with a temporary apprentice whose grin was about to get wiped off his dial. If you think you catch a skrik when you're speeding down the highway and a uniformed figure leaps out of the bushes to pull you in, believe me it's nothing compared to the skrik that he gets. Witbank has a major local sport: dicing outside the Pick 'n Pay parking lot on a Sunday night. People gather from far and wide, to admire each other's engines and sound systems and wheelies, and to split like magic when word is heard that the cops are coming. Traffic Officer Beckett failed to catch any of the dicers, but stopped plenty of ordinary motorists for spot checks. We spent endless effort checking such less-than-central vehicular features as the handbrake, but did nil in the way of verifying the vehicles' ownership. In a society where carjacking creates fear, despair, emigration and boarded-up industries, you'd think it would be obvious to run a routine computer check on the registration plates, but no: 'the systems don't allow for it'.*

4. *A gripping rear view – very artistic, y'understand – of Richard, Morrison and that presenter ou at Deelfontein, formerly a pride of the Karoo but now, um, not. Much of the Karoo's old 19th century brick and mortar is in this sort of shape; some of the Karoo's old 19th century human relationships were alive and only too well. Right here we met a guy who clearly considered it unthinkably impertinent to utter more than two consecutive words without a 'baas' between them. 'Baas, my naam, baas, is Johannes, baas.' The reason we run this undistinguished picture as well as the somewhat more orthodox one on the front cover, is that for the second year running we overlooked the small matter of stills pictures. Abject apologies, especially to critics like Jeremy Maggs at Radio 702 who are going to make us eat dirt. But next year (he vows with fingers crossed) we'll get it right.*

5. *Mendi Msimang, our High Commissioner to the Court of St James, is the kind of guy you'd love for an uncle or a father-in-law. He's also the master of one of the most valuable pieces of real estate in the world, South Africa House in Trafalgar Square. The Embassy's halls and ballrooms and appointment-rooms are as classily spectacular as is imaginable – and barely ever seen. This door was unlocked for the camera's benefit, normal entry is through a poky security checkpoint with all the grandeur of a broom cupboard. I propose we convert the place to the most upmarket hotel in London, use it to pay off the national debt, and let Mendi return to the pomp-free lifestyle he knew in his years as the ANC's alternative ambassador in the city. Mendi and I shared a common affection for Britain and a common view of the major drawback, which we remarked upon simultaneously as we stood on his balcony and beheld the greyness – you keep feeling you're going to bump your head against the sky.*

6. *When we walked in to a squatter camp at Franschhoek and asked for a leader, there was no hesitation. 'Ah, you mean Myra,' said the people. 'Children, go and find Myra.' Myra was Leader with a capital L, although by tacit consent rather than formal voting. She was also Cross with a capital C, mainly with her own constituents who she roundly castigated for laziness, drunkenness, uselessness and for wasting their energies blaming the Boers for their problems.*

7. *Kenny Hlatswayo is mayor of Huntingdon and a pillar of the church choir. Huntingdon is a hundred metres outside the Timbavati, where a world tourism industry is on the rise at rates like R1 000 per person per night. Huntingdon's average income is not R1 000 per person per year. In the Timbavati I had wanted to know how the hoteliers were cutting the neighbourhood in on the action. They said they'd tried, but the locals kept letting them down for example by not meeting vegetable orders. Now I wanted to know from Kenny: why not? Kenny said there wasn't enough rain. Even as we spoke, we were among puddles. We were at Kenny's large new house, under construction. There was a dam in clear sight, not ten minutes' walk away. I said why not build a rainwater tank, or a pump from the dam. Kenny ummed and aahed and scratched his temple, and said there were no resources; the hotel should build those things; the people would become unhappy if one of their own were to tell them what to do. I said: Have you nothing to offer but excuses? Kenny thought a moment, and said: Let us sing. So we sang, he and I and his composer friend Lally, and others joined in, and I was out of tune, and flat, and got the words wrong, but it didn't matter, and we danced our way to the car, and hugged goodbyes and best wishes, and parted as brothers.*

8. *We got into boxing because we thought (which is to say, some of us persuaded others of us to worry) that we were getting too 'political', re blacks and whites and all that stuff. We started off with regular amateur boxing and a lot of voices telling us about building confidence and self-control and turning street trouble-makers into paragons, which was all quite convincing but when I watched a kid get pulled out of the ring with his eyes rolling back into his skull I thought you can keep it. We then graduated to heavy stuff like the no-rules fighting you see here, which had been arranged by a kind of Bouncers' Association to let bouncers let off steam in a nicer way than beating up the customers. Not long afterwards one of the bouncer captains who had invited us was killed in a war with another bouncer gang. I said in the programme and say again now that I suspect that bouncer wars will be a big issue in the near future.*

9. *A Lichinga suburb, about which you can read, if you care to, on page 57.*

10. *Trade unionist Sam Shilowa and Trevor Fowler of the Communist Party. We were on our way to somewhere entirely else when we got stuck in a demonstration, so we took up the camera, got out of the car, and what do you know, bumped into Sam and Trevor. Sam was strong on a 40-hour working week, which to me is a thing for primary school children. Sam said, no, that's what the bosses have. I thought, not the kind of bosses who make factories and mines and industries happen. The two most, ahem, striking things about the day were the extreme pleasantness of the mood and vibe, and the extreme craziness of the 40-hour demand. I tried to get both points across but as per usual the emphases got adjusted by the pressures of the edit suite, and I came out singing the praises of the strikers' humanity, and ignoring their demolition of the national economy.*

11. *Therapeutic, I felt, but I wouldn't think so if I had to do it every day. Many of the homes of Huntingdon were extremely Africanly quaint, and, not for the first time, I tried to float the thought among the locals that no law stopped them from Bed & Breakfasting, and dealing themselves in on the river of Dollars and Deutschmarks that was making millionaires across the fence. Not for the first time, the thought was born to blush unseen.*

12. *Around close-down time on one of the year's chillier nights, I got home from a day as a Witbank traffic cop. With theatre timing, the phone rang at the same moment as Gael cracked open a welcoming beer. The copper-wire cops at last had a bust for us to follow, somewhere round the back end of Randfontein. I scrabbled vainly for a balaclava, Gael bunged an old beret of hers on my head and unwittingly caused much merriment to inter alia Neil McMahon on the Cape Argus who columnised – 'Can this man dress or what?' – thanking me for my contribution to the fashion industry and warning Cindy Crawford to beware of the competition. Mainly I should have been thanked for my contribution to the physiotherapy industry. The thieves had somehow detected our cat-like tread and vacated the premises, leaving us to lug away their intended spoils.*

13. *We tried to tally up the Kaizer Chiefs memorabilia in Pauline Karibe's Alexandra flat, but lost count after the first couple of hundred.*

We went with Pauline and 12 other Chiefs supporters, in a well-populated taxi, to a match in Welkom, trying to get a fix on the life and outlook of the soccer-fan world. Delightful occasion, and a real uplift to see quite how contented and fulfilled so many of the Paulines were, oblivious to the wail and groan that are the hallmarks of public discourse. There were perhaps 40 000 Chiefs fans at the stadium and about 150 bold souls showing the red and white of the local team, Qwa-Qwa Stars. Presumably the future of the premier league is Chiefs and Pirates in one long roadshow, playing each other every week in different provinces before gigantic crowds. Chiefs won, narrowly. I said to a Qwa-Qwa supporter that this must be a slight relief. He said 'No, we'd love it if we could beat Chiefs. If we were ever to beat Pirates, though, we'd break speed limits running for police protection.' I tried, with extremely modest success, to pin down things like the cultures of the different clubs and the relevance of muti and witchcraft. Everybody got terrifically coy on the witchcraft factor, although intriguing hints kept popping out as to how the fanclubs send men to protect the goals against hostile muti the night before the match, how it can be fatal to be caught bringing a black cat to the grounds, and so on.

14. *Beautiful, hey? And clean. In Sydney everything is clean – the air, the water, the streets, the buses, and the basins in the public loos. When I came back and expressed criticisms some people said 'oh, so the SABC forced you to run down Australia, huh' and others said 'ah, how nice that you don't like Australians'. Each comment is as dumb as the other. How can you dislike Australians? That would be ludicrous. All I say is that what they have in the way of cleanliness and comfort is to my mind somewhat offset by the lack of a broader dimension to human purpose. As a re-immigrating friend of mine said, after two years in Aus: 'There has to be more to life than getting old, getting rich, and dying.'*

15. *A free tip: if you look for a job as a refuse remover and are offered a choice between a rich part of town like Sandton and a poor one like Soweto, take Soweto. There, the rubbish bags are seldom too heavy to twirl round your little finger. Sandton people have bad habits such as owning large dogs with incompletely programmed exhaust* *functions, and your body works up a terrible sweat lumbering after the truck while weighed down with full squishy bags, while your heart freezes over at the prospect of a bag breaking open. I spent time as a dustbin man in both places. The best thing about it was meeting Nellie Malike here, who off her own bat had created a patch of public park in the wasteland next to her house, and cleaned and tended it daily. A medal for Nellie, please, and I wish her neighbours would catch on. One of them waited patiently while the truck and the dustmen lumbered past, before nipping across the road to dump her junk in the veld. I asked why, and she thought for quite a while before saying that was the way it had always been done.*

16. *Evening bathtime in northern Mozambique. Jan Pelser and DC Bredenkamp share their soap with a TV ou from down south. See Chapter 5.*

17. *Zimbabwe has a knack of intersecting happily with a brand of intermediate technology which South Africans would consider disgracefully old-fashioned. If you want to draw attention to a roadsign in a place where electric motors are lacking, why then, a little imagination and the wind God grants do the job.*

18. *The Berlin Wall of the Limpopo. Richard in the foreground and technically that is indeed Johan Boshoff in the background, but I don't believe he'll consider a rear view at 80 metres a breach of our no-pictures agreement. See page 132.*

1

2

3

4

5

6

7

8

9

10

11

12

13

14

15

16

17

18

interesting and solid. Joe was stating his case with a welcome absence of the legalese which usually bedevils interviews with his fraternity, and we were humming forth smoothly when suddenly Joe said: 'And of course anybody who buys a second-hand car radio is receiving stolen goods.'

What! There was a second-hand radio in my car, parked 50 feet away. And yes, it had been cheap. Just that I took it for granted that the guy who supplied it had acquired it above board.

For the first time the alternative possibility crossed my mind. For the first time, and with a pair of icy tongs around my soul, I stared at the thought that I my righteous self might also be a candidate for the special place in hell. It was a 220-volt jolt. I spluttered and burbled in one of those awkwardly entertaining moments of spontaneous befuddlement that TV presenters are not supposed to have. 'Oh c'mon,' said Joe. 'You never *sell* a car radio. You just have them stolen.'

Indeed. Wasn't the unofficial coat-of-arms of Gauteng a little pile of broken window-glass in a parking bay?

On reflection I decided that Joe wasn't wholly right. From time to time people did sell car radios – to upgrade, or in salvage after a write-off, or for any of the myriad reasons that people sell anything from bottled air to family heirlooms. But the legitimate sales must be few and far between, and I went on a round of car-radio shops to see how they knew that their second-hand merchandise was kosher. They mostly had nice answers about serial numbers and registrations but the bottom line was that you never know, you just hope.

We tried some pawnbrokers after that, and for them the knowing was more distant and the hoping not necessarily quite as – ah – fervid. They all had registers, as per law, but in some cases even the most cursory glance at the register showed that it was a mere fiction like the register of visitors at the security desk of an office building, where anybody could write

Man in the Moon or J Christ or Modesty Blaise or Illegible Scrawl.

In one place the large and armed proprietor was warmly welcoming, presumably in the confidence that I could suspect much but prove nothing. I felt my skin crawling in the certainty that behind his stockrooms of appliances lay blood and tears and funerals. I argued the moral case as hard as I could, heavily emphasising both to the proprietor and to an unspecifiable segment of the viewers-to-be that those who benefited from thefts and robberies were doing as much to shove South Africa down the drain as those who perpetrated them.

I got quite carried away in my moral indignation, and also in the practical message that the murdering hijacker whose bullets cost his and my children a billion rands apiece in lost growth of the nation was no more than the agent of the dumb beerboep boorjoe schmuck who one minute shrieked for public hangings and the next minute was snapping up cheap CDs and bragging about his ability to secure a bargain.

For TV purposes the point was all messed up by the fact that the proprietor was long-windedly and apparently genuinely baffled by my logic, and I had to take him through it step by step.

'Look, every new murder is the last straw for a new wave of people who decide to emigrate, right?' If only he'd just said 'right', but in fact it took him five perplexed minutes to get there.

'And every emigration means clients departing, businesses closing, factories shutting, skills disappearing, economy-generating people lost to South Africa, right?' Ditto.

'And every closure means harder times for the businesses that remain, so that they are all the more susceptible to the next last straw when the next murder comes along, right?' Ditto.

'So you get into a cycle of decline, with ever fewer jobs

meaning ever more crime meaning still fewer jobs meaning still more crime until the qualified people are all living in Australia and the rest are all living in penury, right?' Ditto, after I'd explained 'penury'.

'But if everybody refused to buy property that they thought might have been stolen, or property which they were not certain had not been stolen, then the whole robbery and hijack thing would come to a halt, right?' Ditto.

If this exchange looks lengthy here, with my spoken word all crispened up and his spoken word wholly elided, you can imagine how lengthy it was in the original.

The unfortunate cameraman, who for present purposes shall remain unnamed, had had his left eye screwed up for half an hour, and was sukkeling mightily with bad light and unprepossessing background and cramped space and the difficulty of varying shot and swinging from close-up on me to close-up on the pawnbroker to two-shot on the both of us, and was heartily wishing I would finally shuddup. So was the sound man, coping with his alternating microphone-boom and the clink and clank of the security door behind us and the disruptive exclamations of transactions taking place elsewhere in the shop.

But the pawnbroker, at least, was acquiring the glimmerings of something like a rush of conscience, combined with the dim recognition that the reason his wife and his kids and his mama and his great-aunt Gertrude in Malvern or Brakpan or wherever were living in constant holy terror of being burgled or worse was not wholly unrelated to his readiness to dole out cash for suspect goods. His brow was furrowing and beads of sweat were popping out and his welcoming smile was converting to grimace, and had it not been for that great ugly camera whirring on and on like a policeman of politeness I think his vocabulary might have seen a drastic change and I would have found myself hastened to the door at gunpoint.

Any case, I wasn't quite ready to shuddup.

'So,' I said, referring to his register, 'when somebody like this S Khumalo here, from London Road, Alexandra Township, comes in with 76 CDs comprised largely of Beethoven, Mahler, Tchaikovsky, the Beatles, Joan Baez, and Crosby, Stills and Nash, for which you pay him a total of R152, what enquiry do you conduct to ascertain that this is actually his own private musical collection that he has chosen to pawn because he has perhaps undergone a sudden change of taste?'

He summoned up hidden reserves of defensive energy, and astutely invoked the New South Africa to his aid.

'Oh no,' he said, triumph and piety all over his mug, 'I couldn't say to a person "because you're black you're not allowed to like this kind of music". I have to respect the individual's choice.'

Hmm. How do you argue this one? I'm the first to agree that, yes, let people be what people want to be, and yes indeed, let them be respected regardless. If a Jason Fotheringham-Windsor chooses to embrace Africa by living in Soweto and consulting sangomas and wearing an Orlando Pirates T-shirt that's fine by me. In fact it's more than fine. The cross-over stuff is acutely welcome as a fundamental means of de-racialising the nation and hastening that elusive day when our debates will be debated according to thought and not according to genes. By the same token, if an S Khumalo of London Road, Alexandra, gets into Mahler or gets into polo or gets into wine-tasting or bridge-parties or stamp-collecting, hooray.

In principle the pawnbroker's argument was rock solid. In practice it was bullshit. He knew it was bullshit. I knew that he knew it was bullshit. He knew that I knew that he knew it was bullshit. I knew that he knew that I knew that he knew, and so on even unto the umpteenth generation. The name 'S Khumalo' was a dead giveaway in itself, being the African version of the 'John Smith', by which a 50-year-old insurance executive is traditionally supposed to check into a hotel when he arrives unexpectedly with a painted blonde popsy on his arm. But no matter what the name might have been there were no two ways; the pawnbroker knew that there was a housebreaking in the recent history of his R152 investment, and was blinding his eye to it.

I pushed the moral issue up to and beyond the point of diminishing returns, even while knowing that I was on a losing wicket. I'd need hours of screen time to even begin to get through to the viewer. I wanted the pawnbroker at least, though, to come away feeling that he deserved the disgust of reasonable people.

The minute I stopped, the cameraman thankfully laid down his burden and said: 'Gee, these are some pretty good CDs you have here. How much?' They were twenty rands apiece. I couldn't promptly renew the entire futile sermon, and left in a disgust of my own. The cameraman was happy as a dog with a bone to acquire a bunch of cheap choice CDs. The pawnbroker was even happier to see me put in my place than he was to ring up his thousand-percent profit, and saw me off with a grin a mile wide. The housebreak industry got another boost to its shares.

In the course of the counterfeiting side of the same programme I had bought two pairs of jeans, one for R400 and one for R40. We took these to the SABS to ask what the differences were. In the name of science the jeans got carved into dishcloth, and the long technical answer boiled down to the assurance that the differences, in terms of durability, quality of stitching, quality of fabric and zip, etc, were approximately zilch.

The dissection was interesting and to my mind inspiring. I like the idea that I am part of a State sufficiently strong and orderly as to provide me the consumer with a lifebuoy amid the swirling seas of commercial confusion. Moreover the SABS mense were a nice bunch of ouens, as befits people who apply high-level skills and abilities to the cause of serving society. However we had stupidly (my fault and not the SABS's) failed to videotape the dissection process itself – the actual seeing of how many stitches per centimetre, how much resilience in the studs, etc.

We arranged to go back there and do a separate programme on the Bureau and its work.

And then we went back again, and back again, and still never produced the programme.

For one thing, it was too subtle. I myself was fascinated by things like the pilchard inspection, but when we watched our tape we became doubtful of our prospects of transmitting this fascination to a million viewers. I felt deeply enlightened watching a laboratory of professional people looking at pilchard tins, tasting pilchards, explaining the difference between the nutritional qualities of the grey broken-up pilchards which swam in ponds of preservative and the pink firm pilchards which filled the tin.

I was impressed by the machinery which pounded away at different makes of vehicle wheel hubs. I was intrigued by the explanations as to which products were automatically and continually examined by the Bureau at state expense as a public service, and which were submitted by the manufacturers at their own expense in search of a seal of approval as a marketing tool. We tested lightbulbs and we tested safety-belts. We tested radios and we tested vegetables. We asked a fair number of the right questions, not least the question why with all this testing available the market still got flooded with for example toys that you could count on to be kaput by the night after Christmas.

While we were there in action in the big building off George Storrar Drive in Pretoria, I thought we had a programme. Back in the edit suite, no one else got excited and truth to tell

I couldn't get too excited myself. We had a nice serviceable education video of the kind that the SABS would have been pleased to show to visiting parties of press-ganged school-children. The cold clarity of the pilchard laboratory, the perverse fascination of the subtle gradations between good radios and bad . . . these things were there in the being there but did not altogether meet the camera's eye. On tape a washed-out pilchard did not look all that different from a fris and noble pilchard, and neither was in glue-your-eyes-to-the-screen league. In addition to which, we were already in tizz mode, all mixed up and not sure what was what, waiting for a flash of revelation and failing to find it in close-ups on lightbulb filaments.

So none of it saw the screen and to this day I feel low and evil when I travel along George Storrar Drive, and hunch involuntarily as I pass the big building lest an aggrieved ex-informant – and they were so obliging and courteous – catches sight of my evil visage and sets up a posse. I can only say sorry to the Standards ouens and promise that *one day* we'll come back and get it right, noting in honesty that *one day* is a flexible concept but that at least the intention is there.

After that failure we failed again, at the other end of the Ben Schoeman highway. We tried to get a fix on the state of municipal politics, and pegged it on the mayor of Johannesburg, Isaac Mogase. The Hon Mayor was courtesy itself, but the programme didn't add up, showing not much but that for a city whose future was in ridiculous doubt the Town Fathers did not seem to be rising very alacritously to the challenge. The council meeting we filmed was marked mainly by (a) the fact that few of the councillors appeared to be making their way through the immense confusion of documentation any better than I was, and (b) the fact that the main activity was dumping on the Democratic Party, which seemed to be asking for the dumping by dropping the broadest hints at the slightest opportunity that they knew everything and everyone else was half-witted.

Then came something completely different in the form of birdwatching, starting off with the CNA's books boffin Abdullah Gallie standing in front of a rack and telling us the extraordinary statistics of how bird books have become a gigantic national craze. Yes, fine, but when we went on the hunt in Mpumalanga we ended up with all humans and no birds, and the Nelspruit Bird Club is another place I'll have to pass with my head down.

By the beginning of the '97 series we had a list of cancelled ventures ranging from the highs and lows of being wheelchair-bound to the highs and lows of being a student at Turfloop, and were much at odds with ourselves and the world. But we had to put something on screen as the introduction to our new series, so we started with a programme we called 'In Search of South African Humour'.

This title was supposed to convey that we were still on a course of enquiry – is there a 'South African humour', or is it all separate sub-groups mainly laughing at other sub-groups; is satire alive, or is it all just recycled old jokes left over from apartheid days – while simultaneously having some laughs.

Some people, like Paul Slabolepszy and Soli Philander, rather nicely combined quest and quip, but the overall package didn't work. Alarm bells started ringing the next morning when instead of the by now familiar flow of loved-your-show comments in supermarket and parking lot I divined a general sense of 'glad you're back on the box, but what was that about?'

The reviews that followed (and there were more than normal, as this was a re-opening) said much the same. John Scott in the Cape Times and David Basckin in the Sunday Tribune – both very fair-minded critics – struck notes of disappointed reprimand, with Basckin in particular making the thought-provoking point that this trekking into ideas was codswallop; we were meant to be trekking to places, to the many corners of the nation and seeing the people.

So we hadn't exactly hit bull's-eye, but we had at least got back into motion. Maybe it was just a matter of stride. From here, anyway, we could only go up. Or something like that . . .

7

Back to School

Something like that. Things looked up on the second episode. I had once before, long ago and minus camera, dropped in unexpectedly on a random selection of township schools. The experience was memorable in many ways. One was the sight of a tiny wizened five-foot-nothing headmaster ambling through his school with his cane flailing, reducing his students to abject terror.

The headmaster wielded his cane in automatic reflex, lashing out with unconscious dexterity at every third or fifth child we passed. Huge hulking Mike Tyson-lookalikes, bulging out of their blazers, would cower against corridor walls as we came upon them, and the headmaster would not pause in his discourse as he whacked away at hands or bare legs or any part of the anatomy that presented itself. As a disciplinary procedure this was new to me.

So was the revelation that aside from the well-known problem of kids whose talents were not being nurtured, township schooling also had an opposite and at least equal problem: kids whose limitations were not being acknowledged.

I spent a lesson in a Standard Eight maths classroom, sitting with my knees in my chin at a desk designed for kids half the size of myself or many of my classmates, while a teacher demonstrated the theorem – Euclid's, I think, or Pythagoras – about the angles on the hypotenuse. One of the pupils was way more in tune with Euclid or Pythagoras than the teacher was. He got the message in no time and spent most of the lesson darting about with energy and enthusiasm to help his colleagues.

In my mind this rang a long suppressed alarm. Here we are in a society frantically short of skills, and here was one set of skills locked up for a year on a course which the boy could clearly master in a month. Is this really the way things have to be?

The teacher treated this kid as an appreciated ally, most of the lesson, but near the end the boy raised the idea that the theorem could as well be proved from the angles outside the triangle as inside. The teacher puzzled this out for quite a while, failed to find a conclusion, and rounded on the boy with a snarl.

'No,' he said, 'you can't do it that way.'

The boy persisted: 'Why not?'

'Because,' said the teacher, 'this is the way it's done in the book.'

More alarm bells. The aim of cultivating the enquiring mind was nominally the Holy Grail of education. This was its reality?

Meanwhile the guy sharing my table was ringing the loudest and least-expected alarms of all. At first I thought, Shame, he's battling. Later I realised this was wrong. He wasn't battling, a term which implies that something winnable lies at the end. He was totally and utterly out of it. He was reproducing in his book the diagram on the board, but with no more grasp of it than I might have copying the letters on a Japanese typewriter. He had no clue. What was worse, he had no clue that he had no clue. He thought he was doing something right. What? The copying? I don't know. But in his head he believed he was on top of it, and to me this was tragic.

He was 19, he told me. A young man, more than a boy. Somebody thought they were doing him a favour, providing him with secondary education. Somebody had thought they were doing a favour pushing him through Standard Seven. I demurred. Until then I too had assumed unquestioningly that a decent society would educate all its people up to at least that level. Now I perceived that no, there was a myth here and a cruelty. If you wanted to be nice to this guy you'd let him go and push a barrow somewhere, and ideally you'd rig things up so that in years to come he might apply himself to night-school. If you wanted to be responsible to your society you would disabuse him of the illusion that he was on some sort of academic track, and thereby save his nation the resentments and animosities he was going to build up about the jobs he didn't get and the bursaries he didn't win.

That unexpected visit had been deeply interesting. Now I wanted to do it again, with camera.

My co-trekkers were not keen, seeing this as one of the 'Egghead' topics whose bees buzzed solely in my bonnet.

I was presumed to be the escaped intellectual, see, having arrived in TV by accident and untutored. Everybody else was a real TV person with real TV training, which told them that what the punters, and more immediately the Channel, really wanted was the Joe Beerboep material; fun-'n-games for the viewer who had his remote on standby to flick you into oblivion if you gave him big words and sociology.

This built a – usually – constructive tension into the plotting of the Trek, with a perpetual tug-of-war between the Egghead and Beerboep philosophies. Frequently my Egghead instincts would be beaten back by the weight of democratic opinion but in the case of the township schools I won the day, mainly because I was patently uptight about the overbalance of

Beerboepery into which I'd already been talked. Aside from the Humour programme we had shot another on Gambling, about which I was less enthusiastic than my colleagues, and when I pushed for something to separate the two the consensus was that the old prima donna was getting ratty and had better be humoured.

So we did it. We did it exactly like I envisaged it, wholly unforewarned, unarranged. In fact we were so unforewarned that I doubt many viewers can have believed it. We went to about six schools in all, of which four made the screen, and in all of them there was virtually the same opening scene, viz:

Camera follows D Beckett ambling through early-morning schoolground in search of Authority Figure. Aha, here looms Authority Figure.

DB: 'G'morning.'
AF: 'Morning.'
DB: 'I was looking for the Principal, please.'
AF: 'That's me.'
DB: 'Uh, we wondered if we might look around your school, and talk to you.'
AF: 'No problem, Mr Beckett, you're welcome.'

With which they would seamlessly lead me into a guided tour of the premises, as if they'd had 16 sets of advance guard rehearse them on The Care and Maintenance of Intrusive Camera Crews. It was so smooth that I could barely believe it was real, and I *knew* it was real. It was impossible that the principals knew we were coming. *We* hadn't known we were coming until we happened upon a school gate two minutes earlier.

Why the principals were so hospitable I don't know, but that they were so hospitable was lovely. May we call it African open-heartedness? I don't know about that either. When I'd tried the same trick in Zimbabwe I'd met a wall of bureaucratic stalling. It might have been merely the luck of the draw. It might have been that all the principals knew the Trek, which their Zim counterparts did not. Either way it was most engaging, and part of the up-side of what became an extremely mixed-message Trek.

The welcome was not only from the principals, but from teachers in classrooms, kids in playgrounds, the lot. Unfortunately the welcome was far from the whole story. When we got into the questions – how're things going, how many kids are at their desks, how many teachers at their posts, how much and what kind of teaching on the go – the answers were problematic.

Schools supposedly start at 8.00 am. Most times we arrived at about ten to eight. Most times kids were still streaming in for another hour or so. Throughout the day we would commonly bump into teacherless classes, for which there was invariably an explanation: Mr Moloi is at a course, Miss Mogomedi is off ill.

Whatever the excuses, there were far more pupils spending far more time twiddling their thumbs than would be tolerated at a white school. At one school, in Kwa-Thema, the day's activities consisted solely of foregathering for morning assembly. After much milling around the assembly took place at about 9.30, and established that classes were cancelled so that the students could attend a funeral.

The funeral was the consequence of a family massacre. A father had gone berserk and wiped out his entire household. Extremely sad, and, as everybody pointed out in shocked tones, extremely un-African. Thus the student bodies had decided that collective African mourning and propitiation of the ancestors was called for. The *student* bodies, note. The principal and his two deputies had had nothing to do with the decision, they didn't even know about it until about 8.30 when they began to wonder why nobody was drifting into classrooms.

The murdered family was from a far side of a town of hundreds of thousands of people, and it seemed that hardly anyone in the school had known the family or even heard of the incident. Numerous pupils displayed nil interest in the notion of collective propitiation. Every one that we spoke to said it was meaningless to them, un-African or not. They were just going home for a free day. Nobody, staff or students, could point us to any individual person who could explain how this decision had been arrived at or who had participated in it. We were repeatedly told 'the student bodies', but despite the fact that we were a very visible and much remarked-upon presence in the premises for several hours – there was no great hurry to leave the grounds – we could not find a flesh-and-blood member of a 'student body'. Principals and pupils alike appeared to picture themselves as puppets in the hands of some distant force which had decided for them. The sense was one of 'another lost day; nothing to be done'.

We did however learn something about the background, and, as the Trek often did, it changed my understanding of a fairly major public issue.

South Africa had been seeing for a couple of years intermittent reports of a schools war in Kwa-Thema. Five students being killed here, three there, in the context of a row between the ANC-aligned student organisation Cosas and its PAC-aligned rival Paso. If equivalent carnage was occurring in a white/black conflict it would be gigantic headlines and massive public knowledge, but since it is all-black and not even linked to that much-fingered bad guy, Inkatha, the reports are tucked away at the bottom of page 7.

We went to Kwa-Thema for geographic variety and because lots of black people get sick of seeing Soweto, Soweto, Soweto always upheld as the pacemaker with everywhere else trailing in its wake. I had forgotten entirely about its private school war until I got there and discovered that the war is the central feature of local life. Something like 50 or 70 children had ended their lives in its course. The school we met had lost 57 teaching days in the last year. There was chaos on the go, local chaos, not a hundred kilometres from Johannesburg and bafflingly private.

South Africans – or at any rate South Africans of my class and clime – tend to think that we know what's happening. If we read enough and listen enough we can keep up. The world is at our fingertips. We receive daily updates on Princess Di's love life ,[1] on the hirings and firings of national rugby coaches, on Kader Asmal's views of life and the universe and everything.[2] We're informed. Then one discovers that just around the corner a war is raging, and one experiences the odd sensation of wondering whether our fingers are actually anywhere near the pulse after all.

It got even worse in the being there, when despite the fact that everybody of every age and walk willingly told us gory tales of the effects, nobody could give us the faintest glimmering of what the war was about.

Next we tried a school at Katlehong and were courteously ushered to the headmaster's desk, upon which a cane reposed.

What, I asked, is that for, in this era of human rights and a big taboo on corporal punishment?

'Ah,' he says, 'that's the law you're talking of. Our culture, on the other hand, says that from time to time we exercise discipline.' The law, he made it clear, was but a thing which came and went, and no rival for The Culture.

---

[1]Thoughtfood for those of us who doubt the existence of that which we cannot explain. When I wrote this paragraph on Sunday morning August 31 1997 I was surprised by a strictly out-of-character mindflash: 'What if she dies before the book appears?' An hour later my daughter told me Di was dead.

[2]Snotty comment, this. Even if Kader, SA's most prolific producer of Letters to Eds, does go to extremes, rather that than the distant silence of so many of his colleagues in our so-called transparent cabinet.

The only decoration on the principal's wall was a certificate from the Boksburg Council, misspelling the school's name but crediting it as the winner of a Keep The Town Tidy competition. We walked through corridors awash with litter – I ensured that the camera saw my feet and the principal's flapping their way through a blizzard of chip packets – and I asked if times had changed since the tidiness competition. 'Not at all,' he said. 'For the next competition we'll do another clean-up.'

This comment, like numerous others, was lost to the microphone because of the vast and continuous racket echoing through the buildings. When I asked about the racket he said it was just because of our presence. When we left we drove around a corner and stopped, out of sight of principal and students, at a point several hundred metres away. The same boisterous racket was echoing on unabated.

At another school, in Soweto, we could both see and smell that the principal had had a rendezvous with Bacchus the night before. He was articulate and friendly despite constant painful winces from his hangover, and he was anxious to give us an upbeat situation report. But the report was peppered with two recurring phrases, the term 'in principle' and the word 'unfortunately'. Almost every sentence would be a proclamation of some great success 'in principle', followed by a rider beginning 'unfortunately'. The debating society was in principle in excellent condition. Unfortunately there had been no meetings since 1994 because of a shortage of teachers to arrange them. The sports function was in principle in excellent condition. Unfortunately there had been no teams or contests for the last year because of 'some mistakes' in arranging schedules. The school's amenities were in principle in excellent condition. Unfortunately all the lightbulbs, and most of the fittings, had been stolen so that in most classrooms it was difficult or impossible to read except on a very sunny day.

The one amenity which in our experience was truly humming was the tuck-shop, a private venture in which several teachers had shares.

Another school, and the principal and the librarian took us to see the library. As we walked in, after a lengthy delay while a key was found, the principal was saying: 'The library is the nerve centre of any school.' This was a majestically inappropriate point to be making in the circumstances, as what we walked in to was cobwebs. The library was a large room with a shelf-studded set of walls, library-like. Nearly all the shelves were bare but for neat handwritten posters offering users guidance in the Dewey classification system. In a back room behind locked glass doors a few hundred books were jumbled in a pile. The librarian, and poster-artist, was a Miss Matabane, who we later discovered was one of those very special teachers whose former pupils talk of with pride when they meet. She was heart-broken about the collapse of the domain she had run for 25 years, but if she had a reason for this state of affairs it was not a reason I could understand. The principal pointed out a hole in the ceiling, through which a computer had been stolen, but neither did this seem to me like a whole reason. I came away not knowing *why* the nerve centre was now deceased, but in no doubt that deceased it was.

To the side of my idealistic brain which would like to see every child receive the kind of Grade A education that my children receive, our snap survey was a fright. To the side, though, which has been repeatedly told that township schooling is gathering speed down the slippery slide, it was not. By and large, classes were happening, teachers were alive and alert, kids were warm and friendly. Truth, as usual, came across to me as a complicated thing that defies glib generalisation.

I knew in advance that I could not re-create scenes like the geometry lesson. Much truth (as I said in *Trekking* and will not belabour here) that is open to a journalist with an ear and a notebook is not open to a TV presenter with half a million rands of video camera behind his shoulder. People respond differently when a camera is present. But instructive glimpses emerged nonetheless.

One was the comment of a principal, the dedicated and livewire Mr Mohammed Lachporria, that people ought to lay off the idiosyncrasies of African spelling and apply a little flexibility to the times that phonetic sounds are translated into written expression.

In principle I'm right with him, and indeed I abhor the indecent speed with which many unilingual South Africans denigrate the failure of their multilingual brethren to achieve perfection in English spelling and syntax and inflection. Unfortunately there does seem to be a slight small problem in building a tolerance into schooling policy, which is that misspelling rapidly turns into non-communication.

I quoted the home-made posters which an energetic artisan named Johannes had fixed to telephone poles all over northern Johannesburg, advertising his services in respect of Licking Roof. While he deserves honours for active marketing, the guy must be losing a ton of business because half his audience genuinely don't know that he's offering to fix their leaks.[3] They think it's an advertisement for an avant-garde play. The poles are full of those, and they're often stranger than this.

Mohammed and I batted around at the question of Tolerance vs Dictionary, not arriving at any blinding conclusion, and then we went off to Mr Nkomo's history class.

Mr Nkomo was pleased to announce that he was now working from the New South African textbook, which no longer depressed people by telling them about colonialism and

[3] Somebody in the meantime has apprised him of his error, and now the posters say 'Leacking Roof'.

Van Riebeeck and such things. It told them about black achievements.

'It must tell you *something* about Van Riebeeck,' I said.

'No,' Nkomo happily replied, 'Van Riebeeck is out of it.'

It seemed to me that no matter how firmly one stood for sensitivity and morale-boosting, the event that heralded not only a third of a millennium of government but also the arrival in South Africa of every modern artefact from roads to mail to statutes could not realistically be written out of history. We had a short sharp debate, which was all but drowned out by rain drumming on the classroom's tin roof (the ceiling had been stolen) and nearly invisible in the darkness (the lights had been stolen) but was fundamentally:

No, he said, Van Riebeeck could go; all you needed was history that made people feel good.

Hey, I said, you make people feel good in defiance of fact, they'll come short.

The debate was a stand-off, but I was still sceptical that Van Riebeeck could have been blotted out. We couldn't read the book in the classroom, so he lent it to me for scrutiny.

I took it home with a foreboding sense of finding the new age gone haywire, sweeping the white presence under the carpet in favour of wishful thinking about ancient lost civilisations and the military genius of Shaka. In fact we wound up with a kind of draw. You had to look pretty hard to find old Jan, but he was there, in a single low-key passing reference. At first my instinct was towards indignation, not that I make any claim on the 1652 connection but I make plenty of claim on behalf of truth and similar outmoded notions. However the book on the whole was by no means out of line, it seemed to me, attempting valiantly to steer a cogent course through the rocks of SA's multiple vantage points upon a complex truth.

Nor was it airbrushing the white role out of sight, merely Van Riebeeck in person, which, when you think of it, might be pretty long overdue. What did he care for South Africa anyway? Zip. He was only here because the Here Zeventien put the screws on him, and he scuttled back home as soon as he could. We've done him enough favours, putting his wavy hair on 300 years of banknotes. He can rest in peace.

After six days of playing schools inspector, I was on the familiar see-saw of African extremity. The good things were great; the bad things were awful. One minute I'd be encountering some horrendous example of incapacity; the next I'd be surrounded by learning and laughter and enthusiasm and ubuntu. That's how it seemed at the time.

Back in the edit suite the perspective was slightly different. It always is. I come away from a shoot with my mental image formed by maybe 30, 40, hours of interaction, of which 10% or 20% is on camera. That 10 or 20% is what forms the editors' impressions, and they then in turn take some 10% of that to pass on to the viewers.

This is part of what is inherently and inevitably wrong with the media. If you think you can take a week of impressions, condense them by 99%, and come out with anything vaguely related to the original balance between right and wrong, good and bad, up and down, please think again. It would be impossible to strike the perfect balance no matter how hard you tried, and the deep dark secret is that no TV producer on land or sea tries that hard. What he does try to do is get good ratings. Thus he wants his programme to be interesting more than he wants its nuances to be accurate. So a stark vivid comment with much gesticulation is instantly at a large head-start over a cautious careful comment mumbled through thin lips, even if the latter is a thousand or a million times more representative of reality than the former.

The schools programme, seen as filtered by the raw footage, reflected the excuse-and-inability factor much more prominently than my mind had sifted it benefiting from the ballast of many hours of unshot inputs, and the consequent process took me a step further on the learning ladder of media impact.

Initially, the programme was cut together by an editor new to the Trek, a particularly knowledgeable and pleasant chap who, whether despite or because of his knowledge, did not perceive the role of the Trek the same way that I did. He put elbow grease and midnight oil into the analysing and processing of what we had, to the point that he, like all the editors and sound mixers and cube-operators ever inflicted with Trek duty, must have wished laryngitis upon me. Sometimes these guys would hear a particular exchange 50 or 80 times over, until they could mimic in their sleep every last syllable and fluff and mumble. (If they got any sleep, that is: one of the purer forms of torture is trying to close down your head after a 14-hour stint listening to stuck records.)

Eventually the editor emerged with a finalised programme, to say it's ready for me to see.

'Fine,' I say. 'Great. I have to leave here in 15 minutes so can we make a date for 5 o'clock?'

'Oh, no problem,' he says. 'You can see it now, it's only six minutes long.'

'Um er gulp, beg your pardon?'

'Yes, you know your big new hang-up about how we should completely eradicate padding?'

'Of course.'

'Well I did that, and the programme makes six minutes.'

True enough I had been on an anti-padding rampage, ferociously pushing the idea that wheresoever we had a segment that said nothing in between two segments that said something, we were to find ways of conserving every possible minute and every possible second. This is neither a simple nor a necessarily correct approach. Of course all TV production cuts out woffle on principle, but where to stop cutting is problematic. If you cut too little you end up sounding like a live talk-show, with lots of dross draping over the sides of the nuggets, and your audience nods off. If you cut too much you end up full of fits and starts and disconcerting jerks.

My hang-up had been that we were not cutting enough. We were invariably leaving out numerous good exchanges that we wanted in but could not fit, and including several flabby bits that we wanted out but could not find a way of cutting out. So I'd been gaaning aan about becoming Supereditors, cutting out all the dross but refining the links with such elegant genius that no disconcerting jerks (at least other than the human kind) entered the picture. It was true enough that I'd been anti padding, but this was basically so we could fill our 24 minutes better, not so we could shed 75% of it.

True, too, we had established that we would run short programmes from time to time, but that was supposed to be a way of leavening the occasional over-heavy Egghead. It certainly was not what I envisaged of my prized Candid Classrooms.

Six minutes. In a state of shock I went to watch it, and six minutes later was in worse shock. In my view what we'd done is wipe out all the punchy bits, as being undiplomatic in the New SA, and wipe out all the touching bits, as being mawkish and sentimental, and cobble together a few bland statements by a selection of the more high-ranking people.

I demurred as diplomatically as possible, and the editor said: 'But the way I've done it is real television.'

And so it was. His was the proper way, I realised, and mine was out of line. Then again . . . there was the famous time that Henry Ford and Lee Iococca had a mighty row at a board meeting, shortly before Iococca quit, and resolved it when Ford took Iococca out the room, down the lift, across the forecourt, and turned back to point at the huge FORD sign atop the headquarters building. 'See that?' he said. 'Now do it my way.'

Who's Trek was this after all? I got it done my way, not least by the painful technique of spending some 40 hours in the edit suite myself, and we delivered and screened a programme which to me was unusually close to what the Trek was meant to be. It had everything from the bathos to the pathos to the hope to the horror, and I thought we'd done as well with our 24 minutes as we could.

Soon afterwards I was going to have to rethink. For the first of what would become several times in this vexed third series of the Trek I got a call from Auckland Park to kindly call in and 'discuss the way your programme is being shot and edited'. It turned out that in the SABC's view we had overcut it. We'd crammed in so many of the punchy bits that it looked wrong, and they wanted us to give it more space. We did that thing. We removed various intricate sequences which had taken several people buckets of midnight oil to produce. We replaced them with fewer and longer, if blander, extracts which would have saved endless hours if we had used them in the first place. I don't quibble with the motivation. If people who are seeing a programme with fresh eyes interpret it differently to those who have had it buzzing through their heads for days, I can accept that the latter have lost their perspective. But what did test the limits of my tolerance was a comment from one of the SABC people when I had delivered the revised version and they had checked it out. 'Much better,' he said. 'You see, all you need is to put a bit more care into the editing.'

As they say, funny old world.

8

Boland Bel-Air

I was in Franschhoek in 1972 and had luscious memories. Of quaint dereliction and crumbling walls and ghostliness. Of glorious mountains and beautiful valley. Of being addressed in Afrikaans and awakened to the novel notion that to some people this strange tongue was not just a matric-passing tool like Latin. Of a beautiful UCT student, her hair in the wind and my heart in the stars.

Also of looking for supper and finding a simple choice: mixed grill with egg or mixed grill without egg.

That was it, take it or try Stellenbosch. We took it. Our plates arrived, twice as high as they were round. Steak at the bottom, a slab the size of a dictionary with a herd of chops piled upon it, a pipeline of poly-extra-saturated wors on top of that, and a pale underfried egg decorating the summit like an angel in a Christmas tree, leaking yolk into the cholesterofest below.

Franschhoek, yes. I remembered it well.

For the benefit of those among us who become jittery at the roller-coaster of change, I am happy to report that two things remain the same:

(1) the name, and
(2) the mountain.

(Oh, the hair in the wind and its effects haven't changed either, but she was at home with our children.)

Elsewise . . . well, it's no news any longer that the humble Boland Boeredorp has transmogrified into Monte-Carlo-meets-Bel-Air. The place is crawling with global jet-setters. Your traditional creaking bakkie is outnumbered five to one by glittering 4x4s. There are 25 restaurants (which offer a hundred brands of designer salad but mixed grill is as easy to find as sheep's head). On a segment of the Villiersdorp road, two big old-style boereplase have proliferated into 58 wine estates (strangely smaller in real life than in image – sometimes just gardens. The trick to being an 'estate' is to carry it off with panache).

In many ways Franschhoek deserves a hearty doffing of the nation's hat. This is growth. This is creation. Nothing does South Africa need more. I walk down Dirkie Uys street, where the rustic desolation once evoked a nostalgia for the ease of the 19th century. Now there are painted walls and varnished windowframes and handcarved doors and neat lush gardens and smart brass letterboxes, and you can keep the nostalgia. What gets the G-spot tingling in my patriotic lobe is the whiff of hope for the 21st century: the images of employment and income and the prospect of having Africa sing the songs of progress.

So, everybody goes rah-rah-rah, right?

Well, no. Not, for a start, the Oom Japie Hugos of this world. Oom Japie was born in Franschhoek seven decades ago, took off at the appropriate time to sow the appropriate oats and so forth, and returned in the early 80s to settle for keeps in the calm and familiarity of the ol' home town.

Calm? Huh! Familiarity? Hah! Oom Japie's timing was a

misplaced masterstroke of the same ilk as the Belgian squire who bought his wife the manor house of Waterloo for her 1815 birthday present. Hard on Japie's heels came the flood. He reckons he's a stranger now, in the ol' home town. If he drops in at the kafee and says goeie middag they'll call for an interpreter. Looking for a main street parking place on a Sunday makes Rosebank Mall feel like Wide Open Spaces. Tourist buses come at you from every side, with a hundred lenses devouring your broekieslace stoep, and if you open your mouth in protest a hundred flashes go off in your face.

On paper Japie's 100-year-old cottage is worth a fortune. In practice, so what? It's the same house, same bed, same stove, same sitkamer. It may be 'worth' a jillion, but all that means to Oom Japie is that his rates go up a lot faster than his pension.

And whereas there are Afrikaners from Cape Point to the Limpopo who sukkel to attune to their country suddenly sounding like Little England, Oom Japie & Co have a knottier difficulty to boot. They have to attune to their valley looking like Little France.

The Frenchification of Franschhoek, locals tell me, started in the proverbial smoked-filled room, in Sandton. This formative moment, as you see from the room being not yet cowed by a Thank You For Not Smoking sign, was at least a decade ago, and it assembled several new Franschhoek landlords in the premises of an advertising agency to brainstorm the question: 'How do we put the place on the map?'

And the answer, in hindsight, was sublime. Go French. This was *Fransch*hoek, after all, home of the Huguenots. True, the Huguenots' purported Frenchness had been utterly immaterial to them for the last 280 odd years, but so what? Shortage of historical background did not stop the policemen of New York from inventing St Patrick's Day and making it a world-wide

Irish institution. The landlords were onto a marketing jackpot, and Franschhoek went French to the point that every eating place or sleeping place, to say nothing of wine-growing place, proudly bears a name South Africans can't pronounce.

For French tourists, there is a different problem. They are très enthusiastique as their bus pulls in to this town of French signboards and French flags and French tricolors on its municipal dustbins, and they bound forth with French intentions such as to kiss the locals' cheeks and proffer French greetings. Unfortunately it's all Afrikaans to the locals, who in keeping with local tradition respond with: (a) 'Huh?', or (b) 'Sorry I don't speak Greek hey', or (c) 'For you only R49,99, dahl'.

Time, naturally, heals. It won't be long before the locals get used to calling the Blignauts Bleeno and the Labuschagnes Labushayn and the De Villierses De Feeyay. Day visitors, as Franschhoeker Robert Kirby points out, need merely be put through the French In Sixty Easy Lessons course to equip them to find their way around the local boutiques and decipher the menu at Chez Stoffel. But quibbles aside, the Frenchness factor is a real part of the Franschhoek phenomenon and an enheartening element of the go-ahead spirit that has made this place a model for a wavering nation.

Which brings us to the bigger catch.

Franschhoek comes in four quarters. There is town, now officially Franschhoek South, which is where (a) the white people live and (b) 100% of the go-aheadness takes place. There is Groendal, now Franschhoek North, the old stable middle-class coloured part. There is Vietnam, the newish coloured squatter camp, and there is Chris Hani, the even newer African squatter camp. None of these places harbours conspicuous affection for any other. All of these places are very conscious that Chris Hani (officially Langrug) has already overtaken all the rest as a population centre and is doubling rapidly.

Chris Hani is a pathetic mess full of the stink of urine and faeces. So is Vietnam. And while genteel Groendal is extremely non-urinated, and strong on china ducks and Tretchikoffs and other trappings of bourgeoism, it is in the biggest way also on the wrong side of the great divide. It, too, watches the boom from afar and says: 'Look at those whites, hogging it all.'

Whereby hangs a large question. Do the whites maliciously elbow the others away from the river of prosperity, or does the fault lie with those who supinely eye the river and say 'but it's out of reach'?

At Franschhoek I found no lack of people with quick fingers, alacritous to point at the other side and say 'the blacks do nothing' or 'the whites leave us out'. More impressively, and surprisingly, I also found several who were ready to do a bit of inward pointing. But while it's one step for the squatter leaders to rather perplexedly concede that 'hmm, yes, maybe it is up to us to make the tourists want to come this way too', that's one heck of a long way from the actual doing of it.

And while back in the gabled estates there are some who apologise for having allowed the collapse of this self-help project or that upliftment programme, this is not all that helpful either. It's got to be more fundamental than obligatory service on the board of a token charity. Either the squatters feel progress some way other than by jemmying the estate windows, or the squirarchy of Franschhoek will soon have hijacking as their staple dinner conversation like their Gauteng counterparts. And it's in the end up to them – the rich, the competent, the capable – to go ahead and get the go-ahead flowing on the other side of town too. After all, if they're so smart, why ain't they secure?

As a metaphor for South Africa, Franschhoek is a fine candidate. The rich get richer and more nervous while the squatter camps get bigger. It's not much help hoping they'll go away. You've got to work – *work* – on the belief that one day the people of Chris Hani, too, will have difficulty finding a loaf of plain brown bread among the profusion of gift shops.

Franschhoek scored pretty well as a programme. I was happy, after about 72 recuts. My colleagues were less happy, after labouring through the recuts. Robert Kirby was not happy either, writing in the Financial Mail that he was glad to have refused to participate. His fears had been confirmed; we had ended up running frivolous trivia like a sequence on an estate-owner who opens his champagne bottles with a hereditary sword.

Now of course no TV presenter will lightly argue with Kirby, whose chief joy is to load his keyboard with grenades and his printer-tray with arsenic and leave you in a state such that it takes six weeks after his column appears before you can pull your head out from under the stone. Nonetheless it is perhaps necessary to respectfully wonder whether Mr K had had his porridge this morning.

The sword-wielder, Achim von Arnim of the Clos Cabrière estate, wielded his mouth as niftily as his sword, with an uncommonly blunt torrent of invective on the central issue, the selective nature of the town's prosperity. That stuff was legitimate viewpoint, apart from being crisp TV. Was I, in the interests of undiluted Eggheadism, to hear his case but censor out the eye-catching sabre-swipe which sent the head of the bottle off into his flower-beds? Might as well have a studio discussion.

To my mind the Franschhoek programme struck a balance. The place is beautiful; there was fun to be had – happily the camera missed the embarrassing moment when I had to dismount after riding further and faster on a horse than I had ever done before – and the whole was wrapped up in a package which encompassed a modicum of thought together with a quotient of entertainment.

And all this had come out of a simple return to our simple origins – go somewhere, look around, tell it as we saw it.

So we did the same again.

9

Diverse Tribe

The leafy north of Johannesburg, when I was at high school and Hendrik Verwoerd was writing the statute books, was English territory as far as the eye could see. Afrikaners were some foreign species, dimly fearsome but eminently mockable – not of course when they were listening, because they might administer a bunch of fives, but when they were safely out of earshot, which was easy because they were hardly ever in earshot.

We'd only ever meet an Afrikaner in the form of an occasional policeman or electrician, who would say things like 'did you got a licence' and 'is your lights burning' which sent my contemporaries into epilepsies of suppressed giggle until the guy was back in his bakkie and the scions of elegance could wet themselves mimicking the accent and the grammar. It mattered nought that he had made an effort in English. That was our right, no? It was also the only way for comprehension to get out of the starting blocks. Our Afrikaans ran to Goya Mora and Buy A Donkey, plus Voetsak Hairyback, a phrase much in vogue in the noble fight against racism, discrimination and prejudice.

In those days the Afrikaner was a straw man – a straw man

with an iron fist, yes, but a straw man in the realm of perception: 'Rope' in one of the bolder slang epithets, for 'thick, hairy and twisted'.

Some time subsequently, the Boer War at last closed shop. Our kids grow up with Boerekinders who win the English prize as well as the mathematics one, and who help them install computer games. Fouries and Venters abound in suburbs formerly the preserve of the Jacksons and Johnsons, and our problems with their use of our language are new problems. Like Liza Doolittle they speak it too well, and they pull rank. If five Afrikaners are in a group and a single Engelsman drifts in, conversation switches in mid-sentence into fluent English. It's one part courtesy but the other part is one-upmanship – 'we could humour you and downscale to simple words and slow enunciation, but it's easier to swap to your language and use it at the same level as we were using our own'.

If you need a top-drawer medic, you'll like as not find yourself in the hands of a Dr Roux or Van der Merwe. Big tax problem? It's Du Toit or Vorster or Cronje you'll be referred to. Trapped into a heavyweight lawsuit? Chances are both your Silk and the other side's trace their lineage to someone who had the postmaster read his letters to him.

Lately you've also started to find that where there's a volunteer feeding scheme on the go, or a night-school for adult illiterates, or a rural self-help project, the moving force can as easily be an alumnus of the Poffadderskuil Hoërskool as an alumnus of Wits. From a city-English perspective, the typical Afrikaner is no longer a grof khaki caricature so much as an ultra-cultivated hi-tech professional whose distinguishing features are a plummy accent and a frantic anti-racism. The wheel has turned the whole circle.

But . . . have we developed a new caricature as misleading as the old one? If in the old days the wheel had loose spokes dangling around its edges, doesn't the new wheel have them too? Politically the image of 'the Afrikaner' has done a total somersault; the thundering *Never!*s of the Old Right transformed into the polite Pleases of the Freedom Front and the Pssts of anxious Nats on the lookout for black allies. The far right could hold its annual convention inside a combi. But was this miraculous transformation quite as miraculous as it looked?

We'd broken the ethnic waters by 'doing' the coloureds. Hey, we thought, let's be rainbow. Let's do the Boere.

We started by trekking an incongruously short trek – to Cedar Avenue in Auckland Park, which would be in the shadow of the SABC if the sun ever shone from the south. There resides a modest well-treed office building called Die Eike, which is the central processing unit of a whole barrowload of Afrikanerdom. The remnants of the Broederbond are in Die Eike. So is the Federasie van Afrikaans Kultuurvereniginge and numerous of its constituent vereniginge. So are the Rapportryers. We started there because I wanted to make a point about changing times.

On one side of Die Eike lie the gorgeous gardens of the Johannesburg Country Club. On the other, until a few years ago, nestled a humble low-rent cottage which was the nerve centre of nearly all the actual revolutionary activism that I ever came across.

Back in that forgotten age of Guilt and Struggle, White Rule and Radicalism, these three neighbours represented three distinct and hostile points of the social compass. If the Broederbonders had nipped next door to the Country Club, somebody would have referred them to the tradesmen's gate. Had they opened the gate of the cottage on the other side, there would have been headlong flight out the back door.

The Club disliked few things more than the moustachioed grey-shoed safari-suit apartheidism of 5 Cedar Ave, but one of those things was the beard-and-sandals treason they would have found if they'd hidden in the unkempt bushes of 6 Cedar Ave and cupped their ear to a cracked window.

At 6 Cedar you wouldn't hear plain ethnic disdain of the Afrikaner Vrot Banana nature. Here there were heavies, racking brains and running through the Tassenberg to advance The Revolution. The only way they'd set foot in the Club was to foment a strike, and the only way they'd be found in Die Eike was doing a Guy Fawkes with petrol in the cellar.

My wife Gael and I were an oddity feature on the fringe of the 6 Cedar landscape. We had a toe in that pond, but we had another toe in the Country Club's rose-gardens, and in the eyes of the zealots that was tantamount to a Hamass activist playing bridge at the Zionist Federation. The international lefties who twirled through 6 Cedar on 'fact-finding' missions would look at us the way Riff Raff in Rocky Horror looks at the bedraggled crimplene-and-houndstooth couple who come to the door for help – the long slow look before he pronounces: 'You seem a little wet.' They would nudge the regulars and cast suspicious eyes in our direction to ask: 'Who let these persons in?'

To the regulars, though, we were a harmless conduit to respectability. They'd invoke our aid from time to time such as when Josie Fanon, widow of Frantz Fanon, the apostle of world-wide black revolt, was on their hands, and they wanted to slip her into our Melville home to throw the Security Police off the scent.

Josie was not the ideal house-guest, but we rationalised that there was too much deep thought going on in her mind, about routes to revolution and the betterment of the planet and all, to leave space for bourgeois conventions like 'please' or 'thank you' or 'can I help wash up?'. Then late one night a car was dropped at our house with a request to deliver Josie and one Rechana to a lawyer in Durban. This was getting very cloak-and-dagger, but there was no moral sin that I could see in driving someone to Durban. I did it, in the hope of being vouchsafed the keys to the wisdom of the Left, but Josie spent the trip reading comics and Rechana spent it glowering at me for being middle class and white and disgusting.

In those days, mental camps ruled. You were in one camp or another, and people like us with a foot in two were uncomfortable and edgy about both. The Club's ethos – obey the law and oppose apartheid, but not in irresponsible ways such as giving the blacks the vote – wasn't right for us. But we weren't sure that the melodramatics of 6 Cedar were creating the perfect world either. I got restive when I heard later that Rechana was in prison in Germany, for blowing things and people up. Still, I would have been no less restive if our sole contribution to The Struggle was to vote Prog and thump dinner tables.

When the 6 Cedar community dispersed – extraordinarily scattered through this world and the next, with early deaths, defections to Europe, to suburbia, to corporatism, and with a few, like Malcolm McCarthy and Horst Kleinschmidt, later returned to fight the good fight as useful citizens of the new order – Gael and I were given a dossier to safeguard. This thing, we were told, was too sensitive to be left in a bank and too dangerous to take through borders. When the time was ripe, it would be reclaimed.

I tucked it in a hiding place, along with other contraband like the mortuary pictures of Steve Biko's body and a smuggled copy of The Struggle is My Life (author N Mandela). Every couple of years I'd remember it and wonder what we were involved in. Were we babysitting the formula for atomic fusion? The masterplan of revolution? The one time the police ransacked the house they missed the cache (and ignored the adage that you do not judge a book by its cover – they took off Radical Chic, Tom Wolfe's rapier-job on American larnies playing voetjie with the Black Panthers). Eighteen years later, with the Special Branch a memory and the glamour of Revolution transformed to the order-papers of Democracy, the dossier's time had not ripened. We opened the sheaf and found a list called 'Potential Sympathisers', with the names and 1977 phone numbers of hundreds of Labour and Social Democrat parliamentarians from around the world.

What an anticlimax. What a joy, to recall those rifts now that they're gone. Like remembering an old toothache; you feel the better for being rid of it than having never had it at all.

And I felt it strongly as I stood at the portal of Die Eike and rang its bell for the first time ever. Back then, these three contiguous properties personified three elements of the fractured land: the Fascists, the Patricians, the Reds. Now you can meet people from all or any of those corners and be at one. We can like each other, welcome each other. It's a genuine wonder – not just in the loose use, but the dictionary definition. While the new nation is correctly said to have bridged gulfs between black and white, its byproduct has obliterated gulfs between white and white. It is a deep and continuing reward, delivering frissons in the flashbacks, such as when confidently ringing a doorbell which would have once spelt trauma.

The idea was to deliver a pithy introductory homily using the three neighbours to sum up the contrast between present and past, and proceed into a short sharp situation-report on the state of Afrikanerdom from the guys who were ex officio at its hub. Having thus applied breadth, and established that Afrikanerdom was wider than the khaki Boer on the platteland plaas, we'd head off to some distant dorp to give a little recognition to the Boer who *was* on the platteland plaas, and presumably in khaki.

A neat plan, we thought, and a way to bring in the Boere from outside the new mainstream without re-caricaturing the whole diverse tribe. But, as they say, to make God laugh tell

Him your plans. The introductory homily wouldn't get pithy, and the situation report was neither short nor sharp, and as always we ended up trying to compress a quart of programme into a pint of pot, so what the screen finally saw was no more than my emerging from Die Eike with map in hand and saying: 'Now let's go somewhere the Boere may not be up to speed on this sophisticated new thinking, such as . . . um . . . what's this "Alldays", in the Northern Province? Wonder where that funny name comes from . . .?'

This was a bit of a cheat. We had already picked on Alldays, precisely for its unlikely English name. We did, though, as implied on screen, get sommer then and there in the combi and point north-west, into the most disillusioning and downbeat Trek yet.

Alldays has a mortuary, a hotel, a new yuppiestyle hunting lodge, a town council, a private school, a CD of the song '*I* will walk five *hun*dred miles and *I* will walk five *hun*dred more', a legend, and a vehicle population that consists of white bakkies.

To a list like that the phrase 'among other things' is an implicit addition, and of course there were other things. There are farms and there is a mine not far away and there is grass and bush and even an occasional stop sign. But that selective list exhausts the features that impacted upon our tour of enquiry, starting with the mortuary. Every dorpie has to be unique in some way, and Alldays' approach – making the district mortuary its most distinctive feature, right in the place where you expect a town hall – is truly original.

So is the legend. The name, we were told approx 200 times over, comes from an English surveyor who powerfully patronised the kroeg. He'd pop in for a quick one after work and drink himself stupid and fall asleep while the Transvaal sun was still shining bright. When he woke up in the morning it was no less bright, and he said 'Gee, you people never have nights here, it's all days.' Which is no doubt a sweet tale in a way, and reflects an accurate concept of local kroeg-patronisation standards, but is a crock of sticky stuff. There had indeed been an English surveyor, but the mundane truth is that his home town in England was called Alldays. (How *it* acquired its name is another question.)

Re the musical repertoire, a dogged single-mindedness was the hallmark. When we arrived at the hotel five hundred miles was playing in the bar. While we checked in it played again. And again. And again. Every time it came to the line 'to be the man who heavahs into you' the bar population enthusiastically sang along. It played through dinner and it played all night and it played through breakfast and it was playing when we checked out some 60 hours later. We felt we'd got the message. The bar evidently did not.

A bunch of local people told us a pile of reasonable and sensible things about prospects and development and the promise of the new age. There was the dominee, there was the hotelier, there was the chairman of the agricultural society and so on.

There was in particular a lady from the Vrouefederasie who gave us two tons of detail about how this women's organisation was applying itself to the uplift – the sewing classes and the literacy classes and the hygiene classes – which had once been the derided business of English liberal bodies like the Black Sash and African Self-Help. This was a genuinely new world she was portraying, with new energies and new effort and a new spirit of getting the blacks on board the train of progress. Unfortunately she sounded like that Soweto headmaster whose vocabulary was dominated by the word 'unfortunately'. The ideas and the aims were there but not much was working. Which is to say, nothing was apparently working other than a couple of home-sewing ventures, which, while surely admirable generators of employment, were not the best examples of selfless contributions to public uplift. They were mini-businesses run by Vrouefederasie members on their own account, paying black women to embroider animal figures on waistcoats or tablecloths for sale to tourists.

For the failure of the other efforts diverse reasons were on offer, from bureaucratic hold-ups over permissions and licences to the paucity of locpop[1] response to the frailties of the Vrouens themselves. One key participant – 'she even speaks their language' – had recently quit in disillusion. One major scheme had spent a year in abeyance for the lack of R3 000.

I said: 'Forgive a stadsjapie pronouncing on what the plaasjapies should be doing, particularly given what we do, but to you the problem is both more immediate and smaller in scale, and for your lives to work out you have to make sure that the lives of the people around you work out. Couldn't the whites here raise R3 000 and end the delay?'

She was as stunned as if I'd said 'raise a million rands'.

'Oh, no,' she said. 'We couldn't meet *anything* like that.'

Well, couldn't they? It's not as if they're living abject lives. Their circumstances are no lesser than their counterparts in the cities. On the other hand, was it fair to ask? There are not a lot of suburban welfare groups digging into their pockets for an extra R3 000 whenever a hitch comes up. In fact, there are not a lot of suburban welfare groups. On the other hand, here is a finite local community, with a distinct and, by comparison, immensely coherent leadership faction in its midst: the whites. If there was a serious will to make development happen, a place like this could be scoring sixes before the big amorphous cities agreed on where to put the wickets.

We met other real people, people who were trying. There were innumerable plans to reawaken fading cattle farms in

[1]Code – originally army – for 'local population' i.e. the blacks.

the form of game ranches. There were individuals, like the couple who ran the smart new general-dealer-cum-pharmacy, who were very much on the side of the new era.

As usual, there was also a good deal of questioning by everybody of everybody else's motives. One fellow bragged about his noble and foresightful rôle in firing up a new black housing development, about to arise in a large vacant patch as close to the middle of town as the town had a middle. He somehow forbore to mention that he had pulled in a tidy profit by selling the land. His townsfolk eagerly filled in the gap, dismissing his claims to social responsibility as a cover for a personal windfall.

Still, for whatever combination of reasons a new South African consciousness was not absent. I emphasise it here. It's not to be ignored. But having emphasised, I proceed to record with honesty that the overall input was not merely depressing. It was odious, hateful and hate-filled.

The first night, cameras down and microphones off, we were invited to join the merriment at the hunting lodge. Fifteen or twenty people were on hand, including some who had already, in working hours and formal context, given me more or less orthodox, semi-politically-correct, perspectives on the state and prospects of Alldays and environs. I approached the evening with a degree of quiet satisfaction that, yes, the pace was different and the details were their own, but by and large a new recognition of new challenges was on the go here just as it was in the committee rooms of parliament or the convention centres of the Sandton Sun.

At first the evening seemed to point the same way. The place was beautifully laid out; beautiful African décor; beautiful hand-carved African furniture; an uncommonly excellent fillet, served to Parisian perfection; a variety of pop classics over the amplifiers, and nil *hun*dred miles. There was a smell of cosmopolitanism too, with a smattering of Britons and

Germans and mining execs from Johannesburg.

Slowly an unease drummed in to my head. For one, the proprietor, Dirk, insisted that we were his guests, with that determined generosity which is trouble at any time and worse trouble when the replete guest may need to become the detached journalist. It was Dirk's mission to impose a free supper upon us, like it is some hosts' mission to impose wine on guests as if a taste for soda is an insult to their hospitality. A certain tension crept in on that account. Then a bigger tension raised its head on another account.

Among the bar decorations was a set of plaques commemorating big kills – a kudu shot by so-and-so, a rhino by so-and-so, etc. One of these plaques, right at the apex, recorded the hunter as what looked like a misspelled version of a black surname. I think it was Kunine. Knowing no Kunines, but plenty of Kunenes, I assumed this was some new provincial official whom the lodge wished to honour (and/or to keep on its side). I made some comment on the name, displaying that I thought its owner was black. 'Oh, no,' said a shocked bar-lady. 'That's an important German guest. No kaffirs get in here.'

From there on the evening sank. Liquor was sinking too, which was not unrelated, but somehow a switch seemed to have been flicked. Until then there had been a guarded observance of proprieties. Not that the K-word and the attitudes that go with it had been absent, but most people treated that kind of talk like they would treat the four-letter words in the presence of a priest: 'Oh! Fu.. oops, sorry dominee, I mean Oh! Dear!'

The bar-lady's ingenuous statement blew the secret, as it were, and opened the flood-gates to a torrent of kaffir-talk. Soon the sole and whole topic of conversation was the blacks. Every so-called joke was about blacks. Every anecdote or tale or item of news or point of argument had something to do with the blacks, and in every case the tone was contempt. The jokes were so unfunny it was hard to believe that anybody could laugh, but laugh the people did, foreigners and Joburgers included. A major theme was Mandela going to heaven and meeting up with Terre'Blanche or Verwoerd or some such character, and coming off second best. One example was to do with Terre'Blanche getting drunk and driving on the wrong side of the road and bashing a car driven by Mandela. Both men die and arrive at the Pearly Gates. Mandela gets sent downstairs because he is so cheeky as to drive a car like a white man. Terre'Blanche gets welcomed in because he has served Earth by reducing the black population.

This was just warm-up. After the heaven series the manne got down to straight talk. 'Why did God make kaffirs so ugly? So people would never forget to hate them.' Uproarious laughter. 'Why did God make kaffirs stink? So they would hate each other.' Uproarious laughter. So it went on.

Did I object? Yes. Did I object enough? No. Why not? Dunno. Partly because I was chicken, but there was a steak factor too. You're compromised when an unpaid-for fillet is boosting your gross vehicle weight and causing small burps of satisfied aftertaste. And the barley factor is not to be ignored. By the time they were in full stride the joke-tellers were mainly in a state such that a breathalyser test would have melted the equipment. Quite aside from the aggression potential, there are limited returns on the delivery of moral sermons in the circumstances.

We left early and unblessed by the backslapping to which we'd arrived (and having paid for our fare). I slept uncomfortably, due not to the bed or the heat but to the awesome sense that this country is incomprehensible after all. It wasn't just that 20 people had been swapping racist jokes. It wasn't just the crudity of the jokes either. It was the absolute acceptability; the fact that once the bandwagon got rolling virtually everybody hopped on, all outdoing each other to be more offensive, nobody a whit skaam. A few hours earlier, many of these guys were minding their Ps and Qs and greatly sensitive to hints of reprimand from an outsider. Now in the veritas of vino they're egging each other forward like schoolboys hissing the headmaster, in a way which forcefully says this is the real thing, this is the hair let down, this is not the façades of proper-speak.

Moreover the whole context was too ironic to make sense. For one thing, while the talk is all kaffirs this and kaffirs that and hate the kaffirs, the environment is a carefully constructed celebration of Africa – African faces in wood and in oil, African crafts, African artefacts, not made by anyone called Van der Merwe. For another, in the lucid phase of proceedings several of the locals had been much concerned to locate themselves as the progressive wing of district affairs, in distinction from the hardliners who were evidently led by one Johan Boshoff. They badmouthed the hardliners with gusto, and the name Johan Boshoff kept coming up as a symbol of implacability. The same name had been coming up the same way from everybody all day, usually in the context of education, where it appeared this Boshoff had caused much trauma by setting up a contentious new right-wing school. When he came up again and again as the bad guy in the eyes of the kaffir-talk crowd, I began to envisage him as a kind of Gestapo Oberst in the sun. If this bunch were the progressives, the opposition must breathe out poison gas.

Throughout the tirade, various black employees were calmly toting plates, clearing glasses, cleaning ashtrays. I have no idea what they were thinking beneath their downtrodden façades, but I winced doubly at their presence. The regulars seemed not to recognise their existence; they were just glass-clearing robots invisible to mankind; but then one of the drinkers abruptly reached out, clasped a guy collecting dishes, hugged him tight in close, yelled: 'My man!',* and then pushed him away with a tap on the cheek like you might give your 12-year-old son.

This was a recognition all right, and no matter how you look at it, a recognition in which affection played some part. Not that it was a classical gesture of friendship; it had bullying and domination and arrogance wrapped up in it too, and was not necessarily an affection welcomed by the receiving party. The guy is one minute wending a quiet slalom with his tray between the flailing hands of gesticulating customers. Next minute a ham-like arm jerks him off course and buries his head in the open shirt and matted hairs of a vast and sweating midriff. It was a far from dignified position for the tray-wielder, not to mention precarious for the tray – which he maintained upright with such desperation that I had to imagine a broken plate would mean half a day's wages. But no way could you erase affection from the equation. The Boer wouldn't have done that to me or Brett or Richard, veritas or no veritas, but he might just have done it to some ultra-nearest ultra-dearest, such as a brother or life-long buddy.

So why now is he doing it to this black guy, about whom he is simultaneously screaming the most disgusting epithets? Does this make sense? If the answer is yes, please send a postcard. I would love to understand.

But the questions and the ironies were the small part of this experience. The great gross naked obnoxiousness was the big one. I'm not among those who insist that the unfolding South Africa has to be about palliness and poodlefaking. I just want it to be about respect. Where was the respect here? Blinding by its absence.

Next morning we set off at a cruel hour to meet the notorious Johan Boshoff of the iron teeth. He had been

*That's Afrikaans, but translation may not be necessary.

'unavailable' by phone, but we knew that half the population had told him we intended calling. His farm was way out of town. The idea was to get there with the dawn, before he was likely to remember any sudden urgent appointments elsewhere which might just last until we'd gone home. We somewhat miscalculated the dawn, being inexperienced students of its arrival times, but the shadows were still long when we turned in to a spectacular farm on the Limpopo.

One day, if and when South Africa gets its act together and goes into full-scale First-World stuff like movie-making, Johan ought to rent out his farm to production companies. They could use it for six different purposes. The roads would do fine for a Rough Rider; the massive stark rock formations for a badlands Western; the daisy fields for an Emma Thompson idyll; the immense plantations with their swarms of toiling figures for either a paean to productivity or a lament about exploitation; the homestead for a setting in Gone With The Wind, and the fortifications for a sci-fi horror movie about World War III.

The fortifications are in fact a paradoxically happy story. The South African side of the Limpopo is lined with an immense African answer to the Berlin Wall – multiple coils of riot-control razorwire with gates like blockhouses, encasing cables designed to deal instant death. This is a legacy of the border war, and whatever problems Alldays and its district now labour under it is an almighty relief that they no longer labour under this one. The razorwire is still there, but now as a mere deterrent to illegal immigration. The electric fence is in theory in 'non-lethal' mode (which I gather is in practice the mode also known as 'off'), and the gate-keeping is, er, shall we say 'relaxed'. The contrast is even clearer in town where public buildings expensively equipped to withstand siege or mortars – with steel doors, heavy window-mesh making interiors gloomy and exteriors paranoiac, scythed fences the height of flagpoles – now loll peacefully open with their locks discarded and their blades rusting. Thank you, Lord, that at least we skipped our armageddon. At the times that we're rudely required to reflect that things might be better, it's a solace to reflect that they might also have been much worse.

It can not truthfully be said that Johan Boshoff welcomed us with open arms. He was 'at the tomatoes', we were told. 'You'll see a white bakkie.' Picturing, through city eyes, a cosy veggie patch in a corner, we made our way in the direction indicated. So far so good. We got to the tomatoes, an irrigated field of a size to land Boeings on. Way off was a white dot which a pair of binoculars might have identified as a bakkie. It betrayed no interest in the combi's arrival at its perimeter, and the combi's prospects of getting any closer were about as good as its prospects of swimming the Limpopo. So I started walking.

This field was *well* irrigated. Every step was a shlurp into quicksand. By the time I puffed and panted up to the turned back of the sole pale complexion in sight, I was caked mud up to my ankles, acutely aware of a million muscles whose existence had passed unnoticed for 49 years, and imbued with a fresh respect for the labourer's lot.

To ignore me any further would have been a declaration of war. Johan greeted, civilly if frostily, living up to every right-wing stereotype from the khaki shorts to the bushy beard to the tree-trunk limbs and the bone-crusher handshake, and said he was duly honoured that we'd come all this way to see his farm and if we now wished to leave that was fine.

I've known similar get-losts before, but mainly in the old days when I secretly disliked the Boere and allowed them therefore to dislike me. This time, it was too much. I was here to listen to the guy, dammit, not to sell him snake-oil. What is more, my feet were barbells and a thousand daggers were dancing inside my legs. The chalice of human tolerance was in need of a refill and I became a tad ratty. I barked and grouched about the sad fate of the alleged tradition of Boere-hospitality. I said that if the Righties were going to treat honest enquiry as enemy action no wonder they made everybody feel sick. I said that if he slammed the door on fair hearings he shouldn't complain that what he got was unfair ones.

The upshot was that Johan would take us around the farm; show us anything we wanted; we could film whatever we liked, except him. And he wouldn't say anything about the school.

Now when you're shooting a TV programme you look at the world through narrowly focused eyes. You're interested in what adds to your programme. A long silent shot of farm scenery might be soothing on the eye, but it does not enhance public grip on why the pillars of the community are, like a gang of outlaws, furtively educating their kids in an illegal school in a barn. Debate took place, more amicable than before, but Johan would not be moved and I couldn't really fault his reasoning. As it was, he said, a couple of dozen kids from the district were receiving a brand of schooling which, no matter how unregistered or unapproved, was in their parents' eyes somewhere close to reasonable. Anything that he might say on a TV screen would, no matter how sensible or innocuous, cause another furore like the one in Potgietersrus. So no go.

After I'd prised a few kilograms of clay from my boots and no longer felt like Charlie Chaplin in snowshoes, Johan offered a guided tour. This was noteworthy for two things. First, the farm was an employment-generator par excellence. I've never seen so many people working in one place at one time, at least not an agricultural place. I didn't ask the obvious question, about wages. I didn't think I really needed to. Whatever the answer was it was going to make me miserable. (Other people around Alldays gave me various estimates of average wages, with the figure five rand a day featuring more than any other figure.)

The sight of a myriad swarthy souls hacking and hewing to deliver foodstuffs out of earth was both depressing and oddly inspiring. On the former count: heaven help us. This is as far as we've got? Half the world is into the pursuit of leisure while half the world breaks its backs in donkeywork with little more reward than to make it through an exhausted night so as to handle more donkeywork on the morrow. On the other count: where would these guys be without Johan Boshoff, and the order and organisation that had gone into creating this farm and its management and its marketing? Would they be their own small peasant farmers, with dignity and property and co-ops and an economy and an occasional trapping of modern comfort, or would they be aching in the ultimate indignity of starvation and wondering why they by the million could not live from the land the way that their forefathers had once lived by the thousand?

Ten years ago I knew that but for one big farmer gobbling tens of thousands of hectares there'd be thousands of small farmers on a few hectares each. But the learning curve is an endless ride, often forcing the mind into directions the heart does not wish to follow. I look at the stupendous order, structure, control and system of the Boshoff farm and have to countenance the likelihood that without it the thousands of lives which it rudimentarily sustains would become not better lives, but even worse.

The tour had another intriguing feature, which impinged slowly and in the same form as the Sherlock Holmes story about the dog that did not bark in the night. As Sherlock found, what happens can be less noteworthy than what doesn't happen. Here too. As I walked and talked with Johan I realised I was not hearing a certain word, to wit 'kaffir'. Nor for that matter was I hearing contempt and belittlement.

Which certainly doesn't mean I was hearing shosholoza rainbow rah-rahs. Johan was sure that Africa in general and its southern tip not least is slithering steadily down the slippery slope. But simultaneously he is very much an African. He wasn't into hating the blacks. He was into differences, yes, but he was also into respect. He wanted to respect them; he wanted them to respect him. Even allowing for the fact that this was one-on-one and free of mob psychology; that it was morning and uncluttered by liquor and raucousness, his tone was a world removed from the disparagement of yesterday and a good deal easier to countenance.

Sadly and sillily, I spent my Limpopo half-morning suffused with TV's dictates. Obsessed with (vainly) urging Johan to tell the camera what he was telling me, I learned not half as much about the private school issue as I would had I been there as a real journalist with ears and ballpoint. Moreover, I accepted Johan's pleas to respect the privacy of the school, and we didn't try to go there either.

Back in town, later, we came across a bakkie-load of the schoolkids at the municipal library – cheery bubbly children, boys in khaki and borselkop and bare feet, girls in gingham dresses like pictures out of Kansas City, 1923. Cumulatively, from their teacher, from Johan, from others around town, I was acquiring a startling impression, of a region and nation littered with secret hole-in-the-wall illegal elitist schools.

People talked of incipient private schools in surrounding towns – Maastroom, Swartwater, Dendron . . . They talked of a great ideological row (Boers will be Boers, 'koppig forever' as one of them put it) between the 'Volkseie' schools and the 'Nasionaal-eie' brand, which apparently mirrored the old Conservative Party vs National Party faultlines. I had already come across some of these private schools in more southerly dots on the map, such as Pofadder and Springbok. Now I acquired a glimmering of an entire carpet of systematic criminality operating unbeknown to the world, providing Afrikaans children with an education on much the same lines as their great-great-great-grandparents received before the time of rules and syllabi and school inspectors.

The pattern, it seems, is for white parents to withdraw their children from government schools and set up their own school in a barn. There might be a single employed juffrou, teaching 10 or 30 children between 6 and 18 years old in a single room. Parents rally round as relief teachers, with one father giving a weekly lesson in motor mechanics and another handling the poetry of Langenhoven or Totius. Initially there was some attempt to get these schools registered and their certificates recognised, but then in 1996 there was an almighty furore over the effort to do something similar on a larger scale in Potgietersrus, and the fuss sent the little farmschools scuttling for anonymity and pulling blankets over their heads.

While we were in Alldays, winter '97, Potgietersrus' seventh successive application for registration was turned down. This was nil news in the national press, Potgietersrus being now yesterday's business. But it caused uproar among the white communities of the Northern Province, whereby hangs a large question.

The perception that the province's white people have of the Potgietersrus school affair is not one which a court of law would accept as gospel. It calls for heavy cross-examination. As a part-truth, though, and as a perception (and perceptions create their own truths, in the form of patterns of response) it has a certain salience. The perception is that the school tried repeatedly to accommodate to the government's demands: that each new application made more provision for more black presence, more facility-sharing with other schools, a greater portion of costs to be paid by parents, etc, but that the school stuck to a bottom line. It wanted its children taught in their language and – although there was much circumlocution around the specifics – in an environment where they felt at home, i.e. basically white. And to the ire and indignation of the whites the government had replied to each application: 'Permission refused, this is racist.'

Well now, the government is dead right. Racist it indubitably is, and as we know this is the new non-racial nation. Indeed, now the world's *most* non-racial nation.

Glance up there at the world's premier league, clustered around the North Sea and the Great Lakes, and wonder what became of the great non-racial ideals of the 70s. Yes, there are wondrously rewarding personal relationships all over (here too, and they weren't invented in '94). But group relationships are something else. In the countries where the march to the colour-blind future was most confident and most purposeful, confused disarray has taken over. The spirit of We Shall Overcome, once so filled with faith that after a crash-course in integration the world would abandon its awareness of race, is silent now. It's not so much that things have gone wrong, as that things have turned out different. It's not that the world is returning to the primitivity of segregation; just that it is re-thinking the nuances of integration. It's looking for a better place beyond stark insistences one way or the other. Nearly everywhere, except the world's most non-racial nation, is re-examining the assumption that where dissidents balk at diving voluntarily into the pool of universality, all you need is to help them along with a prod of the jackboot.

When it comes to the hard cases, the change goes further. From Chechnya to Palestine to Bosnia to Rwanda to Slovakia to Sri Lanka, the seal of global approval no longer requires compression of reluctant groups into the same compartments. It admits and sponsors the creation of new compartments in a frequently frantic search for ways to deter the less comfortable siblings in the Brotherhood of Man from inserting axes or bullets into each other's heads.

Inside this process, and much ignored, is a significant set of new losers – namely the people who *had* embraced the wide world. There had surely in every racially troubled place been racially untroubled people: Czechs living undisturbed in Slovak parts of town; Chechens married to Russians; Arabs participating as democrats in Israel's public life; Croats and Serbs mixing peacefully in the village pub; Hutus and Tutsis toiling at the same fields.

Moreover there are the progeny of past liaisons across the barriers, people who have ceased to be one thing or the other in precisely the way that so many South Africans have ceased to be, for example, 'English' or 'Afrikaans' but are now neither and both. Aha, it is said, but such people are just minorities. Hang on. They may be minorities but what's 'just' about that? They're pushed now into a newly primitive brand of pain. They're forced to make choices that should have been beyond the need of making. Public pressure reintroduces the ethnic splits, and private lives retrogress in the wake. The loyalties of blood reassert themselves and the loyalties of friendship and acceptance and matrimony suffer as a result. This is backward. Can a planet that devises laser surgery and the Internet really do no better with social relationships?

Apparently not. While the comity of nations re-invents ethnicity, and to hell with the tribulations of those who had transcended it, South Africa stumbles into a way of life prescribed by the sociology departments of European universities in the 1960s, and to hell with frivolous obstacles such as human frailty.

Of course it is racist for the Boshoffs of Alldays or Potgietersrus to cocoon their offspring. What they ought to do is share and share alike, and afford the theorists of non-racialism a glow of quiet contentment. They ought to throw open the doors of their formerly white school to their new democratic compatriots, and rejoice in the opportunity to advance the unity of the new nation by having their white Afrikaans children sharing classrooms in proportions of twenty to one with black Sotho children.

That's what they ought to do. Non-racial theory tells us, and so does the Department of Education.

What they actually do is turn to crime, by starting their own schools outside the law.

We learned at school about Lord Charles Somerset, who set out to bash and whip the Dutch into becoming English, and the lesson we learn is how idiotic and oppressive this quest was and how it was bound to fail. Funny how selective retrospect can be. It's common cause that Somerset was way out of line in 1822. Now we have the repeat performance in its foothill stage and the standard response is to clap and cheer. The Potgietersrus episode, in its newsworthy phase, was greeted by howls of righteousness from the leader-writer fraternity along the lines of 'how dare these flat-earth right-wingers try to re-create apartheid'. Much of this flood came from people (of all complexions) who take their own children out of urban government schools when the black proportion reaches 30%, to place them in the traditional larnie private schools which wouldn't even *think* of trying to re-create apartheid, which are *extremely* non-racial and *wide* open to absolutely anybody, absolutely anybody with R15 000 a year to put into the coffers.

From the pool-and-court perspective of the Sachsenwald[2] there is something lip-curling about these calloused Boers, with their hardscrabble farms and broken flyscreens and junkheaps of rusting tractors, barricading the ramparts against an innocent and photogenic black 10-year-old. But up in the place where it happens you do not depend upon the focus of a lens. You see not only the photogenic 10-year-old whose articulate and engaging father, as fearful of the swamping as

[2]The forest planted by early Randlords, covering suburbs such as Westcliff, Houghton, Saxonwold and Parkview and the heartland of the rich and roughly liberal Old Johannesburg Establishment.

any Boer, is outraged by the insult to his daughter and himself. You see also the thousand other faces which the Boers correctly believe will have taken over the school by the year after next. No minorities in these circumstances will behave like paragons of non-racial virtue. To expect them to abdicate the claim to some form of critical mass involves more than hypocrisy, it involves a lunacy. But in the world's most non-racial nation some over-promoted provincial politician knows racism where he sees it and wields his 'Permission Refused' rubber stamp with vigour, turning a crucial segment of his population into embittered enemies of the law.

Thus the Alldays school issue left me with a new awareness of the fragility of the myth. If we draw the non-racial ideal with pencil strokes and delicacy, we may draw a thing that will grow and last. If we slap it on with trowels, history will have a new Charles Somerset to laugh at and say Imagine! The stupidity!

So after two days in Alldays I am a glowering grouch. I am sick of the racism of the whites; I'm sick of the stupidity of the government. I am in disillusioned frame of mind. We set out to meet the local administration.

We have certainly met the former administration, in the form of numerous ex-mayors and ex-councillors and in particular one Ross Thom.

Ross Thom was the town's Mr Big from approximately the time of the Second Rinderpes until precisely the time of the new non-racial democracy. He is now the manager/janitor/bookings-clerk of the Ross Thom Hall, the town's meeting-place, and in moments when the bookings demand is less than onerous he is given to undertaking freelance inspections of the town and environs in his highly distinctive vehicle. Neither white nor a bakkie, this is an aged black Golf equipped with some nine aerials which give it the appearance of a porcupine on wheels.

The Ross Thom Hall is beside the main road, a short walk out of town. Ross Thom sits in the office that adjoins it, and has a total grasp of the comings and goings. He is by no means the only Alldayan possessed of the ability to magically recognise each white bakkie from all its brothers, but he is the only one past whose eyes they nearly all move on their way in or out – and if in doubt the porcupine sallies forth to recce. In the old days, if you wanted to know whether the doctor was in town or who was the dominee visiting or was Oom Wouter at the market, you checked with the switchboard operator. These days the phones are automatic but Ross Thom fills the function.

In Ross Thom's office I listened to deposed ex-councillors talking about their deposers, the new council. It would have been surprising if their views were filled with admiration, and no surprises were involved. The ex-councillors enumerated dozens of areas of decline, from the cessation of road marking services to the cessation of rates collections to the cessation of decision-making and minute-taking. In each respect their complaints seemed convincing. In many respects I thought or hoped that decline might be temporary, a matter of reorientation. In one respect I was stupefied: the totality of the turnaround.

Here the old pattern of 100% white control had not been replaced by a pattern of 60% or 70% or 80% or 90% black control. It had been replaced by 100% black control.

Was this sensible? In terms of respectable democratic theory, of course it was. The district population is of the order of 100 black people per 2 non-black people. The hundred people vote solidly ANC. The two people might divide their vote between the Freedom Front and the National Party. There are six council seats. Of course all six are going to be ANC seats. That's democracy.

On paper, it's democracy. In practice you are waving away

the minority which dominates every bit of commercial and industrial activity, the minority which pays almost every wage which anyone sufficiently fortunate to have a wage gets paid. You are saying to that minority: 'You had your day. Now go home.' You're saying it, moreover, in terms of a foreign theory that does not easily export. You're saying it as if this was an English village, where if in one election 98% of the people vote Tory, why, of course you're going to have a 100% Tory council. Labour and Liberals and Social Democrats can revise their strategies and maybe next election you'll get a Labour majority. This does not apply in a place like Alldays. Your 2% minority is an entrenched and permanent minority, with no place to go to other than to 1%.

No one believes more firmly in universal equal suffrage than I do. You have to have equal citizenship; no special constitutional corners for this minority or that minority. You and I might be different in every way, and fight over half of them, but we had better be equal in citizenship or we fight about that first and fiercest. The trick is to make citizenship not just equal on paper, but in hearts and minds and consequences. Democracy after all is supposed to be about people acquiring power over their own lives, not about the 51% telling the 49% what colour boots they may wear. If you kick one lot into oblivion for the sake of welcoming the other lot out of oblivion, progress is less than optimum.

We left Ross Thom & Co with half an hour to spare before we were due to attend a 10 o'clock meeting of the town council. We thought we'd take the time for a short preliminary chat with the new mayor, who worked at the post office. He was keen to talk to us, but:

(a) a 15-minute delay took place while he went to ask his boss if he could take 5 minutes off work;
(b) a 20-minute delay took place while he went to don the

clothes in which he preferred to face the camera;
(c) just as we were beginning to think he must have gone straight to the meeting, he returned all spruced up and ready. I said: 'Look, maybe we'd better get to the meeting now and do this afterwards.' He said: 'What meeting?'

It turned out he was now the former new mayor. He'd been booted out by some arcane internal dispute. Being not a party to the meeting himself, he shared no part of our anxiety to get there before we missed things, and he was so eager for his moment on the camera that I thought we had to give it to him.

So we stood in the dusty post office yard, him in his Sunday best and me in a pair of striped shorts destined to shortly cause terrible embarrassment to my daughters and sarcastic raptures among the TV critics.

The five-minute interview with the newly former new mayor consisted of an uninterruptible 15-minute tirade of beaming but incoherent goodwill towards all mankind, even including the guys who had just tossed him off his council, topped by about two minutes of question-and-answer on practical matters such as the alleged cock-ups to which the old council had pointed.

The experience demonstrated two things: (1) for anybody to be this generous in defeat was grounds for St Peter to make out the entrance ticket at the Pearly Gates, and (2) for anyone to have this small a grasp of what the council was meant to do was proof that he should never have come within 50 miles of heading the council.

From the newly former new mayor we proceeded to the meeting of the even newer council. We were now 40 minutes late and worried that we were losing out.

We need not have worried, but I didn't know that at the

time and I also didn't know it while I spent another quarter-hour waiting at the council's reception office for somebody to acknowledge my existence.

Three council employees were at work in the reception office, their backs studiously turned to the public window. Other faces came and went, all paying no attention whatsoever to the supplicant at their portals. I suppose I could have banged and shouted, but, let alone that I am uncomfortable in the bang and shout stakes, I thought No, let's see how I fare doing it the civil way.

Meantime I had much opportunity to take in how things worked and in particular to notice a certain central feature, viz, apartheid.

The building had two wings. In front of me at the window was the administrative side. Behind me was the municipal library. The admin block was entirely black. Not a non-black face came or went. The library was entirely white, with numerous white burghers, and nil newly enfranchised burghers, coming and going throughout.

Eventually an official emerged from a side door of the admin section and ushered me to the administrator. It was now after eleven. I said we wished to attend the ten o'clock meeting. 'Ah,' said the administrator, 'most unfortunately the ten o'clock meeting is postponed, as three of the six councillors have not arrived.'

The meeting was rescheduled to 3 pm. I was invited to return at that time. I was introduced to the three councillors who had arrived. They were courteous, and more than courteous in that special way that is the vast redeeming feature of Africa, and suggested that in the meantime I might care to visit the tribal council, some 50 kilometres away. They offered the services of a municipal employee, one Jackson, to take me there.

Jackson left with us, and at the same time the three

councillors came outside to sit under a tree, with Cokes. It struck me as mildly regrettable that the councillors charged with the daunting task of leading this unlikely community into the uplands had nothing better to do than sit under a tree and drink Cokes, but well, maybe it was tea-time.

Jackson took us off to the tribal council. After an exceptionally long and dusty 50 kilometres we arrived at a smart new office building, klinker brick and spic-'n-span. A lot of people were sitting outside under a tree. These, it transpired, were the councillors and staff and members of the tribe's royal family. The building was empty. Whereas it would be lovely to think that this was the pursuit of progress the African way, the indaba under the tree in the fashion of the forefathers, it would also be wrong. The people were lined up in a row, rocking on their chairs, scratching their itches, and watching the cars go by. They patently had nothing, nought zip zero, on their minds. They were perfectly happy to discuss with us. Indeed it was clearly a relief; it gave them something to do.

We pulled the chairs round a rough table, covered with a semi-stripped gearbox, to discuss the affairs of the tribe. I learned that the councillors and the royal family were in many cases one and the same, and that the same people might also be the staff. I learned that the village's problem was lack of jobs, which was hardly news. I raised, as is customary, the thought of the many enterprising endeavours the local leadership might initiate to deal themselves a hand in the economy. I received, as is customary, a lot of long puzzled looks that said: 'What is this likgowa[3] on about? Doesn't he understand that jobs are something for somebody to arrive here and *give* us?'

I learned too that the waiters at the hunting lodge may not

[3]Sotho for umlungu, the Zulu word for white man and the one which every white man knows. Likgowa is derived either from 'bossy person' or 'person who gets things done', according to taste.

have been as impervious as they seemed. When the matter of relationships with the whites came up there was humming and hawing and a number of low-key appreciative comments about this or that likgowa who 'had respect'. Then a long silence and somebody said: 'But most of them call us kaffirs.' Murmurs of regretful assent, and an even longer silence, people looking dejectedly at the ground.

Ja nee. Yesterday one of the whites had proudly told me that he would only employ people who called themselves kaffirs. He would have a throng of applicants for a few jobs and he would draw up a short-list and then say: 'Right, which of you are kaffirs?' Some would say 'Me, baas, I'm a kaffir', and those ones got the jobs.

Is this sick, or what? That the humiliation of the humble becomes a proof of strength to the strong? Johan Boshoff had an interesting theory; that the humiliators were driven to humiliate as a defence against the buffeting they were receiving from the State. There might be something in that but it's not one way. It's a vicious cycle and by no means confined to the rural far north. Whites talk and think in terms of 'kaffirs' and 'coons'. Blacks push for change, by which at bottom they're usually meaning intangibles like respect and recognition and love. But it doesn't come out this way. It comes out as a strident squawk for social re-engineering, and ends up plunging people wholesale into roles they can't fill.

So whites see their breathing space dwindling and their opportunities vanishing, in the name of equal opportunity, and get to see themselves as the new underdogs. So they bolster their injured egos with real or amplified horror-stories about black cock-ups and get smarmy with the bigshots and compensatorily snarly with the little guys. Thus there is more black pressure for more changes, and more white reaction against the pressure, and more pressure against the reaction. So it goes on.

The 1994 spirit of relief and strength and Simunye – we are one – becomes a memory of lost hope, like a wedding day in a divorce court. The black inferiority complex and the white insecurity complex rise in tandem, feeding ever more voraciously upon each other's ever juicier meat. Bah.

We left the tribal council sitting under the tree and got back to town at about 2.30. We dropped Jackson at the town council. The three councillors were still sitting under their tree, with a carpet of Coke cans on the grass. We checked that the meeting was still scheduled for 3, and went off to see a garage owner in the meantime. I had the feeling that if we only returned at 3.05 we wouldn't have missed too very much, but I was determined to be punctual anyway. As it happened, that was easy. The garage owner, to whom we had been much referred and on whom we had frequently called, was magically 'out' once again. I didn't blame him for ducking us. I never blame anybody for ducking the dubious benefit of stating their case to the world through the agency of a TV team which can then take him away on tape and cut him in their time on their terms to their agenda. But it would be nice if more people would do it the upfront way rather than by leaving endless apologetic messages to say they've been urgently called away.

At 3 pm prompt we were back for the town council meeting, and lo, no quorum. The three councillors pursued their programme of rest and resuscitation under the tree. The administrator, when we arrived, got onto a flurry of phone calls in useful Sotho, so I didn't know what was going on. Eventually he announced that the meeting was re-rescheduled to 4. 'Fine,' I said. 'We'll wait.' I don't believe this answer brought him joy.

By 4 o'clock, the waiting room of the admin office felt like a bar at closing time, with a stiffly patient barman flicking the lights and tapping his watch. When I looked outside I saw two of the original councillors ambling off, possibly so as to employ the remaining daylight in vigorous exercise of their leadership role, but then again, possibly not. The third had evidently already left.

We followed suit, and in a rich glowing sunset we paused against a majestic mountain backdrop to wrap the programme. We had to hop a fence or two to get the shot we wanted, and I delivered my parting summary with an eye cocked against the possibility of an outraged shotgunned farmer hovering into range to perforate my trespassing trousers. I said I was totally fed up, with the disgusting vicious racist horribleness in one quarter, with the supine ineptitude in another, and with the hopeless inadequacy of the legal and constitutional structure in which this unpromising package was parcelled.

And that was Alldays. Full stop. End of paragraph. One more completed set of tapes, ready to cause brain damage in the edit suite, and for me a kind of high point of lowness on the Trek. That is: the low points were the programmes where we skirted cores or nubs without striking them. The high high-points were where we hit nubs and they were the kind of nubs that made you feel warm about your country and its people and its progress. This one was a nub all right, but a nub to make you feel bilious.

Then, as we were reeling up the cords and cable, along came the farmer, minus shotgun and minus outrage. We had a small how-do-you-do through his Mercedes window – 'no problem, you're welcome, feel free' – and as he got into gear and inched off he said:

'I'm glad you're doing something on our part of the country. We have many problems here, many fears to be settled and many areas where confidence is to be gained, but beneath the surface there is the seed of an understanding that this is our common land and our common destiny and we all have our roles in making it what we all want it to be.'

Then he was gone, having done nil for the camera but much

for my private morale. There's Africa for you, the downs are excessively steep but so are the ups. One minute you can think the place is sliding into the Atlantic Ocean, or receding into the 13th century while the rest of the world gears up for cyberspace. The next, a chance glimpse or expression or comment or action smacks the thermostat of the soul way up to maximum. That's why on nine of the ten times that an incredulous citizen accosts me to say: 'Do you *really* not want to live in Australia?' I reply 'No I really do not want to live in Australia.'

10

Jozi

After the pain & suffering & weight of depression induced by Alldays, the logical thing to do was to turn to the bright & light & cheerful, such as by investigating the state of river rafting. The trouble is: if logic was my strong suit I would have had a real job.

So early on a cold May morning the following week we stood in the midst of one of the least-bright, least-light, and least-cheerful subjects in the South African lexicon, namely, inner-city residential Johannesburg.

We were in Wanderers street, in front of a crumbling Baby ear shop. Well, it was Baby ear on its north façade anyway. The west side was Babywea. Its stock in trade was babywear, but the signs were in polystyrene letters, and suffering. The shop was decrepit from its signboards down, and I was invoking it to identify an irony.

In my youth these premises had belonged to a nifty smartish restaurant called Rapallo, with creepers up the walls and an elderly Italian violinist who toured the tables to ask for your favourite tune (which whatever you chose, from Jailhouse Rock to Greensleeves, came out sounding like O Sole Mio).

In the early 60s my family had a Rapallo habit. We went

there in my half-terms out of boarding school, before taking in a show at the Empire or His Majesty's. My parents treated me royally, as guest of honour for the night (and it was years before I confessed that all of it, veal and violin and Showboat and Gondoliers and the lot, was chilled by my clammy heart counting down the hours and minutes until the return to captivity).

Now, no Rapallo, no Empire, and no way whatsoever that your middle-class suburban family takes its entertainment in the streets of Joubert Park. Wanderers street is renowned as muggers' paradise. Its flatblocks look like the Baby ear shop. Broken windows abound, often stuffed with rags or paper. A working lift is a distant memory, and it is no surprise to find a static lift converted to a residence. Broken pipes dangle. A four-room flat might have three families of sub-tenants. Toilets and geysers and stoves are overladen, and break, and I've seen teak banisters being used as firewood. The landlord's expenses rocket, and his rents dwindle, and he balks at repairs, so his rents dwindle further and he balks quicker. A large and expensive uplift endeavour, the Seven Buildings Project, was supposedly reversing the decline – applying a loan from the taxpayer to kick-starting a new era: pride of ownership, sectional title, tenants' bodies corporate etc – but reversal was not evident to the passing eye and moreover a spate of current headlines were pronouncing that the project had fallen into deep dwang.

The irony I was identifying is the standard South African story. In the old days there was an ill: no Mr Khumalo was about to seat his family at the tidy clean Rapallo, no matter how neat his suit, how solid his wallet, how keen his taste for veal piccata or O Sole Mio. Even to a schoolboy, this was a nagging worry like a deep low toothache, a perpetual built-in unfairness, an insult which took the shine off all enjoyment of all things Seffrican. And now that the tooth is removed and the shine enabled there is a new ill: everything breaks and sinks and withers.

With Baby ear as the backdrop and Rapallo as the contrast I posed the question: can we have the shine without the sinking, or is the latter the price of the former?

Question posed, we sought answers. It took an hour or more to reach the nearest entrance hall, half a block away, because with every breath we fell into conversation with a fresh set of locals. Part of this protractedness, it's true, was due to the presence of the camera. Part was also due to the growing familiarity of my face (the up-side of that mixed blessing – a media persona – you have friends you don't know). Part, though, was the plain and simple consequence of the prevailing amiability on the pavement, an amiability in some senses applied especially to the rare white presence.

It is true that in a place like this a white skin makes you more likely to get mugged, being more likely to have a pocket worth searching. But it's just as true that a white skin makes you a kind of guest. Most people feel good about you being there and want you to feel good about being there. One paradoxical result is that huge numbers of locals firmly support the exodus of former white residents to paler pastures.

In terms of standard liberation theory the Joubert Parks of the nation were supposed to become the advance guard of the new non-racial society. In practice, not quite. In practice the black population of an area rises very gradually until it gets to about 30% or so, whereupon stand back or get crushed in the stampede of fleeing figures. Truly assessed, the fleeing figures are not only white but also include the original black pioneers who got there in the first place to escape from the township and are now escaping again. But the bulk are white people who are correctly perceived to be fleeing from the blacks, and the correct pseudo-intellectual treatment of this phenomenon is to shriek 'Racism! Racism!' Unfortunately the people of

Joubert Park have widely failed to read the political columnists who purport to speak for them, and what they are actually saying is 'Of course the whites must go. They can't stay here. The hooligans pick on them.'

It's a mass of irony and of unintended consequence – this is Africa – and the biggest irony of the lot is that of the tiny proportion of the traditional little old white ladies who still occupy their flats, many stay on precisely because they're such a small embattled minority that they are pampered silly by their average black neighbour. One such little old lady put it crisply: 'I spent 50 years in a totally white neighbourhood and then 20 years with half and half and now I'm the only white person in the block and I've never been treated so lovingly in my life.' Work that one out.

On our short slow walk down the Wanderers street pavement the unpretty picture began to re-shape somewhat, as distant pictures have a habit of doing once you get close up. We stopped at a barrow to share coffee and some unnameable African foodstuff with the early morning dustbin men and scooter drivers, and I was terrifically reminded of the opening scenes of My Fair Lady, with the flower sellers and the fishwives doing much the same thing in much the same way. In a scripted and choreographed musical every talking part of course belongs to a philosopher of homespun wisdom, where here many of the people were tongue-tied and anyway inconveniently vernacular, but at root this was the same scene. If the Londoners had gone ahead to create a society where the stuffed-cardboard windows and the over-crowded slums gave way to china ornaments and house-proud estates, who was to say the Joubert Parkers could not do the same?

Finally we came to the entrance portal of Branksome Towers, which along with Argyle Court and Stanhope Mansions and Coniston Hall and an odd-man-out named

Manhattan, was part of the renewal project. Among the people congregated on the milling steps was a very articulate trio who introduced themselves as Nomathemba Zulu, Andrew Sihaba and Emily Listener.

Emily Who?

Emily Listener. She is Moretsi to the Dept of Home Affairs, I later ascertained, but she'd adopted the sobriquet as a permanent reminder that 'you must listen to people, especially when they're not agreeing with you'.

Well, Emily for Premier is what I say. She and her cohorts talked for a while on the steps, about crime and decline and so forth, and then invited us to see the building.

It was a walk-up, of course, round and round the old-time mesh lift-shaft rising wrecked and vacant through the staircase as the obtrusive conscience of retrogression. The guys in flat 910 must develop Olympic leg muscles, provided they do not develop early heart attacks. Stacks of people were walking down, we were the only ones walking up. Everybody greeted everybody. A dozen mini-conversations came and went, in half a dozen languages. Is your baby better today . . .? Congratulations on your new job . . . Please leave your rubbish out on Friday, not Thursday . . . Oh, so this is your mother from Lusikisiki . . .

Emily was treated as a combination of favourite aunt and Adolf Hitler. She is the supervisor, it rapidly became evident, and she clearly held the reins tight, not to mention making liberal use of both the spur and the curb. But she was also very much one of the people and involved with the people and a loving matronly presence. In any case the tenants were interacting quite as much with other tenants as with the authority figure, and the feel of the place offered a poignant counterpoint to the kind of flatblock I know better, where tenants peer intently at the liftfloor lights to avoid having to speak to neighbours they have not officially met.

A surprising – considering the unemployment statistics – number of Branksome Towers residents were at work or on their way to work. A surprising number of those who remained at home were working at home. (Though doubtless also 'unemployed' for statistics, and VAT, purposes.) There were one-man industries ranging from the fairly orderly to the extremely unorderly, which is not necessarily the same thing as disorderly. A part-time knife-sharpener, a guy writing, illustrating, and framing verses of the Bible, several leather-workers, an up-and-about seamstress with a flat stacked full of work in progress.

Pretty well everybody talked about improvements taking place, but then, pretty well everybody also talked about conflicts taking place, and particularly a conflict between the two Big Men in their lives, Pressage Nyoni the chairman of the project and Ray Mgidlana the elected local councillor. We went to the horses' mouths in respect of both the improvements and the conflict. Clive Cope and Tim Haynes, the project consultants, compellingly demonstrated assorted reasons to believe the upswing was real. They pointed out that much of the continuingly bleak public and media perception of the area was because the buildings needed paint jobs, but that actually paint was a low priority as against things like new drains, of which they were impressively and very touchingly proud. They lugged us round the plumbing in enthusiastic detail, putting Richard's camera skills to the interesting challenge of making sewerage pipes look interesting.

Pressage and Ray were just as feet-on-the-ground in terms of facing up to the practicalities, such as handling the emotive issues of varied rental rates and direct – i.e. unit-for-unit – billing. Both guys were altogether charming and even self-effacing. Pressage had stuck on his wall an utterly vitriolic anonymous fax obviously emanating from someone in the Ray camp. Ray, who was also a director of Sanco, the outfit most responsible for creating the boycott philosophy of the 80s, would have brought joy to Genghis Khan with the ferocity of his new insistence on Pay Up and No Excuses.

However . . . well, I put bluntly to each of them that I was smelling a bad dose of the African Disease coming on. When the elephants fight the grass gets trampled, and it seemed to me that for the umpteenth time we had here a case where two strong leaders, unable to reconcile their differences or to adopt the notion of co-operation within disagreement, were in danger of wrecking a public project on the rocks of private ego.

Normally I am quick on the draw in protest against ascribing racial characteristics to individuals. I hate the tendency to assume that because many blacks are late for meetings therefore this person or that person should be expected to be late, or that because many Indians evade tax therefore this person or that person should be expected to be diddling his tax, and so on. On this occasion I was making the assumption myself, and given the awesome history of African power-struggles I am not rushing to apologise. Had this been a row between a Van Zyl and a Gibson I would be inclined to expect that sooner or later a modus vivendi would be found. Being a row between a Nyoni and a Mgidlana I was gripped with fear that the death of the endeavour lay at the end.

Of course both Pressage and Ray firmly insisted no, no, no, nothing like that. Each had a dozen cogent reasons why their case was right and the bad guy's was wrong. Fair enough, that's democracy, but there were just too many distinctive odours of the African Disease in the air, such as when I was called to a room choc-a-bloc with people who promptly, and clearly primed, went into an almighty denunciation, with much song, dance, chant and animal-kingdom metaphor, of the other side and its leader.

I became fairly preachy with both Ray and Pressage, on

how they were not allowed to let personal rivalry spoil a worthy project, and I thought at the time that this was one occasion when a sermon by the presenter was right and proper. The sermon, and the intriguing combination of assenting, dubious, and defensive responses from its two addressees, would, I felt, have a salutary impact on a much wider set of conflicts than their own, and I came away feeling that if there was one really worthwhile thing I ever did on the box this was it.

Which might have been right and might have been wishful. No one will ever know because the whole issue fell victim to the Television Disease. When we cut the programme, as usual with hopelessly more material than we could possibly condense to 24 minutes of screen time no matter how much agony occurred in the edit suite, the big moral issue was long and confusing and visually static and generally non-TVable, and it ended its days in the proverbial cutting-room dustbin.

When we left Joubert Park, to take in other aspects of city centre life, we left with heart-warming ululations and farewells and a firm injunction to come back on Friday night. Why we had to come back on Friday night was not vouchsafed to us. It was some kind of secret conspiracy, although from the tone in which it was presented it was not for a Spanish Inquisition or a Nuremberg Trial.

We Trekked around inner Johannesburg. We went to Hillbrow, latterly known to the bourgeoisie as Hellbrow and as the place where the druglords' New Business Division injects you with addictive substances on arrival, which is lousy marketing because the druglords' existing client base thereupon murder you for the gold in your teeth and you wind up as a customer of the city mortuary which is foresightfully located right on the spot.

We watched a streetfight between stoned urchins and we watched the intervention of a young Afrikaans Christian activist from Potchefstroom who, brushing the urchins' knives away like straws, klapped them into temporary peace and relative sobriety. We spoke to legions of antique European immigrants who told us this place was not hell, it was worse. We went to a nightclub so full that prostitutes plied their services vertically and so noisy that a cannon could have gone off unnoticed. We played basketball with teenagers who made me a chump and whose way of teenage rebellion was to be so clean-living that they embarrassed their parents. We met Hope Papo, super-vigorous local councillor whose mission in life is to restore Hillbrow to order and whose views on the penalisation of vandals, public urinators and thieves make the Spanish Inquisitors look like the Prisoners' Organisation for Human Rights.[1]

We went to the innermost inner-city, the mighty grey post-modernist battleship that is Bank City, FNB's headquarters. I have a soft spot for Bank City, partly because it is a symbol of business (read 'white') faith in Johannesburg; partly because it is beautiful. Bank City is urban class writ large. The huge open courtyard with its ponds and fountains is South Africa's closest approximation to the great Venetian piazzas, albeit rudely dissected by the six speeding traffic-lanes of Simmonds street. Walk round its edges and you're walking under high classical eaves, the pavements set between agreeable shopfronts and rows of agreeable trees, in welcome contrast to the normal Joburg practice and in particular the practice of the other gigantic bank complex, at the far end of the same Simmonds street, where the solid high unshaded concrete leaves a passing pedestrian feeling deeply shut out, like perambulating the perimeter of a prison.

[1](After Hope had waxed ferocious for several minutes, and I could imagine the nation's hairiest right-wingers bouncing on their sofas in hysterical applause, I took perverse delight in asking a final question to which I already knew the answer: 'Oh, by the way, Hope, what is your regular job?' and hearing Hope's reply: 'Organiser for the Communist Party'.)

Had Bank City with its 5 000 salary-earning occupants and its myriad contractors and suppliers defected to sanitised white Sandton as it might easily have done, that would have been tantamount to the keystone nail of Johannesburg's coffin. For those among us who reject the view that central Johannesburg is destined to become a Lagos – bankrupt, scruffy and full of broken street-lights – Bank City is the repository of much gratitude and much hope.

It's not necessarily that FNB stuck to town out of sheer dedication. That the city centre remains a commercial hub is largely due to an emotional tug in two particular minds. Harry and Nicholas Oppenheimer feel that their companies owe a loyalty to the city, and it could be career-limiting for any major province in the Anglo-American empire to disregard this factor. But it was also the city's good luck that FNB decided on its centralisation plans in the early 80s and not ten years later, by which time there would have been a good deal more push to run to Sandton. As it is, with half a billion rands of investment in Simmonds street, FNB has got to make the best of it. How were they shaping? That's what we asked, of numerous FNB employees on the piazza, and although there were many horror-stories about muggings and assaults there were just as many 'fine's and 'okay's.

Moreover even the muggees and the assaultees were keener to talk about a totally different worry than about the safety angle. They wanted to talk about smoking. Bank City had recently become smoke-free and it transpired that practically every face on the piazza, or at any rate practically every white face and quite a few of the unwhite ones, belonged to a bank-worker taking a smoke-break. They were every age and gender, colour and seniority, bound by their common exile in the cause of the filthy weed, and they were having a djol. It struck me afresh that much as tobacco might send you earlier to your grave it also lends itself to more conviviality on the route. Also that if their main problem with Bank City was the No Smoking rule they were living in something less than mortal terror.

We left them to wander through the streets of what the papers regularly if improbably describe as the world's crime capital, and the most dramatic event we saw was a shouting-match in Zulu between a fat mama with a pavement stall and a couple of kids ten floors above who were irritatingly squirting water at her. Things did not look that different to the Johannesburg of Rapallo days except that (a) those days the kids ducked out of sight after squirting the water, and (b) then 9 out of 10 people were white and now it is 1 out of 20. These, like the other 19, were getting about their business without visible agitation, and at least half of those we spoke to were into the fine-and-okay mould.

Once again the close-up view was less horrendous than suburbia's well-oiled exaggeration factory would have it, and when we left, shortly after nightfall when we discovered that our sun-gun light was giving wobbly output, I was feeling on balance quite mellow about my city's health and welfare. Not, I emphatically assert, that I am blind to the vastly excessive crime that does exist even if it failed to leap out and perform for us. Not that I am sanguine, either, about the housing decay, the threats of more of the same, and the barriers to effective turnaround.

Jozi, as the current occupants call Johannesburg, or Joeys as my contemporaries called it when it was the hub of our daily lives, is a very long way from the perfect city, but nor is it the unmitigated cesspit that the bourgeois instinct is so keen to label it. That is the crux. It's not as bad as we tell ourselves it is. The barbarity and the savagery are real. The ineptitude and the new political distortions are real. But the normality and reasonableness of the ordinary average person in the street is the biggest reality and the most readily ignored.

There's a choice here. If the minorities keep hyping

themselves into gloom, keep run run running from the blacks, we will end up with guarded ethnic ghetto-havens on the north edge of Johannesburg, the south edge of Cape Town, the east edge of of Pretoria, the west edge of Durban, and so on, and with Lagos in the cities. And what then? The expansion goes on, and we run again. Sandton and Claremont and Pinetown and Waverley and their equivalents across the nation become the new downtowns, the new places to abandon in favour of new ghetto-havens, and we run eternally, until the children of opulence are in Toronto and the children of dispossession have jungle growing through the flagstones. The other choice is to engage, to say, Yes, we are Africans, we embrace Africa as ours, we claim it no less than any others claim it, we give it love, we belong in it. We use the cities, we combat the ills, we maintain and sustain the order and structure that we seek, and we create a society where it is natural and normal, safe and secure, for the lifts to work and the windows to have panes, and criminality to be not only punished but also ostracised and despised.

On came Friday night and our blind date with Joubert Park. Friday night as it happens was the 50th birthday of my friend Rob, in a glorious mansion with a stone squash court, a world or three kilometres removed from Wanderers street. We got there and greeted and congratulated and conversed, and at an early hour we explained that I was leaving and why. Much concern from the guests. How was I going to get there? Gael was going to drop me (I'd meet the crew there and they would bring me back). Major consternation among the guests. Going at all was upsetting enough but to let Gael drive back alone was outrageous. Had I recently taken out a life policy on her or what? There were proposals for back-up cars and for menfolk to accompany her and for Eagle Watch to wait for me, and a generally dim view of my sense of responsibility.

Even without the consequently heightened level of paranoia

I was not unsympathetic with the concern and the logic behind it. A bad thing can easily happen to a woman alone in Joubert Park at night, and although rationally bad things can equally well happen to both of us at any time and any place, you're more conscious of it when everybody insists that you're asking for it. But we believe in living our lives on our terms and not the terms of the barbarians, and after a virtual fight for the right to get in our car we waved goodbye to a lot of people going tut-tut and treating us as if we were on a suicide pact.

As soon as we were in Joubert Park the paranoia evaporated. Of course we knew the barbarians *could* strike, but they could also strike in Westcliff or Houghton. Here amid the to-ing and fro-ing of a thousand pedestrians we couldn't get nearly as agitated as from behind the walls of mansionland. Not for the first time I was grateful that fate forces me to perpetually dangle a toe in waters which, absent the dangling, I would be sure were full of piranhas. (Although I admit I rang Gael on her way back and tried to keep her talking. She laughed me off and hung up.)

My crew, in the form for this occasion of Richard Burnett, Len Nzoyi, Michael Modena and Brett Shaw, was waiting in Wanderers street and rumbling the rumbles of mutiny. Not only was I biting into their Friday night; not only was I delivering them to the maw of Joubert Park at the drunkenmost-but-one time of the week, but now I was late to boot. And so I was, what with Rob's party and the consternation factor on top of that. Griping happened, and an element of wondering about whether we really wanted to be here, but although Article I of the TV Crews' Trade Union Rules says 'Gripe hard when you gripe', Article II says: 'and then do the job'. TV crews are inherently game, or what would they be doing there?, and Shaw Pictures crews are gamer than most.

So we load up lights and mikes and all and schlep up to the

designated rendezvous, a third-floor flat.

Ja well. Nobody home. So we schlep downstairs again, but then meet some wholly unknown character who authoritatively informs us that we are meant to be at a different flat, on the sixth floor.

Confusion also happened. We were traipsed through several flats in three buildings and roundly ignored while voluble vernacular discussions took place. Then we were unceremoniously deposited in a bedroom and left there to admire the furnishings in suspicious isolation for a very long time, while we mulled the thought that we had somehow become an unwanted embarrassment. That is to say, some of us mulled that thought. The majority view was more along the lines of 'feathers to these rude persons, let's split'.

The majority view was drawing extremely close to the point of democratic triumph when the bedroom door opened and disclosed a welcoming committee, who greeted us with copious fanfare and then escorted us right back outside to the street.

On the pavement a braai was on the go. As we had surmised, the occasion was a party. What we had not surmised was that we were to be joint guests of honour, sharing that role with an intercom box.

The people, we learned, had half-expected us to chicken out, and therefore were only half-prepared for the eventuality that we did not. Thus the great delay, but now we were introduced to the novel experience of a braai on a city street, among the exhaust fumes and the tramps.

We were also introduced to the intercom, and this was some introduction.

Margate Court had today installed its new intercom, an object of great pride and a symbol of turning. From today you could buzz the buzzer at the entrance grille and your host could let you in from her flat – 'like the whites in Killarney' as one resident said with satisfaction. From today, no sneak thieves and no troublemaking gatecrashers. Today marked the start of Margate Court's rise in the world. That the starting point was a security system rather than lighting or plumbing or heating tells its own tale, but a start was a start.

People gathered round the intercom, crushed and squeezed in the narrow foyer, and sang its praises. And when I say 'sang its praises', I mean *sang* its praises. Having sung to the intercom, and sung to each other, and sung to their leaders, and heard their leaders exhorting good behaviour and home-owning responsibility, the people sang to us. The embarrassment returned, but we could hardly claim to have been unwanted. And then they fed us, like kings. Singing and dancing gathered pace. Beer and chops never tasted so good. Our worst worry was that so many people were coming to greet us and offer inaudible good wishes, drowned by the music, that we were in full-time handshake mode and could barely do justice to the chops. The singing and the dancing became catching, and in a while we were in there with the rest, dancing and keeping tune to Tswana words which we (well, 80% of us) mouthed without understanding. We could be fairly confident that they weren't to do with Revenge on the Oppressor.

The pavement became a contagious celebration. Even Richard, not usually classifiable as a sentimental soul, was caught by the spirit and kept bemusedly observing that this was too good to be believable. Which was very literally true. It wasn't just that the food was good or the music was good or the vibe was good; it was that here was an affirmation of South Africa coming at us from where it was least expected, and telling us why we belonged.

11

Copper

Alfred Woodington sold me on copper wire. Alfred was an activist in the Struggle era, and the author of the most impressive piece of personal peace-keeping I ever saw.

It was at a foundry in the East Rand. P W Botha was President. Love and brotherhood did not prevail. There was a strike. A few thousand extremely agitated working men were gathered in a scruffy patch of wasteland, and the fertiliser was about to hit the fan. Speakers were taking the microphone one after the other to urge revolt. Not that I properly understood their text, but when phrases like Phambili[1] iStruggle! and Phansi[2] iCapital! recur five times per sentence one can infer that the gist is not a treatise on the virtues of balance. When they got around to Bulala AmaBhunu[3] I noticed that on the perimeter the police were drawing up in break-their-heads formation, and it was minutes or seconds before the world's press got itself a handy evils-of-apartheid horror-story for tomorrow's Page 2 lead.

---

[1]Forward – what did you expect?

[2]Down.

[3]Kill the Boers – by whom were equally meant all whites including those who used to say: 'Not me! I'm English!'

Whereupon a coloured guy took the microphone. He had a doleful expression and eyes lidded as if listening to a long bad joke at a very late hour, and I didn't expect fireworks.

Which was right in its way, because what we got was anti-fireworks. With a few short punchy references to common sense, reality and the law, this Comrade Woodington got the Casspirs to simmer down to an idle and the strikers to simmer down to a grumble, and deprived the East Rand's undertakers of quite a bit of business.

In post-struggle times Alfred became security manager for Spoornet, and one of those not altogether common people who put as much dedication into building the new State as they had into demolishing the old one. He was upset that Spoornet's work was increasingly sabotaged by the theft of copper wire, and he enlightened me on the crime's particular peculiarity: its extreme imbalance between the damage caused and the gains made.

If I steal a shirt from your washing line, you have lost a shirt and I have gained a shirt. If I steal ten rands worth of Spoornet wire . . . well, I gain the price of a breakfast, at the personal cost of a sore shoulder (even that much wire, with its insulation, would exercise a weight-lifter) and at the personal risk of getting fried. (A wire-thief who errs ends his days as petrified carbon, welded to the cable.) Also, the thief's ten-rand gain might mean the nation's ten-million-rand loss. A train stalls on its way to harbour. A hundred containers miss their ships. Twenty other trains are banked up waiting . . . Add in the knock-on effects – mass rail rescheduling, foreign importers switching future orders to Brazil or India, Company A gets liquidated meaning Supplier B loses custom meaning B's Supplier C bites the dust, a new domino wave of retrenched ex-workers unable to pay school fees or lay-bys or the mealie-mama on the street corner . . . The total cost of my breakfast is literally incalculable. Meanwhile come dinner time

I might try the same trick with Telkom wire and for the same gain leave half a province incommunicado – including, ironically, its cellphone users, as despite all their magic cellphones still depend on landbound links.

Alfred had faith that if we showed the crooks the error of their ways they would desist. At first I took this view to be very quaint and ideal and unreal, but Alfred's feet were closer to the ground than I imagined. No one, he said, was claiming that a sudden mass Damascus conversion lay in wait, but if we could not believe that some people in the copper-wire food chain were susceptible to logical or moral appeal, what hope was there for any good anywhere ever? Moreover we were not only addressing ourselves to the tragic hungry desperado who stood to end up like a frieze from the Last Days of Pompeii, but to the ladder of allegedly law-abiding citizenry which stood behind him.

There are thousands of little scrap-metal bucket shops which act as the pawnbrokers of suspect wire. Some, no doubt, are dead straight, but it would be rash to take them for a majority. The ethic of most of the industry is to say: 'Oh *no*, I would *never* buy a *stolen* item, but there is no way of telling', and it is virtually impossible for the law to find, according to its own criteria of reasonable doubt, that among those who say this are the many lying immoral bastards which everybody knows there are. The big and 'respectable' firms will indeed (sometimes) turn away the oke with flapping soles and ragged trousers who pitches up with a chunk of cable over his shoulder, but when the same chunk comes back processed and molten at a slightly higher price from a bucket-shop, it becomes a matter of 'But what can we do? We can't accuse our suppliers of receiving stolen goods.'

Conductor factories in turn buy from the big-time recycling dealers and manufacture new cable to be sold to, inter alia, Telkom, Spoornet and Eskom. It's an immaculate, if perverse, circle. The cable users buy back their own stolen metal whose theft might have effectively cost them and their nation ten thousand times the price. By buying it back they guarantee the market and thus make sure that the theft goes on – indeed it has geometrically escalated in the last five years – and if there is any fundamental answer to this weirdity it is not one yet visible to the naked eye.

And so we got into copper wire, and into several unexpected by-products such as a blow-me-down introduction to the size and power of the metal recycling process.

To some people, industry is a noisy and dirty thing and a regrettable lapse from the way the world was meant to be, with green grass and burbling brooks and bucolic tranquillity. To this person, industry is beauty. Without industry you might have the bucol but you wouldn't have the tranquillity. You'd have a world of dongas and land wars. To me there is an exhilaration in the sights and sounds of heavy machinery providing human work by processing material to provide more human work in the cause of providing humans with heating and lighting and plumbing and access. The recycling industry delivered plenty of the machinery, and the sights and sounds that go with it. It also turned out to be a vastly larger arena of activity than the customary public image of battling little back-pocket establishments conveys. In the case of some metals, recycling the old is bigger business than mining the new, and a big recycling works operates on the scale that one more readily associates with a mine. Moreover the sheer technological grandeur of turning bits and pieces of old scrap-iron into solid fresh ingots was altogether breath-taking.

The same can not easily be said of every aspect of the activity. More than once I was acutely reminded of Charlie Chaplin in Modern Times, taking an almighty swipe at the drudgery of production-line work. Charlie plays a wage-slave whose job is to snap two nuts tight every few seconds for eight hours a day. That becomes his life, and when he goes home at night he snaps imaginary nuts as he walks. It was pretty telling, and that was in 1936. In 1997 I watched with horrified fascination as Charlie Chaplin came to life. In one place a fierce and mighty furnace raised the temperature of a building big enough to house a Boeing fleet to intolerable levels. Several guys had Chaplinesque jobs and one in particular had virtually the identical job. With rhythmic precision, fifteen times a minute, minute after minute after minute, he whacked two hammers simultaneously on two flanges. I'd have hated to watch him walk home. As they say, the only thing worse than being exploited is not being exploited, sitting on the dock of the bay wasting ti-i-ime away. But while I stick to the view that having a job is a huge step up on not having a job, this kind of sight is also a harsh reminder of how far we have to go to make a job something more than a necessary evil.

At another of the big operators, the boss, very new age and all, happily introduced me to his new empowerment (read 'black') co-director. Having thus satisfied the New South African requirements the boss conducted a tour of the premises while the co-director trailed behind with all the relevance and significance of a twig hooked on a back bumper.

At one part of the plant, several dozen labourers were stuffing unwieldy metal parts into a heated pit where a giant hydraulic hammer pounded them into shoebox cubes. The redeeming feature of this activity was that the labourers were building up Schwarzenegger bodies. Not that many of them had the time or energy or basic awareness to begin to contemplate entering the muscleman glamour-stakes, but they would at least impress the township chicks on a Sunday afternoon, which I guess is the only time they might ever care about anything other than sleep. The un-redeeming side was that they were broiling, they were exhausted, they were breathing thick dust and shavings, and they were in constant danger of losing a finger or hand – or, with a moment of lost balance, worse – to the pounding hammer.

I was riveted by this process and watched for quite a while, not least in a spirit of 'there but for the Grace of God go I'. Then I said, awkwardly positioning myself so as to address both the boss and the trailing co-director, who I had repeatedly but successlessly tried to bring into discussion: 'I'd be interested to know what prospects of career advancement there might be for any of these guys.'

The co-director looked, as per normal, at the boss. The boss looked at me, the sort of look you might look at someone asking about the prospects of spring following summer. He turned to the labourers, and stared at them for a long moment, and turned back to me, and said: 'None.'

Aargh. Is this what the brave new world is to be about? A charade of status for the few; the many to be two-legged draughthorses?

Questions of labour and reward exercised the mind rather morosely, but another angle of the copper wire hunt was, with one hitch, marvellously encouraging.

Alfred – recent revolutionary, recent non-citizen, now suddenly installed as manager wearing jacket and tie – had to do a fair amount of negotiating and introducing among tough Spories[4] who not long ago would have klapped him if he'd ventured into their rec room. Most of them – like the cable-fixers we met at a forsaken chunk of veld where a train was halted by a wire-break – had no forewarning. They'd never met Alfred. He had to explain who he was and why he was bringing a camera crew to invade one of their hitherto least-public activities, and this could have called for quite some explaining. It was very possible that the Spories might take umbrage at any tie-wearing head-office dude moving in on

[4] Railwaymen.

their act, let alone 'n voormalige terroris now suddenly re-incarnated as some brand of makhulubaas.

These moments cause their small irregularities to the heartbeat. Rationally and officially I spurn the racist view that I because I am white I therefore have some link to the actions past or present of other people who are white. Emotionally, though, in the face of the clear and present possibility of somebody being made to feel hurt or slighted, I do a quiet prayer that the white guys will behave right.

These Spories behaved right, all right. They responded like heroes. I wanted to hug them. They were perfect: friendly but not gushing, co-operative but not pushovers, polite but with none of the fawning that you find in the dining-rooms of elegance when a Provincial Minister is inveigled to lunch.

That's what I love about South Africa – the fullness. It wouldn't be the same if these people, this cross-section of humanity called to this barren veld by common interest in a crippled railtrack, had come from the same place as I came from, and thought the same way in the same vocabulary. Maybe there's a litmus here, for those who tickle at emigration's urge. If you imagine a world where everyone was pretty much like you – same values, pronounced 'mall' the same way, etc – then if that looks like paradise you may as well opt out of all the growing-pains here. If it seems a little pallid, maybe not.

The Spories explained their line-fixing problems willingly and ably, and in baffling detail, as people with technical skills usually do. When we left them it was to meet Telkom's 'secret weapon' – which, we understood, was about to be exposed for the first time to the eyes of the world, through our agency. Duly appreciative, we awaited the revelation.

And waited, and waited. We were in the .... Building in ...., between .... and .... and not at all far from the .... But that's all I can tell you because we are sworn to secrecy. No kidding. It sounds like the age of Total Onslaught come back to life, but that's the deal. Privileged to see the weapon, we weren't to say where it was. So I can't properly finger the rude bastards who non-greeted us on our arrival there.

We got to a kind of ante-room, and there we sat. Something was awry with the arrangements. Alfred was busy sorting it out and all of us were busy being ignored. Here was a roomful of ten or twelve people, all at control screens but not all too busy to talk, to each other. To talk to us would perhaps have meant that lightning struck. Certainly, nobody did it, or caught any of our eyes for the merest split second, as if they might be turned to salt.

Was this some racial thing or what? Or a resentment at being leapfrogged? Or the plain old colourless creedless rudeness which can so easily be taken for some form of prejudice. I don't know. I rather liked Alfred's way of handling it, which was to whisper not a word to us, whether by way of excuse or complaint or skinder, but to briefly, and only once, apologise for the delay and then go forth on his own to sort things out. When we finally got to meet the weapon we also met several other bouts of the original upright Sporie treatment, so I didn't get too paranoid about the rude guys but I would love to understand them. It's bad enough anybody being rude to anybody, but when you add the sensitivities of race to the issue it's worse. True, reconciliation on its own doesn't put a chicken in anyone's pot or a guarantee in his pension, but it's a fair start and I can't see that anybody ever loses from it.

The weapon turned out to be Supercomputer; a magic new system which sounds an instant alert whenever a line is being tampered with at any part of the far-flung Spoornet empire. It can identify the endangered line right down to the centimetre, but thereupon a problem arises. Computer technology has not yet got to the point of reading the thief's fingerprints or

ID book, let alone slapping on the handcuffs. I hope it might have struck fear into any SABC3-watching wire thief to know that he triggers an instant alarm, but it wasn't helpful to us in finding any thieves, TV-watching or other.

We were on standby night after night. The closest we got was immediately after the act. One night we went bundu-bashing with a Telkom wire-detective, who projected a double-dose of that I-do-it-for-my-country feeling that you often get from people like firemen and tax collectors and policemen, a determination to do the right thing regardless of whether everybody else is ripping off the system or profiteering from short cuts. We found a sad little collection of ruined cables and a sadder homemade furnace where the freezing crook had vainly tried to burn the insulation away before he was frightened off – presumably by the sounds of our arrival. The next day we narrowly missed a pitched battle involving a large armed and organised gang with ten-ton trucks, who had reeled kilometres of cable out of underground conduits. I think the police were glad we hadn't been there to get in the way. Maybe I was too.

One of the copper-wire cops also gave us the best example I ever had of the way people speak differently to a camera to the way they speak to a human being. We had been walking through an industrial area full of patently criminal bucket-shops. He was griping much better about how impossible his job was and how the whole industry was a cesspool of crime.

I said: 'It seems to me then you may as well wind up; go and do something else and just accept that wire theft is out of control.'

Put like that, of course, things sounded different. He stopped abruptly, hunched a little, glowered at me, and shoved an admonitory finger practically up my nose. 'My china,' he said fiercely, 'that's what you bleddy think, my china. Let *me* tell *you*, my china, that these ouens are in no bleddy doubt that we're here, hey. I tell you, my china, when I *gaps* just one oke on a Monday morning, for the whole bleddy week the whole bleddy industry is like little bleddy angels, with Mandela looking overr their shoulderr.'

'Gee,' I said, 'you give me a good answer. Would you say it on camera, just like that?'

'Sure,' he said. Richard wound up the camera. I said again: 'Just like that, right?' 'Sure,' said the cop, and he drew himself up, patted down his hair, brushed his lapels, and earnestly informed the camera: 'If a suspect is apprehended there is a beneficial effect upon law and order.'

The copper wire programme delivered a startling number of purposeful responses. People offered solutions – technical ones such as moving to glass-fibre and other valueless conductors; scientific ones from people like a professor of chemistry who had a new DNA way of branding metals with irremovable identity marks. There were ideas for trapping crooked dealers, ideas for mass campaigns to re-charge the nation's morals, and so on.

These responses were doubly noteworthy. On the one count, for displaying the quantity of people who want to make a contribution. On the other, for displaying the difficulty of effectively marshalling the energies involved. Months later, now as I pen this page, it strikes me that of all the many people who I put in touch with whichever branch seems most relevant to their idea, nobody ever came back to say that results had followed.

12

Stepmother

Shortly before we went to England, Saint Nelson made one of those statements which demonstrate that saints are not necessarily economists. The world, he said, was morally obliged to invest in South Africa.

We were going anyway. Keith, the big thinker in the Trek's engine-room, had come up with England, reasoning that if after a year we were still getting daily comment on our Australian jaunt, well, let us also apply the skew view to that other focal point of our public's geography. I, the parochialist who would be as happy to burrow forever under Karoo desert or Boland loam, bought the idea not least because it was a decade since I'd touched base with the Mother of Empire. Plus I was surprised to discover that Keith, man of unknown parts, had a house in London, so wherever else the pound sterling would be swallowing seven at a time of our ravaged rands at least it would not be in hotel bills.

The trouble was, we didn't want to replicate the Aus formula of wrangles with emigrants. We needed a different theme, and the President's demand for world support gave us the clue. How were we, newly re-admitted to the Comity of Nations, shaping up? Where and what were our exports? How was our standing? Were people at the hub saying: 'Ah, plucky brave South Africa, how can we help?'

I'd suspected, of course, that we might be less than centre stage in the British mind. What I hadn't suspected was quite how far from centre, and quite how unpromising a role we occupied in the minds which noticed that role at all.

We started at Chase Manhattan, speaking to a youthful New Zealander who, on behalf of an American bank in London, shuttled tens of millions of dollars a day this way and that around the emerging world – one minute creating a factory and a livelihood for a thousand peasants in Patagonia, the next minute damning an entire Armenian industry to stillbirth. How did he respond to the injunction from the First Citizen of the Planet?

'In an ideal world, I might perhaps work for President Mandela. In the world as it is I work for my clients.'

Well then, what prospects might his clients perceive in the emerging market at the tip of Africa?

Not a lot, was the short answer. Expensive labour, low productivity, Africa had minimal appeal in a candidature which included burgeoning Asia, stabilising Latin America and the re-orienting ex-Iron-Curtain. But for South Africa all was not lost: 'There are still a lot of white people running things down there.'

What!

This was funny. This was also flashback territory. Back in apartheid's prime I spent some time in England, and on my second night there I went to a James Bond movie in a party which included a Nigerian girl. I was talking to her as we climbed a classy carpeted staircase when I had a jolt: She can't be in this cinema! It passed in a split second but I never forgot that momentary spasm of South Africanism smiting me.

Now, 1997, the spasm smote again. You can't say this!

Not on camera anyway. In South Africa everybody was supposed to pay lip service, at least, to the national quest to de-whiten the running of things.

The newspapers had just been bragging, even on the flight over, about how 8,6% of the Johannesburg Stock Exchange was now black, and how this was progress even if too little, too tardy, still a long way to go.

Back home, we'd all been sucked into the vortex of the equalisation ethic. We were accustomed to an aggressive spirit saying 'bring the blacks in', and a defensive apologetic tone from every firm or university or club or council which had not 'transformed' enough: 'We're sorry, we're getting there, look at our figures, here are graphs.' Nowhere in South Africa was anybody sharp and smart and fast-track casually telling a TV camera anything like 'thank heaven for the whites'.

We went looking for evidence of South Africa in the British marketplace – and had to scratch our heads a bit. Where does one start? Heavy industry? Computer stores? Music shops? Toy shops? Motor showrooms? Not exactly. It boiled down to minerals or wine or fruit, of which only the latter two were accessible to the lay wanderer. Thus we layly wandered, and were sadly humbled by what we found. In one suburban bottle-store the immigrant Spanish proprietor welcomed our query most expansively: 'Ah, Zoussafrique, vairy good wines, vairy vairy good.' That was nice, we said, could we see the racks? He led us through to the bowels, past the huge wall of French, past the numerous half-walls of Spanish and Italian and Portuguese and German, past the quarter-walls of Russian and Korean and Chilean and Bolivian and Chinese and Australian and way down at the end, at calf height, displayed a sign saying 'Africa'. The rack had five bottles in it, of which three were from Egypt and two from the Cape. 'Vairy, vairy good wines,' he repeated, grabbing one of the Egyptians and holding it forth.

Two or three similar experiences, and then we wander to the Big Daddy of Brit department stores, Marks and Spencer. Here again are our few lonely bottles, lurking in a lost corner beneath the products of countries which you never thought of associating with wine. I ask the friendly manager what else of ours she has on hand. She takes us to the fruit, and is embarrassed to have to scour shelf after shelf before finding a Cape apple. 'It's sad,' she says, 'as long as I've worked here people wanted South African fruit and wine, and because of the boycotts we had trouble providing it. Now that there are no more boycotts, the demand isn't there any longer.' For what reason might this be? She super-politely says that it's not that our standards have gone down or anything, but, er, everybody else's have gone up.

We proceed down the road to that most London of institutions, the fruit barrow. A delightful large young woman is manning the stall, a bit of cheerful repartee for every customer, a bit of news-swapping, family greetings, fruit advising. She could be Eliza Doolittle's great-grand-daughter. Her dad or granda' might have been Desmond with the barrow in the marketplace. About 23 generations back, one could see, her forebears were serving Dick Whittington. Not a lot had changed, including not the barrow, which if you came across in a museum you would study with interest. (Coming across it sommer right in the street, of course it's just an old barrow.) She was an education in herself, as a model of stability in a turbulent world. We're told all the time: change, develop, progress. She said: Not me, I'm happy. She's happy with her so-called 'station' in life, and has no need of the aspirational hype which does so well out of telling us to strive, to compete, to be dissatisfied with where and what we are. She's happy too with her girth, and unbothered by the expectations of the health and beauty priesthood. We have things to learn from her. I loved her.

One thing we could learn is why she doesn't have more SA produce. She hadn't realised how little there was, until she started hunting through the barrow at our request.

'That's funny,' she said. 'I used to have quite a lot.'

So what had changed?

'Doan't raartly know, love. Let's ask Bill.'

Bill – husband or brother, we took it – had no hesitation about raartly knowing. 'Qua'ity's way off,' he said. 'The blacks fu' it up, innit?'

There it was again. Flat stark statement of the unstateable, presented in cool matter-of-fact manner as if it was a mere platitude.

I argued with Bill, not least on the practical grounds that even if general decline was on the cards it had hardly had time to get under way. He insisted that he'd been visited by a new South African marketing officer – from what organisation he did not know – who 'had no i'ea what he was doin', and di'nt even speak English proper'. But his evidence wasn't just pegged on this incident. He sounded exactly, accent aside, like a Ventersdorp farmer of circa 1993. 'You lo' capi'ulated, of course Africa takes over.'

Bit by bit this theme became the dominant feature as I saw it of Brit attitudes to South Africa. Practically everybody we spoke to came up in one way or another with the same bleak perspective. Not many, though, put it on camera, and especially not many in the suit-and-tied, socially conscious quarters which are meant to speak with expertise. There, it was common enough to make this sort of reference in casual conversation and then when the tape was rolling to calmly say the opposite; to plug the official line of 'ah yes, noble South Africa, stepping confidently into a bold new age'.

This double-talk became a touch irritating to me, and also forced me into the shaky and undesirable position of having to myself state a harsh perception that was barely substantiated by my interviewees. It was my voice saying 'These Brits are full of hypocrisy about the new South Africa.' Very few British voices were displaying the hypocrisy, to the viewer.

I should have ducked it, you might say, and sensibly speaking you are quite right. But for good or ill one non-negotiable feature of the Trek is that if some unspoken outlook or attitude seems to me to be an indispensable part of whatever jigsaw we're trying to unravel, I must speak the unspoken and run the risk that viewers think I'm imagining it or stirring it.

This problem, we were learning, was built in. It recurred whenever we got into seriously sensitive territory, which usually meant race relationships.

Its first big bite had been more than a year before, at the troubled University of Durban Westville, where I had acquired the clear impression that a large factor in the troubles involved Indian students feeling displaced by a new African domination. There was an all-African SRC; liquor was served at student functions; beef and pork were on the canteen menu. Plenty of Indian students talked, in private, of having lost their own sense of belonging in pursuit of the attempt to give African students a sense of belonging. Simultaneously there were African students who felt they didn't belong nearly enough; who objected to the Indian flavour of certain courses, the Indian predominance of lecturers, etc. It was touchy stuff but it was certainly big in many minds. Was anybody saying so for the benefit of the screen? Not on your life. So I said it myself and unleashed an outraged storm of how-dare-you complaints which frightened the channel and made me wonder whether I had done right. Over the next year or more, though, I'd keep meeting UDW people who said thank you for opening the lid and helping make an air-clearing more possible. This solid trickle of low-key appreciation made it worth while and boosted my determination to keep taking the risks, which kept on coming. In Franschhoek, in Alldays, among coloureds in

Cape Town, the race issue had popped up in more ways off camera than on, and I had had to distil the former. Now it popped up in England in the most full-frontal form of all, and I did the same.

Moreover, as often happened with some or other central point which I wanted to be sure would not disappear, I made the same observation three times. I would deliberately repeat myself to the camera so that if in the cutting we dropped Sequence A or Sequence B, for reasons of poor sound or soggy context or whatever, we would have the option of Sequence C. Sometimes, though, the editors would adjudge two sequences both to be unsoggy of context, and unless I was on hand to squawk that it made me feel like a chump or an obsessional, it could irritatingly happen that the same comment would meet the screen twice. On the England programme, extraordinarily, we ran not only Sequence A and Sequence B, but half of Sequence C. So there I was thumping the tub to unintended excess on the perfidy of Albion, like a prosecutor who in the absence of evidence pushes the rhetoric button way up to maximum. Highly embarrassing, and it did not pass unnoticed. John Barker in the Natal Mercury, for one, took me firmly to task.

Well, John, I take your point. I just don't know the answer. I don't think it is to shy away from stuff that is clearly real albeit unexpressed, and no matter how cautious I am about identifying the unexpressed realities there will always be people who do not want to believe them. I can promise little but to try harder.

Ironically, part of John's problem was addressed in the original programme we submitted to the SABC. But the SABC returned this programme to us, too, with a firm order: Cut Bill.

We had half-expected that Bill the fruitseller's short hard sentence would go down ill. For one thing the sentiment was, um, abrupt, and for another there was once again the dreaded F-word, which caused us more problems than any other word in the language.

Clearly this word belonged in Bill's routine lingo just as it is now in the routine lingo of huge numbers of South African TV-watchers. But at the same time it is legitimate for public discourse to stick to rules that private conversation may breach. Nearly all of us, after all, use some words over a beer among peers which we wouldn't use if the Bishop/Imam/Dominee/ Rabbi called for tea. We avoid certain usages in the presence of our mothers or in some quarters of society our wives. Indeed some of the more quaint and antiquated among us even protect our children's ears from harmful invasion, although when we overhear teenagers among their peers we wonder why. We remind ourselves of our own grandmothers, who used to protect us from damn and blast and the like, which to us weren't even in the league of swearwords. Today's generation has moved into yet a further league which leaves no conceivable barrier standing, at least in terms of the traditional anatomical functions and their products.

In any case, rationally the offensive swearwords should be the words designed to put people down, and particularly the words designed to put down the ethnic groups who have clear collective memories of underprivilege. (You can call the WASPs anything you like and they'll laugh it off, because they've never been ethnically sat-upon.) It's hard to see a logical objection to processes which every one of us practises, except perhaps that the expletives derived from those practices have now become so wholly all-purpose that they obscure communication. Afrikaans parlance is even worse than English, and it is quite possible, in circumstances where escape is not an option, to spend hours on end hearing bar or braai talk where two short words feature more frequently than all 100 000 substantive entries in the Groot Woordeboek put together.

They can mean anything from extreme affection ('Fok! Waar die fok kom jy vandaan, jou ou fokken kak') to extreme aggression ('Fok! Fokof jou fokken kak, of jy gaan kak') to thousands of notions inbetween including surprise, weariness, shock, pleasure, disappointment, drunkenness, madness and/or ailment in general, largeness, smallness, and all superlatives of any nature whatsoever. Meaning is conveyed entirely by tone, and one of the wonders of modern times is that mankind has toiled on and up through centuries of civilisation in order to master simultaneously the science of laser surgery and the return to the language of the missing link.

It ought rationally to be linguists who object to the traditional expletives, rather than moralists, and especially the kind of 'moralist' who happily mouths terms like 'coon', 'kaffir', 'coolie', 'hairyback' etc. But human affairs have never been wholly rational terrain, and the fact is that plenty of people have a gut revulsion at gutter talk. Me too, for that matter, although I am one of the many hypocrites who at some times dislike the loose use of terms to whose loose use we at other times contribute.

So for whatever combination of the interests of protecting sensitive ears, defending the language, and preserving a dignity, the policy of the Trek is that the four-letter words get deleted unless there is some particular reason not to delete them, e.g. when I am asking a squatter leader (with the public toilets clear and large in the background) why his people shit in the veld. That's dictionary definition, and euphemisms such as 'defecate' or 'move bowels' would be artificial. So far we have had no occasion to employ the other four-letter word in its dictionary definition, but plenty of times where someone is using it in some emphatic context. (Quite often it is literally the only word they know for the emphasis they're wishing to convey, as in the case of Myra, the iron-lady coloured leader in Franschhoek, who thought at length before arriving at a resounding single-syllable enunciation of the way her people thought they'd been treated by the Boers.)

The general idea is to leave 'em alone where they fit, and to bleep 'em, or excise the passage altogether, where they do not, the borderline being determined by ad hoc debate in the edit suite. I tend towards the prudish side of this spectrum. In fact maybe I am the prudish side of the spectrum. One result is that frequently I lose. Another is that when I win, and we do administer the bleep, we are technically contravening SABC policy.

When we started on the Trek there wasn't any policy, as far as I know. The SABC was operating on the general assumption that naughty words were no longer streng verbode like in the old days, but were not nice and generally AWP, Avoidable Where Possible. It seemed to me that this was a satisfactory way of conducting affairs, and neatly in line with the overall idea of an empowered society. You were here in a small way empowering whole legions of producers and commissioning editors and programme managers, who between them worked out what was right and what was not.

Sometime in '95 we suddenly acquired a new policy. It got handed down from some unknown locus within the Realms of Power, and what it said was simple:

Henceforth shalt thou chop bad words out of programmes broadcast before 9.00 pm, and shalt thou not chop bad words out of programmes broadcast from 9.00 pm even unto close-down.

This being now **POLICY**, it was obeyed as policy is obeyed in policy-driven organisations, with exotic results such as that on at least one occasion (not on our channel) a fairly rough film which started at 8.30 had the bleep-machine doing overtime until 9, and a string of unadulterated expletives thereafter. Another minor consequence was that a couple of times, while the policy was still fresh and in new-broom mode, we elected to run our 9.30 programme with disclaimers in the credits pointing out that bleeps were our own concession to family viewing and were not to be blamed on creeping censorship by the corporation.

The appeal of Bill's pithy one-liner was precisely that he was saying out loud precisely what so many of his compatriots were saying behind their hands. His verb was a marginal case in terms of our logic. I was for bleeping it, but was outvoted in absentia and what we delivered to the SABC contained the full phrase.

And so it came to pass that a few hours before the programme was to be run, it was back in the edit suite with Bill on his way to the discard heap – in toto, no refined debate about language vs sentiment: Bill out. Fullstop.

You would think, no doubt, that I ought to indignantly protest about oppression of artistic integrity and so forth. In which case I regret to have to disabuse you. I swallowed it meekly, partly because half of my mind was uncomfortable anyway and partly because the whole of my mind was shaken by having two programmes sent back in rapid succession.

So viewers were left even freer than they would otherwise have been to imagine that I was inflaming the Brits' prejudices, but for me this was an unignorable feature of the expedition. In and around Africa – in Mozambique, in Zambia, in Mauritius – I had already seen a view of South Africa which flew in the face of our own belief or hope that our new foundation was the basis for ascent to the broad uplands. Africans and Indians of our own continent took it as read that now we were part of 'real' Africa we were bound to sink to the norms of Africa. Here was the same perception digested through the eyes of Europe. Were we to dismiss all this unappetising evidence as the sour malice of distant spectators? To me it seemed increasingly compelling to ask whether there was an Emperor's New Clothes factor, with we South Africans playing the blinded courtiers.

* * *

English speaking South Africans grew up with Britain's cultural baggage as our own. 'Pussycat Pussycat where have you been', we chanted in our nurseries, 'I've been to London to see the queen.' There was the grand old duke of York and his ten thousand men; the bells of Old Bailey saying when will you pay me; the games of Roundheads vs Cavaliers, where we vied for places among the long-haired romantic monarchists and treated the stolid republican team as the bad guys.

Nor was English descent a necessary qualification. I have a vivid childhood memory of the neighbourhood's domestic servants sobbing heartbrokenly at the death of an English king (and would never have guessed that half a century later their grandchildren would sob the same way at the death of an English princess).

On the face of it a visit to England was a pallid and predictable excursion, devoid of the adventure of a visit to, say, Thailand or Siberia. In practice, I found it entirely fascinating, not least because the presumed familiarity turned out less familiar than the presumption.

Small surprises came thick and fast, sometimes in unforeseen ways like discovering how radically English weather breaks the unwritten rules Africa takes for granted, such as that you can freeze and swelter at different times of the same day.

We were there in midsummer. It was balmy enough, and less wet than reputation would have it – mostly hovering in the no-man's-land between drizzle and dryness. Some of us Highvelders had sleep problems, finding it hard to suppress the recurring uh-oh-I-overslept feeling when you have six hours of daylight before the shops open. So I took a couple of

3 am strolls and found that it might have been noon. Same sky, low and grey, and same temperature, comfortable but disorientingly constant.

Size, too, was an unexpected surprise. You don't expect size to be a surprise when you're expecting size to be a surprise, right? It's not news that London is big. One knows that London has four times the people of greater Johannesburg, so one assumes that if you multiplied Johannesburg by about four you'd have something comparable to London, and that is wildly wrong. You could put ten Johannesburgs into central London, and throw in ten Sandtons for good measure, and still lose them. There are numerous street corners where you can confront more sheer bulk around you than you could see from every corner in Johannesburg taken cumulatively. Nothing is less than four storeys high. Business and residential areas overlap abundantly. Almost the entire city is richly alive from early morning until the small hours.

When London talks parks it does not mean rare and dinky napkins of grassland like Joubert Park or the Zoo Lake. It means frequent mighty swathes of gigantic green, which puts in mind the question of what greater Johannesburg will look like when it, in the lifetimes of most of us, is a conurbation stretching from Vereeniging to Pretoria. Will we too have open public land, measured in square miles, where the urban masses take peaceful and pleasant recreation of a Sunday afternoon?

When I pose the question I know what answer springs to mind. 'Sheesh, not a chance, there would be muggers behind every tree, beercans and broken glass all over the lawns, you'd get hijacked at the parking lot; forget it.'

Which is doubtless what the gentry of London also said, when their parks were new. Except they called the muggers 'footpads' and the hijackers 'highwaymen', and their offending litter was the entrails of poached deer.

It seems to me that once you make things happen, and

keep them happening, sooner or later they'll start to happen right. The trouble is the getting going. In Britain at least two things helped create the ambitious parks. Kings could decree and snap fingers, which made venture planning a good deal easier than when it is encumbered by the brakes and blinkers of democracy. And the crucial executors of the decisions had a vested interest. This was their home, there was nowhere to go, they were pretty sure there was a tomorrow, and another tomorrow to follow it. Our future planning misses out on both counts. I'm happy to forgo the kings and the finger-snapping, but I worry a little about the executors and their commitment.

Here was another unexpected contrast. In Britain there is a pervading sense of people being on top of their jobs. At the Hammersmith police station we ask for someone to speak to us on crime prevention. We are referred to a sergeant. I am a tad disappointed. What can a sergeant tell us of the big picture? He starts telling and it turns out that the answer is: everything. He's in charge of crime prevention for a borough bigger than any South African police area, and his grasp is total. With calm confidence he outlines plans, strategies, triumphs, threats and statistics. At home I would have been referred from a sergeant to a captain to a superintendent to a director to a commissioner, and been lucky to find a commissioner with half the command of his subject. This is surely related to the very different scale of activities – when your precinct's average annual murder rate is one, you can put in more thinking time than when you are opening new murder dockets every day. There is a sense of the law being on top and its breaches being aberrations, in horrible contrast to the South African spirit of the law as an embattled rearguard in a retreat against the tide. Partly a consequence of this sense and partly a reason for it, there is also a prevailing spirit of personal competence. The sergeant doesn't find it at all overwhelming to carry responsibilities which in our structure would belong to a much more elevated rank. Partly, too, there is the affirmative action factor.

The London police are just as anxious as our own, or even New York's, to de-whiten their collective face, and they distribute huge quantities of politically correct recruitment brochures to say so. But the idea that you then bend the rules to boost the black component of the upper echelon is completely out of court. That kind of thinking is not in the average Briton's vocabulary at all, let alone the forefront of his vocabulary in the way that applies here. There are no fast-track provisions whereby chosen people zoom through the ranks at giddy speed in order to be presented as symbols of empowerment, and I am sure this has much to do with why every office-bearer of whom you ask a question will simply give you the answer. The phrase 'hold on while I ask my supervisor', increasingly the hallmark of South Africa's civil service, is unknown in Britain.

And their extraordinary orderliness is unknown here. Our police sergeant, having told us how new technology made his job so much easier, invited us to nip down the road to the borough's town hall and watch the surveillance systems in action. We did that, and learned that most of London, and a high proportion of the nation, spend much of their lives being spied upon. The Hammersmith control room had about 50 screens, tracking streets, shopping malls, railway stations, parking lots, etc. The operator is in instant contact with the police; he has a zoom control that can take his picture from a crowd scene to a moustache or freckle at a touch; everything is on tape. A potential thief may well be identified before he pounces, and have a couple of plain-clothes police on hand when he does. Alternatively, if he's on the getaway the hue-and-cry automatically catches the operator's eye, and it won't be only a freelance Rambo or Crocodile Dundee who takes up the chase; it's also that chain of unseen cameras with their damning evidence. Only problem, said the man in charge, is that operators tend to nod off because there's no longer enough crime to keep them alert. No wonder.

The totality of surveillance sounds like a future-shock prediction by Aldous Huxley or George Orwell – Big Brother is Watching You – and of course there has been some human-rights, creeping-tyranny protest, mainly apparently from old-timers brought up on Orwellian warnings. The protest never got more than lukewarm, though, and you can see why. Technologically it may look like a totalitarian horror-story but the social attitude behind it is diametrically opposite. This is not about clandestine dictators suppressing dissenting thought; it's a society so advanced that it couldn't care which way you think as long as you don't nick nobody's handbag. As the operator said, if there's a march down High Street it means nothing to him whether they're gays or anti-abortionists or communists or fascists. What he's looking for is the face in the crowd which might take offence and express it by stone or fist. The worriers worry that all that equipment *could*, given an unfortunate twist of the social screw, end up as a terrible instrument of suppression. So it could, and perhaps we should never be too sanguine about the propensity of mankind to screw up, but when you contemplate what it would do for South Africa to have every mugger perpetually aware that a camera might be videotaping him, I'd take that risk.

A different risk about London and videocameras was our risk of falling into cliché. The horseguards in their tin waistcoats, the Trooping the Colour, the punks with bicycle spokes in their noses and gold paint on their hair . . . you saw this stuff in every travel agent's window. I wanted to go somewhere new. The team, Keith and Richard and Brett, maintained that London without the cliché might as well be Manchester. That would have been okay by me, truth to tell, but I'd learned the hard way that Keith's TV nose made for better ratings than my somewhat more sombre approach. Compromise was reached. I bought my cup of tourist birdseed and stood in Trafalgar Square with a thousand unhygienic pigeons clambering over me like every holiday snapshot since the box brownie was invented, and I put a brave face on the terrifying task of manning a soapbox at Hyde Park Corner and shouting the odds.

Cliché or not, Hyde Park Corner is an institution to love. A society which sends bobbies to protect the right of every nutcase to let off steam is precisely a society which never has gangs of renegade colonels sending tanks to occupy the radio station and imposing a new tyranny until the next gang marshals new tanks.

The soapboxes on either side were both dedicated to the matter of World Government. The one on the left said we had none and needed it badly, the one on the right that we had plenty and didn't need it at all. Both were seriously intent on raising mass movements among the camera-clickers en route from Buckingham Palace to Madame Tussauds, and both might have been there 50 or 100 years ago or presumably 50 or 100 years hence.

Our soapbox-donor was a different matter – a black guy who seemed mainly set on having fun. His stint at the Corner was evidently to him what a Sunday morning round of golf or visit to the bingo hall might be to other people. His props consisted of a large upturned map of the world – south at the top and north at the bottom – which gave the impression that he would be strong on rights for the Third World and down with northern hegemony. In fact he was talking about penises. He was into some sort of male-liberation case based on the male genes being inherently superior to the other kind, which was evidently all summed up in the properties of the penis. When I, with Keith's prodding elbow doing injury to my ribs, rashly raised a heckle, he deflected it to the delight of the audience with some neat aspersion-casting on the presumed properties of my relevant organ.

Discovering that I was South African he changed tack, into a racial diatribe that you would not expect to encounter outside the pages of an Evelyn Waugh novel. He, he claimed, was super-English, born in England and therefore superior and civilised. I was a savage from Africa and should kindly stay in Africa and wear animal-skin.

If he'd been some sort of half-black or mulatto, this would have been one thing, but he was as negroid as anybody and thus his perception was all the more startling. To a South African ear it was also oddly liberating.

In our set-up there is no such thing as an untrammelled black voice. You'll never see any black person, not even a crank or showman, stand up in public and tramp all over the ordained black line. All blacks are supposed to share certain basic views, such as that their core problem is the way they've been treated by the whites, and nobody dares say otherwise. There can be variations in emphasis, but too weak an emphasis can itself bring on charges of treason to the black cause. Mr Mandela himself has famously dumped on unnamed 'black journalists' for 'disloyalty'. So now we know. Black journalists are expected to think with their genes when it comes to public issues, and reserve their brain cells for perhaps working out their accounts. And white journalists are evidently exempt or debarred from the same loyalty, here in the new non-racial society which the deluded among us imagined was about a common loyalty to a common State.

In South Africa it often seems that black humanity is irrevocably condemned to be black first and human second. We've lately been able to look across the Atlantic and see a determined assault on the chains of blackness being led by black academics, but at home we've become used to the idea that dissent is a thing to be whispered behind cupped hands, and furiously disclaimed if it leaks into the public weal. To hear a black mouth loudly and unabashedly proclaiming heresies from a speaker's soapbox (more literally, an upturned beer crate) was a refreshing indicator that we might also yet get to the time when freedom means freedom to step out of line.

As the penis specialist warmed to the South African theme he became less jocular, more heated, and stepped ever further from the line. I, he said, was the most stupid kind of African of all, a white African. We were so stupid that we had made our Mister Dee Clirk give in to the black Africans who, little did we know, had nil interest in all the non-racial democratic twaddle that they had pretended to go along with for the sake of getting on top so they could kick us out.

It turned out that there were dozens of South Africans in the crowd. We might be 1% of the population of the world but we were a good 30% of this its most cosmopolitan corner, largely comprised of an Afrikaans tour group from a platteland dorp – I think it was Lydenburg. A woman with a caricature ox-wagon accent blew her top at all this treason talk, and furiously advised our speaker that he wasn't fit to touch the feet of the finest gentleman on earth, President Mandela. The speaker failed to agree, and pandemonium occurred. In no time the World Government audiences had dwindled to nil as the congregation flocked to watch a group of Boere sounding like Father Huddleston harangue a black man who sounded like Eugene Terre'Blanche.

It was a bit cheeky in the circumstances to ask our Terre' Blanche for the loan of his box, but he obliged warmly, and enthusiastically took up the role of chief heckler. Keith abundantly acquired the colour-sequence he'd been after. It was with difficulty that I dissuaded him from the intention to run it in toto, but in the event the inevitable places where mike or camera had not been in the right place at the right time advanced my case. We eventually gave it some 10% of the total screen time allocated to England. It delivered at least 90% of the public feedback. So it goes.

After a week in England my notion of South-Africa-in-the-world was badly deflated. We had found practically no evidence of a place at all, other than that of the alleged 80 000 restaurants in London, with thousands of Thais, Israelis, Chinese, Indian, Laotian and Italian (which nobody any longer expects to be run by actual Italians) a total of two are South African. One of these is in any case a Nando's, which while a fine South African success story is problematic as proof of South Africa's general exportability, being entirely built around a Portuguese metaphor upon which its Joburg Jewish proprietors have no claim other than as a smart slice of marketing.

We had also bumped into numerous expatriates who had roundly turned their backs on South Africa, frequently after a hijack or barbaric assault, and whose basic message to the nation was 'you whites should get out while you can, put on your overcoats and come and enjoy civilisation'. In terms of the Seffrican connection the message was bleak. But as regards the state of England it was great.

Britain when last I was there had been very much the sick man of Europe, grimy and hangdog, filled with aggro and decline, with racial tension and industrial tension and unmet contracts and vanishing customers. At that time the world was saying that Britain was on the skids and Britons themselves were saying they were on the skids. Now, a decade later, Britain is a nation with a spring in its step. Its politics, which were so recently before so crisply class-bound, so bitterly pro- and anti-Thatcher, so full of Right versus Left animosity, have progressed into a cool ho-hum set of acceptances. Although we were there right after the general election, there was a total absence of the victors' normal crowing 'we smashed 'em' and an equal absence of the vanquisheds' mournful 'the country's ruined'. Practically everybody, including those who had hated Maggie with passion, was saying 'ah well, she did put a few things right'. Practically everybody, including those who were still exhausted from working on behalf of the losing Tories, was saying 'ah well, it was time for a change'. Ideology-wise, the average citizen could barely tell Labour from Tory, both of whose class linkages had crumpled into a jumble of free choice. The notorious them-and-us-ism had faded into dimness.

We repeatedly asked our British contacts to take us to the most benighted parts of the city, and caused them much brain-racking and confabulation. They delivered a housing estate (oddly enough, containing a Bloemfontein road and General Botha pub) where we met several smart and cheerful black yuppies on their way to gym or night-shift; the only sight of the Third World being a family O'Flaherty whose thurrteen bratty kids were the stroppiest gang of blatant pickpockets since Fagan.

We didn't believe that this could really be the bottom end of London, and since everywhere we were coming across was pretty well middle-class – even the tough areas from the nursery rhymes being straightened-out and smartened up – we kept looking. Finally we learned that the new desperation area was a place called Brent, which the ditties had never heard of, way up north around Wembley stadium. We got there and an achingly sincere Brent councillor poured out his woes, which were largely to do with the sub-economic housing schemes of the leftish 60s having proved to be all wrong and inhuman. The schemes in question looked just like the coloured flatblocks of Newclare or Athlone, which, while by no means quaint, would be considered halfway up the South African scale of accommodation. Now they were getting demolished to start again.

The councillor was regretful that things were turning out all contrary to plan. Whites were quitting the area in droves, not through actual racial tensions, which were negligible, but because a job application carrying an NW12 address was automatically taken to come from a black no-hoper. Meanwhile the area was separating out into Indian, West Indian, and African quarters, posing the challenging new problem that the Indian schools were increasingly delivering much better results than the national norm, and the African schools much worse.

Brent was salutary evidence that the English garden was not all roses, but at the same time it demonstrated that if this perfectly habitable-looking spot was the lowest point of the social heap, the heap on the whole was in a pretty good place. Indeed all the signs demonstrated the same thing.

Unemployment was down to 4%. British teams were triumphing in sportsfields around the globe. Theatre was on a roll. Construction and refurbishing was wildly active. Symbolically the sun shone upon Britain and the real sun was trying hard to follow suit. To me there was a very core lesson in this, which is that it is quite possible for a society which today feels awful about itself to feel fine tomorrow. A combination of the right policies and the right attitudes and the right commitment can cause a nation to elevate itself by its own bootstraps. When I listen to the wailing and groaning and prophecies of decline that abound at home I feel that our traditional stepmother up there with the grey skies and the safe streets has not yet reached the end of what she has to teach us.

13

Synthesis

A thread runs through this book, you will have noticed. There is an underlying question: Are we coming right? Are we, the people of South Africa, making a success of our nation?

For many South Africans the answer is categorical, whether Yes or No. Some take it for granted that of course we are coming right. We're liberated, the bulk of our people are at last coming into their own. Prosperity obviously lies ahead, once the legacies of the past are overcome, and it's verging on treasonable to doubt that.

Others take it as just as obvious that we are slipping down the tubes, following Africa into retrogression. For this faction, to question the inevitability of decline is naïve – at best a whistling in the dark, at worst a deceit.

I am uncomfortable with the categorical alternatives. Compelling as it is for the newly liberated majority to assume that liberation has to lead to fine results, it is also unrealistic in the light of the continental track record. But the prevalent despair among the minorities seems to me to underrate the potential to get things right. The same people used to insist just as categorically that there was no resolution to the political conflict – 'the script is written', they insisted, 'the die is cast', they insisted, 'the irresistible force of black nationalism is bound to clash with the immovable rock of white nationalism' etc. Their last prophecy of doom was made wrong by human action. Now they seamlessly slide into a new prophecy of a different doom, implosion rather than explosion. If they were wrong once could they not be wrong again?

As well as wrong, the categorical alternatives are harmful. Many people develop the assumption that since things are destined to come right anyway, they are under no particular obligation to *make* things right. Many others assume that since decline is on the cards there is little point in exerting yourself to reverse it.

Personally I favour a humbler answer, to wit 'maybe'. In the preceding chapters I touch on innumerable areas where in the course of the Trek I have encountered daunting evidence of the potential for collapse, and many others where I have been emboldened by the potential to succeed. I conclude that we may come right but we are extremely far from a guarantee.

In the course of asking the question I form a view as to what might lessen the down-side potential and strengthen the up-side, and find it hollow to leave the issue at a 'maybe'. The 'maybe' begs the next question: how do we turn it to a yes? For my money it's mainly a matter of removing a delusion, the delusion of racial parity.

National delusion is not new. There was the famous Nonquase delusion, that if the Xhosas starved themselves the whites would get out of their hair. There were repeated colonial delusions to the effect that if you stomped hard enough on the Afrikaners and/or blacks you would create a Little England in the veld. There was the apartheid delusion that you could unscramble the omelette into pristine ethnic eggs. Now we come to our own times and the rainbow nation, and to the delusion that the task at hand is to make all the stripes of the rainbow equal in every way.

The much-identified chief sin of apartheid was that it set out to engineer society into colour-coded apartments. The central quest of the new State is, in the name of redress, to engineer society into a revised colour-coded racial parity. I am sure that this quest is a delusion as impossible as any of its predecessors, and as ruinous. In this chapter I explain why, and suggest a better alternative.

Which is an invidious thing to do. A delusion after it has died is a wonderful thing to attack; everybody rolls up to kick its corpse, especially the people who themselves once believed it and are thus doubly angry. But a delusion in full swing is hard to see as a delusion. A delusion in its own time is a holy cause, and its adherents become irritated if doubt is expressed. I believe that for those of us who wish a contented nation to emerge over the years ahead it is necessary to shout Whoa! Foul! The earlier and the louder the doubt is expressed, the quicker the shock wears off, the sooner we limit the damage.

* * *

History, they say, repeats itself, and I have been this route before. From about the time I could first pretend I needed to shave, I believed that to make sense of this nation the starting point was that we had to all be equal citizens. This meant universal equal franchise, or what was then called 'one man one vote'.

In the eyes of many good and decent people, prisoners of the delusion of their time, this was a shocking, horrifying thing to say. It wasn't just 'left', it was worse. 'Left' was to want to let blacks sit on bus-stop benches. To want to give them the *vote* – '**What!** You mean same as *us*! Same **queues** and *every*thing!' – no, this was 'ultra-left'. It was radical, communist, 'pro-black', 'ideological' and so forth not only to the Boere but also to the average English-liberal who was *of course* against apartheid but was even more against 'capitulation'.

I got used to all these appellations, all of which were wrong. I had no ideology other than a sense of fair play and a wish for a successful South Africa. I was by no means 'pro-black' insofar as that term implied the corollary 'anti-white'. I was hardly 'left wing' in any sense more doctrinaire than a human respect for the underdog.

But reason was irrelevant in the face of the vast disgust with which enfranchised people expectorated upon the proposition that 'one man one vote' was the starting point of stability. For them it was tantamount to a call for suicide, and that was not because Afrikaners or white South Africans had any specially odd streak running down their backs. They were doing what came naturally. Imagine how anti-apartheid Britain would have reacted had their issue not been to grant independence to their colonies, but to invite 500 million Indians, 100 million Nigerians, etc, to become joint Britons with the British, enjoying person for person the same rights over Britain as the 50 million British.

When white South Africans objected in those days to the idea of 'majority rule' or 'one man one vote' it was not because they were sjambokking thugs who ate black babies for breakfast. It was because they were terrified. Of course there were the primitives, English as well as Afrikaans, pin-striped as much as safari-suited, but there were also the decent people, and they also came in all castes and walks, and it was hard to say to them: 'Look, until every black person is just as much a citizen as you, you haven't got a ghost of a chance of coming to rest.' You might as well be saying: 'Look, slit your wrists.' It caused them pain, but it was necessary, because until we had hurdled the hurdle of equal citizenship, everything else was going to jam against it.

Then we came to the political miracle, and now even the most morose pessimists acknowledge that whatever problems we have or are still to meet, we are vastly better off than if we were still tinkering with qualified franchises and Fourth Chambers and the other artifices of white hegemony, and bombs were going off in parking lots.

People who, while the delusion lived, said 'how dare you speak such treason', now say things likes 'thanks for having rattled our cage'. My magazine Frontline was twice banned for advocating a political dispensation very much like the one which my persecutors embraced euphorically a decade later, waving their new seskleur flags. Now the former censors say: 'Oh, you did so much to change my thinking.' At the time they said: 'This must be suppressed.'

And now we have the new delusion. When the pendulum dropped, it dropped with a vengeance – naturally enough, since it had been frozen for centuries at one edge of its swing. It flashed, for a brief shining moment in 1994/95, through the point of equilibrium, the point sought by Martin Luther King's dream for 'a day when my children shall be judged not by the colour of their skin but by the content of their character', and then it sped up the other side where it now refreezes.

Just as much of Africa had done before us, and is now frantically undoing, South Africa went over the top on liberation. We established a new national ethic that said: 'Since we are now all equal, we had better make sure that this equality is manifestly reflected in our racial statistics.' We took the admirable notion of human equality, and rammed it into the unreachable notion of racial parity.

The two are not only not the same; they are mutually contradictory. Human equality is about people; racial parity is about groups. Human equality paves the way to growth; racial parity causes decline. Human equality builds self-confidence and mutual respect. Racial parity entrenches complexes, self-hate, and mutual resentment. South Africa faces a fundamental choice: are we to better the lives of multitudes, or are we to sacrifice tomorrow's health on the altar of today's egos? Our reigning national outlook says: 'we achieve prosperity through parity', which is like saying 'we acquire children through celibacy'. It is one or the other, and by default we have taken the parity route.

We adopted as a national mantra the idea that but for our unjust past, races would be equal; that in the natural order of things all races would be equally represented in every sphere. Labour Minister Tito Mboweni says: 'The composition of the workforce must reflect the composition of the population.' Moss Mashishi, now the head of an empowerment conglomerate, spoke against me at a Wits debate when he was a student leader and put the same point more firmly: 'This nation will remain distorted until 80% of actuaries, neurosurgeons, and financial directors are African.'

The mantra is not always spelt out; it is more often the unstated basis upon which the nation conducts its affairs. When tenders are accepted or licences granted not by price, calibre of materials or quality of workmanship, but for the number of black people in the tendering consortium, that is an outflow of the ethic of racial parity. When companies or councils acquire higher applause for recoding the colour of their executive bodies than for increasing their profits and taxes or improving their services, that is for reasons of racial parity.

This process is widely taken to be inevitable and obligatory, but for varying reasons. Generally white people see it as a forfeiting of cutting-edge effectiveness in favour of showing goodwill, being fair, securing public contracts, or going with the flow.

Many black people take it as unquestioned that the natural state of the world is for all the races to be functionally equal in every respect, and that but for white oppression there would be black and white people running corporations, computer consultancies, architectural practices etc in identical proportions and with the same effects.

Proceeding from this premise the only way of understanding what is happening in South Africa now is by ascribing a dreadful clannishness to the whites. You will as a logical consequence of that premise assume that the recovery of the natural order will mean a flowering, with legions of black accountants and engineers arising to bring a cornucopia of creation that multiplies the nation's wealth and work. You will be stupefied that the whites, currently in control of the economy because of their past oppression, appear so unwilling to permit that flowering. You will hear them say things like 'we're trying our best, please note that our black admissions ratio has gone up from 32% to 35%', and will be staggered. How can they think that this is anywhere near fair or adequate? You will see companies bragging about appointing a black director, and will interpret this as adding insult to injury. There are meant to be many black directors – not perhaps 80% all at once, because the whites must still apply some training and bridging to make up for their past neglect – but the pace you see will be woeful, indeed virtual sabotage, for which there is no explanation other than white selfishness. No matter how much goodwill you feel towards white individuals you will be deeply offended by the whites' collective obstructionism, and find yourself supporting laws to accelerate the transformation process.

That is, if your lodestar is the premise that racial parity is the natural order, that the world is *supposed* to deliver electronics experts and garden labourers in proportion with the 'composition of the population', you will rationally, and not out of a sense of revenge or animosity or 'gimme', see your country's main need as to speed up the replacement of the 'old guard' by the new, for the sake of jobs and prosperity.

If, however, your premise is fallacious, you may be required to confront some very hard alternative routes to the creation of the prosperity you seek.

It seems to me that the premise is fallacious, and that it goes to the core of why the new South Africa has become such an all-round disappointment.

There are things it is hard to say to people nursing raw nerves, but which must be said anyway, because once you start bending truth to suit fashions or sensitivities you are weaving a tangled web.

One of these things is that the seeds of racial disparity were not sown in 1948. They were sown way before 1652. When two races met at Table Bay one came to the meeting in possession of artefacts which the other lacked – the nail, the screw, the drill, the loom, the chimney, the sail, the wheel and the written word, and if necessary this list could be 50 pages long. This was, technically and organisationally, a greatly more advanced society than the other. That much is uncontested, but it is now assumed that at some subsequent time the gap has or should have disappeared.

Why do we assume it should have disappeared? The answer is that it is very unsettling to modern sensitivities that there should be a gap. It is sentiment that declares the gap should have gone. Logic says that if you climb half the hill in the time I climb a quarter, by the time I get to half you're likely to be at the top. If African culture proceeded X far along the road to development while Dutch culture proceeded 2X, then when African culture gets to 2X the best place to look for the Dutch is at 4X. Ah, it may be said, but they should have imparted their skills. As a matter of fact they did some of that, but even if they imparted with superhuman dedication were they expected to jam brakes on their own development in the meantime? While Jan taught steam technology was Kleinjan not allowed to bone up on internal combustion? We know that if we look at the aggregate African capacity to build a steel factory or a power station, we are not looking at the same thing as the aggregate European or Asian capacity.

This is objectionable stuff to be dealing with. But there is a truth here that has been lost in the anxiety to observe the pretence of racial parity.

Humans are equal; we have our five billion separate individual characteristics and an identical core humanness, but when it comes to racial aggregates and their functional characteristics, if you look for parity you condemn yourself to perpetual frustration. It is not there to be found.

As to why not . . . those who are so inclined can and will argue forever. Is it culture or genetics or oppression or climate or geography or all of these? I don't know, it is no part of my concern to find out, and I distrust all the interpretations I hear – from the glib bar and shebeen versions to the hi-falutin' academic ones. My concern is a simple one: to make the best of the concatenation of people we are. It is measured by simple criteria. If in my old age I can drive to town and find there liveable lives being contentedly lived amid work and endeavour and confidence and order, we'll be succeeding. If a grim squalor of wrecked buildings, ruined services and failed dreams, no.

Many bricks will go into building the target we want – education and health, policy and investment, all our joint interactions on every front. But if we build on a dud keystone they will falter. The keystone that makes sense to me is human equality and human respect. In the old days it was ignored in favour of the delusion of compartments. In the new days it is ignored in favour of the delusion of racial parity.

South Africa's best hope is to ditch the target of racial parity and re-establish the ideal of human equality. I hope we do it now and with good effect, rather than too late and with wrong effect in the fashion of Zambia[1], Mozambique, Uganda[2] etc, where after 20 years of impoverishment and misery we swing the pendulum back to its first wrong position and beg for economic recolonisation.

Marx and Hegel give us a useful tool in the theory of the dialectic, which says that in a time of tension the Thesis, the existing situation, will run its course and come to be seen as all wrong, and will be supplanted by the Antithesis, the exact opposite in every way. In due course the Antithesis will also fall into disfavour, and give way to the Synthesis, which will contain bits of the old, bits of the new, and bits of its own.

We've had Thesis, compulsory division into rigid compartments. We have Antithesis, compulsory compression into a single flat tray. We come up for Synthesis – one nation, free and open and actually tolerant, respecting the application of skills more than the complexion of the holders, recognising individuals rather than a race or gender rank order of preferred South Africanness, judging 'not by the colour of the skin but the content of the character'. The sooner the Synthesis, the better the prognosis.

However, when Synthesis is first floated it looks heretical. It will be variously said to be derogatory to blacks, to be racist, to be retrogressive, to be impossible or to be utopian. All of these accusations will wither in time, but it does take time.

It is said for example that racial jealousy and statistics-rivalry is inherent in the way the world works. In fact we have under our noses an excellent example of a non-parity, human-equality relationship. Jewish South Africans are grossly over-represented in the professions, the command-posts of industry, the mansions. To the rest of us this causes nil pain and

---

[1]Of the 187 Zambian privatisations which are currently giving rise to a new 'hope for Africa' mood, I believe that 186 have gone to outside companies.

[2]A businessman operating in Uganda tells me that to get contracts there the first requirement is to have no 'empowerment partners'.

sometimes a certain relief. If the hand holding the surgeon's scalpel belongs to a Doctor Goldberg, we have that little extra faith in the right cut being made the right way in the right cable, and in the likelihood of decisive intervention if something goes amiss. If we contract with a Jewish business we have a slightly higher expectation (which is not always met) that the right goods will arrive at the right time and the right place in the right condition. We take it as an untroubling fact of life that on aggregate the Jews get their act together better than us, but that doesn't give us complexes or chips on shoulders, and doesn't make us feel small vis-à-vis any particular Jew. It is a fine relationship, and a model for what the black/white relationship could be when we come to the Synthesis era.

It is said, then, that to build black confidence is vital, and racial parity is the route to it. Certainly the confidence is vital, but it is strictly Antithesis thinking which assumes that you build black confidence by creating black failure. When the conduct of an economy is based on colour more than capacity you will occasionally encounter people who rise superbly to the demands but you will frequently encounter people who wilt. No South African needs to be told that wilting is a large feature of our communal concourse, but the straightforward two-plus-two connection with the philosophy of parity is seldom acknowledged openly. When people, of whatever colour, see black companies crashing or local authorities floundering, they tend to blame the individuals involved. They should rather blame the public syndrome which systematically squashes square pegs into round holes for the sake of racial parity. If the nation acquired a fetish to ensure that left-handed people of Irish descent were fully represented as postmasters, I might be put in charge of a post office. When the service declined you would blame me, which would unfairly assail my confidence. If the scale was large enough you would develop a loaded view of every left-handed Irish postmaster. You might find us most pleasant and personable people, but you would never be able to deal with us without being inflicted by the odious thought 'oh, oh, here's a guy who is running a function into the ground'. You'd think the same even of those left-handed Irish who might be perfect postmasters. You would be unable to recognise their calibre, because your subconscious would be dominated by the statistical probability that they are out of their depth. You'd feel bad about it as if ashamed that you were catching yourself in some primitive anti-Irish or anti-left-hander trait. If you yourself were Irish and left-handed you'd feel doubly bad. In fact none of the ill effects – the postal deteriorіation, your guilt complex, my inadequacy complex – are either your fault or mine. They're the fault of the delusion of parity. Free us! Let the delusion be broken. Adopt a policy of human equality, and take it seriously. For the price of a slower rise in the statistics of Irish postmasters, we'll find self-respect and we'll find mutual respect. Also, more confidence in the postal system.

It's only now, in the heyday of Antithesis, that confidence is taken to depend on the statistics of racial representivity. Synthesis sacrifices representivity in favour of personal confidence, which accordingly ceases to be a pseudo-confidence constantly dropping through the holes in its floorboards.

Synthesis is in all ways a better place for us to be than the place where we are, but to get there is a two-way street. If you want the black establishment to shake off the chains of racial aggregation, the employer caste had better do it too. Do they? They say they do, of course, but the shaking-off is less than total. An example:

A friend was complaining that he couldn't find the right person for a job he had to fill. I asked how many applications he had had. He said 'three', and after a pause added 'and 21 blacks'.

I said that sounded like 24 applications. He said, earnestly, 'Oh no, it's not an affirmative action post.'

There's the nub of it. You get your PR agency to wordsmith a mission statement about how passionate you are for equal opportunity and employee development. You inscribe it in Gothic script, and frame it and hang it on your foyer wall. Then you find a general manager who will show the flag at the Provincial Legislature's cocktail party, and there you are, buttoned up. The New South Africa is accounted for.

My friend was taken aback when I said I expected him to interview all the applicants. He said it was pointless, he knew the blacks. I said he didn't know these 21. He said none of their applications was right. I said he can't judge by paperwork: just as many people in the new age have outward qualifications exceeding their inward abilities, so are there many whose actual capacity is ill reflected by their paper skills. He said it would take days. I said if he wants a downturn in the new distortion, he'd better pay. The price is to put effort into displacing the distortion of racial statistics by the reality of personal fulfilment.

He did it, and he appointed a black woman, for the right reasons. He looked for capacity alone, and he looked much more laterally than he would have liked to. She didn't fit his bill to a T, or even to an S or R or Q or P or O. He's had to adjust structures and job definitions. He has to do more mentoring than he wants, and take more headache pills. But he believes he has the person on hand who in the long run will do more to make a particular function hum than any alternative applicant would have done. He got her by looking past the moulds and at the individual, closely.

Were this approach a bigger feature on the options table, there would be a slower ingress of black faces into the management of firms and factories than we now see, and it would largely be rung-by-rung ingress rather than the shooting-star brand which is the flavour of the moment. From the perspective of 20 or 50 years hence, it would be an enormously major relief. We would obviate the usual African fate of after a generation of decline selling the residual assets of the ruined State at firesale prices to foreigners. It would spare us the resentments of a class of bourgeois blacks with expectations raised beyond the meeting of them. It would keep and attract skills. It would mean more livings being earned and fewer livings being begged or stolen.

Unfortunately, for today's industrialist who wants to do the right thing by today's criteria, to say nothing of procuring licences and government contracts, 20-year perspectives are cold comfort.

It's now that he is doing business, and to do business now he must demonstrate his empowerment credentials. Thus he might rig up a 'consortium', filled with (preferably well-known) names beginning with M and ending with vowels. This consortium will display a well-divided set of share-ownership percentages, but will not make public the management contract by which one member of the consortium will run the enterprise, in effect paying the others a fee for the use of their names.

He might alternatively deliver an executive committee showing the same names bearing classy corporate titles, but neglect to mention that these titles are duplicated by other titles whose bearers are not on hand at the presentation. The 'empowerment' (now in vogue to replace the newly dirty-worded 'affirmative') Director of Product Development will have a non-empowerment counterpart called Director of Marketing, with a very similar job description but with 40 people in his department instead of 2.

Industrialists who perpetrate these subterfuges treat them as cost factors, parcelled away in the same corner of the mind as the donations budget and redeemed by the same warm fuzzy feeling: at least you are giving salary and status to a nice guy.

The total bill is actually rather higher. The resources and the headspace going into show-purpose charades means less left over to go into real advancement in unglamorous arenas. The token appointee becomes messed up by having too little to do; by failing to win the respect of his peers; by a sense of guilt for playing along with the sham; and by the inexpressible knowledge that he is out of his depth. The message to white aspirants is: to get a fair shake, get out.

Every real effect of the distortion is ill, from wealth creation to race relations to psyches. But the distortion goes on because of the fear of appearing offside, and we become trapped in a vicious cycle. Transformation leads to wrong results, so black sentiment thinks there can't have been enough of it and pushes for more, so institutions boost their showpiece quotas, which means more loss of competitive edge, which means more closures and fewer investments, which means more disillusion with the inadequacies of transformation and more demand to rectify these by creating more transformation. Blacks become embittered by unfulfilled expectations and whites become alienated by a sense of unwantedness. The faith and amity that shone so brightly at the time of the Mandela election ebbs into the cracked foundations of the new delusion.

It's sore to now recall the euphoria of 1994, perhaps the most marvellous moment the clock of history has ever seen, and the millennial privilege of being part of it. For ten minutes in there we were large, we were strong, we were proud, we could conquer the world. We forgot that we'd spent our lives declaring that the political predicament was insoluble. We revelled in relief and togetherness. The flag was plastered on the Boers' bakkies and the townships' taxis alike. We believed in ourselves, the totality of our newly united selves. We set up a terrific, exciting, new social contract. The new establishment said: 'In place of all the insult you gave us, we offer you a non-racial state.' The old establishment said: 'Great, thanks, we'll give it a go.' Most golden of ages, but awfully short. It ended when we broke the social contract.

Both sides reneged. The new establishment set up a racial rank order of South Africanism. The old establishment went into a sulk and gave up on the blacks.

We need to renew the contract. We need to recover faith. We need to move to Synthesis. A fine time would be around now.

* * *

It's the head that must work out ways to adjust the mixture, but the motivation is in the heart. I've spent my life wanting to see this country fulfil its potential. I love the country, not just the beaches or mountains or game parks, but the people. I'm enriched by the people around me, most particularly the people not like me. I'm enriched by the challenge of seeing an awkward human concatenation melded into a strong and progressive whole, where we relate all round on a basis of confidence and respect.

The Trek is due to return to the screen shortly. There, and wherever I can, I will keep pursuing the target of a nation which will feel good about itself, today, tomorrow and beyond.